Book One in *The Vesta Shadows* Series

BRIDES OF ROME

A NOVEL OF THE VESTAL VIRGINS

By Debra May Macleod

CS Assigned ISBN–13: 978-1514831687
ISBN - 978-1-7750608-2-6

This book is a work of historical fiction. Apart from the well-known actual people, events, conditions and locations that appear in the narrative, all names, characters, places, conditions and incidents are the products of the author's imagination and/or interpretation of history, or are used fictitiously. Any resemblance to current events or conditions, or to living persons, is entirely coincidental.

Cover photo: Woman in Roman clothing with shield and helmet © FXQuadro
Image ID: 266929526 Provided by Shutterstock.com

Inside illustration: Letter V logo © Steinar
Image ID: 206140168 Provided by Shutterstock.com

Inside image: Denarius showing the Temple of Vesta
Statue of Vestalis Maxima / Virgo Vestalis
Original Press Photo Temple of Vesta, circa 1930
From the collection of Debra May Macleod

Cover design by Rita Toews

VestaShadows.com

PROLOGUE

THE CAMPUS SCELERATUS

(THE "EVIL FIELD" JUST INSIDE THE CITY WALLS OF ROME)

113 BCE

Licinia tasted sour vomit threaten to rise in her throat. The green cypress trees that dotted the landscape and the blue sky overhead swam dizzily in and out of her field of vision as she struggled to maintain her balance. She swallowed hard, but her mouth was dry with the thick summer heat and her own stark terror, and it felt like a blade piercing the back of her throat.

A blade. She had prayed to the goddess for a blade. Even criminals and gladiators met death by the quick work of a sword or dagger yet she, a revered priestess of Vesta, was denied that mercy. Her guards had been as kind to her as their station permitted, yet not one of them had dared to smuggle a blade into her room no matter how much she begged.

Not one of them had been brave enough to provide her with what she needed to end her suffering at once, even when in her most panic-stricken moments she had offered to dishonor herself and her virginal service to the goddess by pleasuring them, however they wanted her to do it, in exchange for even the dullest of kitchen knives.

No doubt they had seen her supposed lover flayed alive in the Forum.

Blood soaked through the fabric that was wound loosely around her body, the scourge gashes on her back once again opening up. The Pontifex Maximus took her arm and pulled her toward a gaping black hole in the ground.

Around it, stood several somber priests and two of her fellow Vestals, the docile Flavia and the duteous chief Vestal Tullia, their eyes moist and their palms up in supplication to the goddess.

The black hole was at her feet now. Licinia looked down into the void and felt a rancid mist of cold, dank air rise up from its depths and cling to her face. At once gripped by terror and filled with a macabre fascination, she blinked at the blackness. She could just barely make out the first rung of a ladder that extended down, all the way down, to the pitch black end of her life.

"*Tu etiam protege me, dea,*" she heard herself cry out. "Goddess, protect me!"

"Mother Vesta goes with you."

It was Tullia who had spoken. It was against custom for her to speak to a Vestal condemned to death for *incestum* – breaking her vow of chastity – but the Pontifex Maximus was in no mood to remind the austere Vestalis Maxima of decorum. This ugly business would be finished soon, but he still had to work with her. No point making matters worse.

The Pontifex Maximus stepped back and nodded gravely to the executioner, a war-torn Hercules of a man whose body took up the space of two men. He hesitated for a moment – this was a *priestess of Vesta* after all – and then extended an uncertain hand toward her, urging her to descend the ladder and praying to Mars that she would go willingly.

She rounded on him suddenly. "Do not touch me," she spat. "I serve the immaculate goddess." He pulled his hand back.

"You have served the goddess well," said the Vestalis Maxima. "May you continue to do so."

Licinia felt her throat tighten, but she inhaled sharply to stop the tears. She looked at Tullia's face – expressionless in the glaring sunshine – and then gathered the bottom of her robes in one arm, holding the folds of drapery aside so that she could descend the ladder without tripping on them.

She slipped one sandaled foot into the black void and felt the cool, clammy air envelope the bare skin of her foot and shin. A chill ran up her spine as her foot found the top rung in the blackness. Her other foot followed. She stepped down to the second rung, feeling the raw wounds on her lashed back tug and bleed anew. She stepped down again. The black dirt was at eye level now and her fingers were stained with soil as she clung to the earth. To life.

It was so strange to be at this angle: staring at the sandaled feet of people who, when this duty was done, would ride back to Rome in their litters with fresh air still in their lungs to continue with their day, talking, eating, sleeping and waking in the morning to the light of dawn. How foreign and impossible those things seemed to her at this moment.

Her body immersed to the neck in Hades, Licinia turned her eyes away. She didn't want her last image to be the crookedly-tied sandals of a priest. What idiot slaves he must have. Either that or they secretly despised their master.

She peeled her eyes open wide, hungry for light as she descended down the ladder, rung after rung, into the ever-blackening pit until her feet landed on solid ground. She looked up. The opening to the world above looked like the disc of a full-moon shimmering white against the black sky.

Licinia's heart pounded so hard that her chest and back ached from the pressure. She stood like a statue in the dark, feeling the spindly legs of an unseen insect scurry over her foot, and terrified to look around her. That would make it all too real. And she wasn't ready for that yet.

The ladder moved upwards quickly, too quickly for her to grab onto it. She watched it rise and then disappear into the glaring lightness above and, a moment later, saw a basket descending to her on a long rope. She reached up to catch it in her arms and then removed the items before those above could remove the basket as quickly as they had removed the ladder.

A loaf of bread. A jug of water. An oil lamp that burned with a small but steady flame.

As she stared into the flame, she heard a grating sound in her ears and felt soft earth fall onto her hair from above. Her tomb was being sealed.

The full moon above gave way to a half moon, and then to a crescent as the last sliver of light disappeared and she was left with only her pounding fear and the flickering flame. Tullia was right – Vesta was with her. The Vestalis Maxima would have undoubtedly lit the oil lamp with the sacred flame from the temple.

She cradled the small oil lamp in her palm and turned around slowly, as one who knows a ghost stands behind, to look around the silent black pit.

The pit was larger than she had expected, more or less rectangular, with smooth dirt walls. A few steps to her left stood a small couch and on the ground in front of it…Licinia cried out. A body.

It was wrapped in robes similar to Licinia's, but those lay dishevelled and rotten against decayed flesh and exposed bone. The arms and legs were splayed and the skull was visible, as was a patch of straggly long hair. The mouth was open.

Feeling the blood leave her head, Licinia slowly lowered herself to her knees. If she fainted – and she was close to it – she would drop the oil lamp and her only source of light would be lost.

She inhaled a few breaths of the stagnant air and felt it stick in her nostrils like a foul film.

Something caught her eye and she glanced to her right. Lying against the dirt wall were two more bodies. These were arranged in a more dignified state, their decaying robes wrapped carefully, respectfully, around them. Dry bone was visible through the fabric.

You have served the goddess well. May you continue to do so.

Setting the oil lamp gently on the dirt floor, Licinia crept toward the splayed body of the Vestal. She gently wrapped her hands around the bony arms and folded them across the torso, and then drew in the decomposed legs.

Gingerly, she pulled the old, delicate fabric around the body, doing her best in the dim light to wrap the Vestal with dignity. Once done, she rolled the body until it lay restfully against the other priestesses.

She moved with purpose back to where she had set the jug of water and bread, carrying them to the oil lamp and sitting cross-legged in front of it. She tore a small piece of bread from the fresh loaf and held it above the oil lamp, sprinkling crumbs into the flame.

"Mother Vesta, your humble priestess, who has served you these fifteen years with purity and reverent duty, honors you with this offering. Please light my way to the afterlife."

The heat of the summer day was a distant memory now as the skin on her bare arms prickled in the cold air of the black pit. The deafening silence of her deep tomb throbbed in her head, yet through it she heard the words of Anaxilaus, her Greek physician.

Do not prolong your suffering by drinking the water they give you. Show Hades you are ready and he will take you sooner. Even he can have mercy...in his way.

She knocked the jug over and watched the water seep into the dirt, trickling into the underworld.

Forgive me goddess, she thought, *but my last offering must be to Hades*.

CHAPTER I

RISE

ROME 45 BCE

"Have you heard the song that his soldiers sing about him?"

"No, but I can imagine…"

"It goes like this: *Home we bring our bald whoremonger! Romans, lock your wives away! All the bags of gold you lent him, bought him ten more tarts to lay.*"

The women chortled in unison, winding their way through the chattering crowds, bumping into bodies and lifting their *stolas* to avoid dragging them through the dirt on the cobblestone. The Forum Romanum – crowded and crazy on a slow day – was on this historic day a giant moving mass comprised of gawkers of all classes, all come to catch a glimpse of Rome's new dictator.

Dwarfed by the elaborate multi-colored temples and basilicas that towered above and encompassed them on all sides, the women wound through the mass of people – merchants, shoppers, slaves, prostitutes, politicians, filthy children – to pass before the circular, white-marbled Temple of Vesta, goddess of the home and hearth.

Several large bronze bowls surrounded the temple, inside each of which burned flame from the eternal fire of Vesta that was housed within the temple's sacred inner sanctum.

The women gravitated toward one of the bowls. It was an overcast and cool February day. Surely the goddess wouldn't mind if they warmed their mortal hands over her immortal flame.

The one who had sung began to sing again, "*Julius Caesar, knows how to please her –* "

She stopped abruptly as a white-robed priestess descended the steps of the temple and glanced their way. High Priestess Fabiana, who had served as Vestalis Maxima for the past twenty years. "Forgive us, Holy Lady," the songstress said, lowering herself onto her knees as her companion instinctively did the same.

As the chief Vestal stepped off the marble step and onto the cobblestone of the street, two Praetorian guards – elite bodyguards of Imperator Julius Caesar – materialized seemingly from the shadows to stand on either side of her, their gold armor and scarlet red uniforms flanking the Vestal's white robes.

The more senior Praetorian removed his helmet and bowed his head. "Great Lady," he said, "shall we accompany you now?"

"Yes," said the Vestal. Her voice was lighter than her seventy-six years. "Thank you."

The splendid trio moved toward the adjacent House of the Vestals, creating a domino effect of men and women who quickly dropped to their knees before High Priestess Fabiana. A chorus of murmurs went up.

Please ask Mother Vesta to protect my son who serves in Gaul...

Preserve my family...

Bless my daughter's marriage...

My child is sick, please ask the goddess to save him...

The Vestal pulled back a fold of her white robes to reveal a handful of palm-sized wafers. As she glided past the kneeling supplicants, still flanked by the gleaming Praetorians, she dropped a *mola salsa* wafer – used as sacred offering to the goddess Vesta – into the cupped hands so desperately held up to her.

After the spectacle had disappeared into the anteroom of the House of the Vestals, the songstress turned to her awestruck companion.

"Forget those sweat-stained gladiators clambering in the sand," she said. "I'll be picturing that shiny pair of Praetorians when my husband rolls on top of me tonight."

* * * * * *

Julius Caesar sat straight on a cushioned marble bench inside the lush open-sky courtyard of the expansive three-story, fifty-room House of the Vestals. Smiling, he rose to greet the high priestess as everyone else – senators, other Vestals and a throng of patrician guests – bowed.

"Caesar," Fabiana matched his smile, "Or shall I now call you King?"

Caesar smirked. "Are you trying to get me killed, Lady Fabiana?"

"If I wanted you dead, you'd be dead. Now pass me a cup of wine."

Caesar took a gold cup from a slave's tray and handed it to the Vestalis Maxima. "Priestess Fabiana, I need your help."

"I know," the high priestess said matter-of-factly. "You have been appointed – rather, managed to appoint yourself – *dictator in perpetuum*. Dictator for life. Congratulations, Imperator."

"It's for the good of Rome," said Caesar. "You've dealt with the Senate. A bunch of rich old men waxing poetic about the virtues of the Republic, and for no other reason than to put more coin in their purse and squander more land. Under my command, Rome will be more of a republic than it has been in decades."

"Some aren't so sure. Some say you are King Tarquin reborn."

The Praetorian who stood at Caesar's side widened his eyes and tightened his lips. Had anyone else said those words to the dictator, their head would be on a spike in the Rostra by now.

"Tarquin, with all his arrogance, would have made a better senator than king. You will see, High Priestess..." He looked distractedly over the Vestal's shoulder as a flourish of whispers and muted excitement swept through the gathering. "Ah, but now enough talk of kings. I see Queen Cleopatra has arrived."

Cleopatra VII Philopator. The notorious Queen of Egypt had already been in Rome for a year, living in Caesar's country house with their young son Caesarion and providing a well-spring of scandalous gossip the likes of which Rome's upper crust hadn't enjoyed in generations.

As she always did, she strolled into the courtyard as if it belonged to her, cutting a swath of superiority and style through the chatting cliques of patrician Roman matrons and men. Her long gold gown clung to her slight waist, curving over her hips and extending down her legs to feather the ground. Her arms were bare except for the gold bracelets that snaked around both upper arms.

Her dark hair was pulled back into a tight bun and on her head was a gold diadem with the symbol of her monarchy, a cobra, in the center. Like her, the cobra gazed down at the world, regal and ready to strike at any moment. Polished white pearls were nestled into her black hair to create the type of striking contrast the queen was known for.

With her hook nose and large eyes, she was no exotic beauty. Pretty at best; however, her slaves knew precisely how to accentuate her allure and shroud her flaws behind cosmetics, dress and gems. She moved with the grace of a cat and purred when she spoke.

Caesar and Fabiana rose, Caesar taking the queen's hand as she floated toward them.

"Majesty," he greeted. "I'm delighted you could join us."

"It is your great day, my love," she said. "I am honored to share it with you." She turned to Fabiana, her smoky eyes lined with black kohl and her red ochre painted lips narrowing into a tight smile. "And in the company of Vesta's high priestess, no less."

"It is good to see you again, Queen Cleopatra," said Fabiana, not bothering to sound convincing. She was getting too old for that.

"Has Caesar told you of his plans to build a great library here in the Forum? It is to be modeled after the Library at Alexandria. Thousands of scrolls for study, a museum, public gardens…"

"…and of course a special building for the Vestal order," added Caesar.

The old priestess laughed out loud. A warm laugh. "The priest Lucius tells me you have promised to build a massive temple to Mars as well. Where will you get all this marble?"

"Well, if you refuse to ask Vesta for it on my behalf, I shall ask my own ancestor, Venus. Or I shall ask Cleopatra to petition Isis for me."

"Immortal women love you as much as mortal ones," smiled Fabiana. "You shall have your marble, no doubt. And I will be glad for it, Julius. Learning belongs among the temples."

"We can agree on that much, Great Lady," said Cleopatra. "Priestess Fabiana, tell me truly – what do you think of Caesar's dictatorship? You are his kin so you must know his heart. Is it not for the good of Rome? I have been in your city for a year now and even in that time I have seen things improve. Caesar's policing force has made the streets safe. His accounting has lowered taxes for the common people. The friendship between Egypt and Rome has filled Roman bellies with Egyptian grain. You have even adopted our calendar…"

"Queen Cleopatra has given us much," said Fabiana. "Perhaps Her Majesty should be dictator of Rome as well as Pharaoh of Egypt?"

Caesar slapped his leg and laughed out loud. "She could do it, too." He picked a stuffed olive off the tray of a passing slave and pushed it in his mouth, eyes widening as he spotted a familiar young Vestal.

Like all Vestals, she was dressed in a white stola and white veil that covered her hair. Her personal slave, an auburn-haired Greek beauty five or six years older than her, stood behind.

"Ah, Lady Pomponia…come closer, you are also celebrating a great day, are you not?"

"Yes, Caesar, I am surprised that you would remember such a thing."

"How could I forget?" He gestured for a servant to hand Pomponia a cup of wine. "Cleopatra, young priestess Pomponia is today celebrating ten years as a Vestal."

"Ah, that is significant?" asked the queen.

"Vestals serve the goddess for thirty years, Majesty," said Pomponia. "We study for our first ten years as novices. After that, we are dedicated full Vestals who tend the sacred flame and perform public rituals."

Caesar swallowed a mouthful of wine from his gold cup. "Lady Pomponia and I have a history," he said casually to Cleopatra. "I was the person who selected her to be a Vestal when she was only a child of seven. I was Pontifex Maximus – chief priest of Rome – at the time." He turned to Pomponia. "I remember the day you took your vows," he said. "I can still see your long hair hanging from the Capillata tree, right over there in the gardens."

"It's grown back," said Pomponia. "It's long again." And then too informally and without thinking – "Caesar, where is the Lady Calpurnia?"

She realized her error immediately. Everyone knew that Caesar's wife Calpurnia avoided public functions if there was a chance her husband's Egyptian mistress might attend.

Pomponia swallowed so hard that Quintus, a young priest of Mars who was standing an arm's length away, raised his eyebrows and looked at her, scolding her with his eyes.

"I'm afraid Calpurnia is ill," said Caesar.

"I will sacrifice to the goddess for her health," said Fabiana.

"Thank you," said Caesar. "How kind." His glance shifted to Pomponia's slave who stood quietly behind her mistress, head down and hands clasped together. "And how are you, Medousa?"

"Imperator, I am well."

Cleopatra's smile tightened even more. "I have not known you to be so familiar with slaves, Caesar."

"This one is special. I chose her myself for Pomponia on the day she took her vows." Caesar reached out to touch the pendant of Medusa, the beautiful snaked-haired gorgon that hung around the slave's neck. "I named her Medousa for the charm she wore," he said. "Medusa, to ward off evil." His fingers traced a circle around the pendant.

Pomponia wasn't sure, but it seemed as though Cleopatra's entire body had tensed.

Caesar turned to Fabiana with a sad sigh. "*Tempus fugit*," he said. "Times flies. What I wouldn't give to have those ten years back. I was in battle, but my armor fit better."

"Ten years ago I could still walk up the temple's stairs without hearing my knees crack louder than the sacred fire," said Fabiana.

They all laughed.

Pomponia exhaled and looked over her shoulder, trying to avoid eye contact with her companions for the moment. A few feet away, she noticed Rome's great lawyer and senator Marcus Tullius Cicero who waved politely at her. She smiled back.

She liked Cicero. Not only had he successfully defended the brother of the Vestal Fonteia years earlier, but she had once sat next to him at the games when she was a young girl.

The spectacle had included the slaughter of over twenty elephants. Pomponia could still hear their cries. Screams, really. It took them so long to die. They had clambered together, the older ones trying to protect the younger ones.

We are of one mind, Lady Pomponia, Cicero had said to her. *The games have their purpose but I derive no pleasure from this either. In fact, I am compassionate…I have often suspected that animals have much in common with mankind. Surely such butchery does not please the gods.*

A political animal through and through, Cicero was one of the few senators to attend Caesar's gathering at the House of the Vestals. Like most senators, he revered the Roman Republic and looked down his nose at Caesar. Unlike most senators, however, he was willing to wine and dine Rome's dictator to stay in the game.

Pomponia tensed as Marc Antony – Caesar's brilliant but boorish general – swaggered up to the senator and threw his arm around him.

"So Cicero," Antony bellowed. "Still pissed at Queen Cleopatra for stiffing you on those books? It's all anyone can talk about! Gods, you'd think this town would have bigger problems, eh? What with our new dictator and all…"

"A misunderstanding," said Cicero. He pulled his head back, obviously avoiding the wine stench of Antony's breath.

"That's a good man," barked Antony. "Forgive and forget, eh?"

"The choice of the wise," said Cicero, knowing Antony neither forgave nor forgot. "*Mea sententia,* General Antony."

With Fabiana, Caesar and Queen Cleopatra now immersed in a conversation that fluttered between politics, wine and astronomy, Pomponia quietly made her retreat.

Moving across the gardens with Medousa in tow, she took refuge in the peristyle that surrounded the courtyard and stood in a slant of shade cast by a tall statue of a long-dead Vestal priestess.

And although she didn't give him the satisfaction of returning his chastising gaze, she still felt the critical eyes of the young priest Quintus watching her.

Politics were exhausting.

* * * * * *

The last guests had departed and the Vestal priestesses sat languidly in the courtyard as slaves noiselessly cleaned around them, returning tables and couches to their proper places and fishing litter out of the pools.

"It's getting cool," Fabiana said tiredly. "I think I shall retire for the evening."

"Caesar will never forgive me," said Pomponia. "He thinks I was trying to be clever."

Fabiana smoothed the veil around the younger Vestal's face. "Caesar has known you since you were a child," she reassured. "He knows your heart. And he is worldly enough to tell the difference between youth and malice."

"Why did he choose to meet in our gardens today? Why not celebrate at his home?"

The old priestess sighed. "He was sending a message to the people. He wants them to believe that he has the support of the Vestals. You must remember, Pomponia, Vesta's eternal flame is what gives life to Rome itself, and we are tasked with keeping it alight. Regardless of what changes happen in Rome, regardless of what dictators or disease or devastation come and go, the sacred flame burns on. It comforts the people. It lets them know that the goddess is with them and that they and their families will go on. It lets them know that Rome will go on. It is the one constant in a changing world. That is why he sought my help."

"What did he want you to do?"

"To stand in the Rostra with him during his speech tomorrow," she said.

"Are you going to do it?"

"No."

"Why not? If the people need us, what harm can it do? Is Caesar not family to you? He has always been a major benefactor of the Vestal order."

"Our duty is to the goddess, not to Caesar," said Fabiana.

She pulled off her veil with a sigh, revealing the close-cropped gray hair beneath. It was not something the conservative Vestalis Maxima would have done ten years ago, but the gardens were private enough and her seventy-six years had loosened her stern adherence to tradition.

"The Vestal order is the oldest and most revered priesthood in Rome's history," said Fabiana, "but that hasn't stopped a few people from using it for their own purposes." She folded her white veil in her lap. "We must never allow others to use us as pawns. We must protect the sacred flame...and each other." She paused and then continued. "Someday I will tell you the story of the Vestal Licinia and you will understand." Fabiana arose slowly. "I'm taking my old bones to bed now. *Bonum nocte*, my dear."

"*Bonum nocte*, Great Lady."

Pomponia pulled her *palla* around her. It was cooling off more quickly now. She cast a glance around for Medousa, but she was nowhere to be seen. Oh well. She was likely busy in the kitchen, cleaning and washing. Pomponia could put herself to bed tonight. She pulled off her own veil and thanked the goddess that she wasn't needed in the temple until morning.

She slipped from the greens of the elaborate gardens, through the peristyle and into the grandeur of the Vestal's home, a three-floor structure that rivaled the luxury and wealth of any palace in the Roman world.

She stopped to unfasten her sandals and then strode barefoot across the cool orange mosaics of the marble floor, finally disappearing into her own lavish quarters.

Outside the House of the Vestals, on the cobblestone street of the darkening Forum, Julius Caesar's large, gold-gilded litter sat idle with several Praetorians standing guard around it. The curtains were drawn.

Inside the lectica, Medousa lay naked on a smooth cushion. Her eyes were fixed on the rich red tapestry that hung from the ceiling. The back of her neck burned as the chain of her Medusa necklace dug into her skin. Caesar was clutching the pendant in his hands, twisting it around his fingers ever tighter.

He prompted her to spread her legs further and she obeyed as Rome's dictator thrust between them, at last enjoying the pleasures of sole power.

CHAPTER II

AND FALL

ROME 44 BCE

The morning of March 15, 44 BCE – the Ides of March – began as any other. Breakfast. A sacrifice of salted flour to Vesta. Dressing. Prayers. Tending to the sacred fire in the temple.

By mid-morning, Pomponia's stola was damp from a fearful sweat. A line of perspiration formed along her veil, dripping into her eyes. She blinked the stinging away.

Julius Caesar was dead. Assassinated as he arrived at the Senate for his duties. The cry had gone up in the Forum Romanum – Caesar is dead! – and then silence had fallen like a stone. The streets emptied as people fled home to their families and locked their doors.

Who was in control of Rome?

Pomponia and four other Vestals stood in the inner sanctum of the round Temple of Vesta, circling the sacred fire that burned in its hearth, palms up in prayer to the goddess. *Mother Vesta, your faithful priestesses ask you to protect Rome.*

The crackle of the fire answered their low prayers and echoed off the pristine white marble walls. Pomponia closed her eyes and felt the heat of the eternal flame lick the back of her hands.

High Priestess Fabiana burst into the temple. "Get the will," she said breathlessly. "Bury it in the courtyard, behind the statue of High Priestess Tullia. Put some flowers on top of it." She shoved a scroll into Pomponia's hands. It had Caesar's seal on it. "Put this in the vault in its place."

Her chest pounding, Pomponia rushed to the hidden chamber in the heart of the temple, the place where no one but the Vestal priestesses were allowed to go.

With trembling hands, she opened a small but thick marble-inlaid iron door and pulled out Caesar's authentic Last Will and Testament which was encased in a cylindrical scroll box. She replaced it with the decoy copy.

There's no way the assassins will break into the temple, she thought. *It would be an outrageous sacrilege. They would lose the support of the people.*

It was customary for Rome's most important men – generals, dictators, certain senators and consuls – to keep their wills secure in the Temple of Vesta. There was no safer or more sacred space in the Roman world. Indeed, in the seven hundred years that the Temple of Vesta had stood in the Forum, there was not a single violation of the tradition or of the temple's sanctity.

And considering Rome's violent past, that was saying something.

Pomponia wrapped Caesar's official will in her palla. She moved hurriedly through the temple, hearing Fabiana whispering hushed instructions to the other Vestals around the sacred fire. She looked back. Fabiana nodded curtly to her. *Do it. Hurry.*

She pushed open the bronze door of the temple and raced down the marble steps – directly into the solid chest of the priest Quintus.

"Do not touch me," she scowled. Of all people. The last thing she needed right now was to deal with his predictable disapproval. Every public ritual, every ceremony or festival, it was the same thing: Quintus, Priest of Mars, finding a reason to scold Pomponia, Priestess of Vesta. She was in no mood for his finger-wagging. "Move," she said. "I am tasked by the Vestalis Maxima."

"Priestess Pomponia," said Quintus. His face was pale and tense, but his demeanor was as high-handed as ever. "For your own safety, I shall accompany you."

Pomponia looked up. In addition to its usual watch of six well-armed Roman soldiers – one soldier per Vestal, both day and night – the temple was being guarded by some twenty priests of different ranking from a number of religious collegia.

Quintus's superior the Flamen Martialis, High Priest of Mars, was present. So too was the Flamen Dialis, High Priest of Jupiter, as well as the Rex Sacrorum, King of the Sacred Rites who honored Janus. All held daggers.

A number of Praetorian soldiers also stood guard. For the moment, they had no master. Caesar was dead. Yet their duty had led them to the Temple of Vesta to watch over their general's will. His estate had to be protected. His true heir had to be named. His final wishes had to be honored. If his assassins got their hands on it, none of those things would happen.

Clutching the scroll box in her palla, Pomponia scurried toward the adjacent House of the Vestals as Quintus stayed at her shoulder, matching her pace with long strides.

She noticed for the first time that he wasn't in his priestly robes or a toga, but rather wore a simple tunic. He had come in a hurry.

His hand rested on the dagger at his left hip as he strode alongside her, his eyes making quick assessment of the Forum. A dirty child ran by with a barking dog in pursuit. Fruit rolled out of a basket that had been dropped on the ground and left. A few shifty-looking men slunk behind columns, either waiting for news or waiting for an opportunity to profit from the anarchy.

Rome was a beast with its head cut off, a beast that would destructively convulse until, like the Hydra, a head grew back.

Pomponia and Quintus burst into the courtyard of the House of the Vestals to find an unkempt slave within it. He was drinking from one of the pools, his cupped hands draining water into his mouth and splashing water on his face.

Quintus drew his dagger. "Get out," he said.

The slave turned around. It was Marc Antony. Quintus lowered his blade. "General Antony," he breathed. "What is happening?"

Antony sat down heavily on a marble bench beside the pool. He wore the face of someone who was thinking a thousand thoughts at once.

"He's still lying on the Senate floor," he muttered. He looked up at Pomponia. "Send some temple slaves to get his body…have them deliver it to his house. Calpurnia will be waiting…"

"I will send Medousa," said Pomponia. At the whisper of her name, Medousa emerged from behind a column in the peristyle. She nodded at her mistress before darting off to find help. Pomponia watched her leave. *Was that a smile on her face? No, just fear…*

Antony squinted his eyes and shook his head in disbelief. "I laughed at Calpurnia this morning," he said. "I *laughed* at her. She's a superstitious old bird, I'll give you that, but she was so damn sure of herself. She warned him not to go today…said she had a dream that he would die." He looked squarely at Quintus. "A *dream*! Gods, it's absurd, is it not?"

"It doesn't matter anymore," said Quintus. "His body will be taken to Lady Calpurnia. You must hide."

Antony stood up so fast that Quintus jumped, his hand instinctively touching his dagger. The Roman general held his hand out to Pomponia. His eyes were on the cylindrical object wrapped in her palla. "Priestess Pomponia, give me Caesar's will."

She hesitated, but then Quintus nodded at her, his eyes commanding her to do it. She suppressed a scowl. Even now he was giving her orders. And although she hated to do it, she obeyed.

* * * * * *

Charmion, Cleopatra's advisor and servant, swept into the queen's luxurious bedchamber in Julius Caesar's country house, utterly dispensing with protocol and gracelessly dragging the three-year-old Caesarion behind her. He was in the middle of a royal temper tantrum, but she paid him no heed.

Cleopatra dropped the glass perfume bottle in her hand. It shattered into pieces on top of a golden Roman Eagle mosaic that stretched across the floor. "What is it?" She held her breath.

Charmion tossed a pile of dirty clothes onto the queen's bed. "Majesty will put these on," she said. "The prince must also wear them."

Unquestioningly, the queen pulled her dress over her head and dressed as Charmion outfitted the squirming prince. Two rough wool tunics, stained and stinking like manure.

"Caesar is dead," said Charmion. "Assassinated."

Cleopatra set her jaw but said nothing.

"You will leave on horseback. A litter is waiting a few miles away. We must make our way back to Egypt without delay." Charmion wrapped a frayed rope around the prince's waist to fasten the tunic.

"When did it happen?" asked Cleopatra. "How long do we have?"

"It happened this morning, perhaps two hours ago. We have minutes."

The door to the bedchamber opened. Both women tensed; however, it was only Apollonius, another of the queen's trusted advisors.

"You and the prince will go with Apollonius on horseback," said Charmion. "I will go with your decoy in the royal litter."

Finally, a trace of fear – "No," said the queen, "you will come with us."

But for the first time in her twenty-five years of service to the Pharaoh of Egypt, the slave known as Charmion did not obey her queen.

* * * * * *

The throngs of people in the Forum Romanum parted for the procession of Vestals like knife cutting a loaf of bread in half. Such deference wasn't just respect, it was also the law. Anyone who refused to make way for a Vestal priestess or litter, or who accidentally or deliberately touched the sacred body of a Vestal, could be publically whipped and executed.

The Vestal litter moved off the Via Sacra – the sacred road that wound through the Forum – to set down beside the Rostra, the great speaker's platform from which some of Rome's most historic speeches and announcements had been delivered.

Medousa pulled back the curtain of Pomponia's lectica and the Vestal gracefully climbed out. "We could have walked, for all the trouble," said Medousa. "It would have been faster."

"The Vestalis Maxima wants a show of ceremony today," said Pomponia. And then added with a bite – "But if you think it wise, I can ask her to consult with my slave next time."

"As you wish, Domina," murmured Medousa.

Pomponia studied her. "Medousa, we're here for Caesar's funeral rites – a dark time, nay? – yet here you are, behaving as if Apollo himself just granted you your freedom and asked for your hand in marriage."

"I am stricken with grief, Domina, and not thinking straight."

An official-looking slave bowed to Pomponia and led her to a raised platform alongside the Rostra, upon which High Priestess Fabiana and two other Vestals, Nona and Tuccia, sat upon red cushioned seats.

The elder Nona sat rigidly but Tuccia, the Vestal who was closest in age to Pomponia, reached out to squeeze Pomponia's hand in warm greeting. Pomponia once again gave silent thanks to Vesta that she was chosen to attend the ceremony while two other Vestals had to remain at the temple to tend the sacred fire.

She settled in beside Fabiana and was about to say something to her, when she noticed the high priestess's red eyes. To Fabiana, this wasn't just a state funeral for a dictator. To Fabiana, it was the funeral of a family member. Caesar had always been something of a pet to her, and everyone knew the affection the general had for the Vestalis Maxima.

Pomponia couldn't remember the last time she had seen such a crowd packed into the Forum. Men and women – dressed in the finest of togas and stolas to the most threadbare of tunics – stood shoulder to shoulder, peering over each other's heads to stare up at the Rostra.

Upon it, the body of Julius Caesar lay on a marble altar, covered in a purple cloak that moved noiselessly in the slight breeze. Near the head of Caesar, a larger-than-life wax effigy of the dictator stood on a pedestal. No less than twenty stab wounds had been carved into the wax statue, with the red lifeblood of Rome's great general and Imperator oozing from each one.

Antony commissioned that in a hurry, thought Pomponia.

Yet despite the dramatic imagery and the occasion, the multitude in the Forum was strangely silent. Uncertainty and expectation hung in the cool March air. At the moment, Rome seemed to be less in a state of violent turmoil and more in a state of dispassionate wait-and-see.

But then Marc Antony appeared. He strode across the platform of the Rostra as if it were the world's stage and he its star actor, dressed in a rich, deep purple cloak that matched the one covering Caesar's body. Wide gold cuffs encircled his wrists.

To Pomponia, he was a different man than he had been the day before in the Vestal courtyard, disguised in a foul slave's tunic and slurping water from the pool like a stray dog.

On the Rostra, the black-robed priests of Pluto, god of the underworld and divine brother of Vesta, solemnly moved aside for Antony. Fragrant smoke from their incense burners rose up to the gods, creating the sense that the expansive marble platform was a sacrificial altar. Antony's message was clear. Caesar had been sacrificed.

As he approached Caesar's body with slow, severe strides, Antony suddenly extended his arms and dropped to his knees, wringing the purple death cloak in his hands and looking up to the gods with moist eyes.

Like waves on water, gasps of emotion moved through the mass of people.

"*Bona Dea*," Fabiana whispered under her breath. "He plays the people like a lyre."

Pomponia checked herself. Her eyes were moistening. She had so much to learn from the high priestess. She sighed and glanced around, noticing for the first time that Quintus stood on the edge of the Rostra, dressed in his priestly robes and holding the Aquila, the Golden Eagle of Rome.

Normally, an enlisted legionary soldier of high-ranking would hold the Eagle as a military standard; however, Quintus had a somewhat unique standing. Not only was he a priest of Mars, god of war, but he had also served in Caesar's army in Gaul, discharged only after being seriously wounded in battle. He was conscious of every step now, careful to conceal a slight residual limp at all times.

At the edge of the Rostra, at Quintus's feet, a pretty girl – quite obviously pregnant – looked up at him and braved a small but flirtatious grin. Pomponia had seen her before: Quintus's young wife, a girl by the name of Valeria. She carried on her hip a small child, their first daughter, who grinned up at her father.

They're proud of him, thought Pomponia. But then Quintus shot his family the same chastising glare that she knew all too well, and they stopped smiling and looked away.

Pomponia rolled her eyes. It was no wonder that so many Vestal priestesses chose to remain in the order instead of getting married after completing their years of service to the goddess.

After several weeping moments, Antony stood on unsteady legs. "My fellow Romans," he announced from the Rostra. "You were loved by the man who lies on this altar. A great man whom you knew only as a great name – Caesar! Sacrosanct Caesar who served as Pontifex Maximus, High Priest of Rome! A man – nay, a god! – who defended Rome's honor in barbaric lands, who spent years in bloody battle for the glory of our eternal city and her people!"

In one swift movement, Antony lifted the purple cloak that covered Caesar's body, took hold of the bloodied toga that lay underneath it, and held it up. The white folds were drenched in Caesar's blood and the rich fabric was in shreds from the assassins' daggers.

"*Lupus est homo homini*!" cried Antony. "Man is a wolf to his fellow man! This hero, this god, this great leader of Rome and devoted father of her people, faced a thousand enemies in battle and survived their swords. Yet he could not survive the betraying blades of those he trusted as friends!"

The muscled arms of the robust general held the bloodied toga even higher. He looked up at the wax effigy of Caesar as if he were gazing at the face of a god.

"O inviolate Caesar, what good did your clemency do? Your bravery in battle? Your love of Rome? Only to be slain by those you embraced as friends! Even Jupiter and his heart of stone must crack at this mortal story of tragedy and treason!"

Holding the torn toga close to his chest now, he ran his fingers over the dried blood. "Caesar's blood, which was so often shed in war, now stains his toga in peace!" He choked back a sob and then, as if overtaken by a sudden swell of vengeance, bored his eyes into the crowd. "Such treachery! By Jupiter, I swear that I shall avenge him!"

At that, Pomponia followed Antony's spear-like gaze as it settled on a number of senators, including Brutus and Cassius, who sat rigidly alongside the Rostra. Their faces were blanched with disbelief.

This was not the diplomatic, unifying funeral speech that Marc Antony had promised.

But then just as quickly, Antony cast his piercing eyes upward, to the heavens. He outstretched his arm, gesturing to the strange star that had mysteriously appeared in the sky shortly after Caesar's assassination.

"We have all been amazed at the brilliant star that hangs in the heavenly canopy above, that shines with equal light both day and night. The finest Roman, Greek and Egyptian astronomers cannot explain this star – but we the people know what it is!"

Pomponia glanced up. It was a strange sight: a star with a tail, one that hung suspended in the sky night and day. The priests had been beside themselves with speculation and study, and augurs had been taken on the hour since it first appeared. No one could explain it; however, Antony seemed to have an explanation in mind.

"It is *Caesaris astrum*," he shouted, "star of Caesar, soul of Caesar!"

A mad cheer of wonder and jubilation swept through the Forum.

Antony didn't let up. "Gaius Julius Caesar, *divus Julius*! Once a son of Rome, now a god of Rome! And now, his place among the gods can be seen above us!" He placed his hands on his chest as if to stop his heart from breaking. "We must pay tribute to such celestial rebirth, nay? The gods demand it. I therefore decree that the month of Quintilius – the month of Caesar's mortal birth – be re-named July in his honor!"

A second cheer – this one pulsating with a volatile mixture of grief, anger and awe – surged through the crowds of onlookers. History was being made on the Rostra before them and they were witness to it. They were a part of it. They loved it.

Antony pressed on. He could never have hoped it would go this well.

Taking a great breath through his nose, one that inflated his sizable chest even more, Antony extended his arm and a soldier slapped a scroll into his palm. Pomponia recognized it instantly – she had hidden it in her palla, after all.

"I have in my faithful hands the last will and testament of our great father," said Antony, "kept unmolested and true by the Vestal priestesses in the temple." He unrolled it before a starving crowd that was hungry for more. "It was the last wish of the divine Caesar that the Roman people, whom he loved as kin, take pleasure in the life that was denied him."

Antony nodded to a group of soldiers alongside the Rostra and with some effort they hauled a gold chest onto the platform. Antony plunged his hand into it and then held up a handful of coin, letting some slip through his fingers to land on the marble platform of the Rostra. "To each and every Roman citizen, the divine Caesar bequeaths seventy-five drachmas."

Another wave of gasps – shock, joy, despair – moved through the mass of people.

"And to the people of Rome the divine Caesar also leaves his private walks, orchards and country estates that they may use for their pleasure…may they bring you as much peace as they brought our great father!"

A shout went up from the crowd, and then another. Jostling. Pushing, shoving. A forward thrust of thousands of bodies, all moving toward the Rostra.

Antony's rapier gaze settled once again on Brutus and Cassius, two of Caesar's assassins. It was clear from their ashen complexions that they knew it was all about to come apart. Roman riots formed faster than storm clouds. The two men stood up slowly, cautiously inching toward their litters.

That's right you bastard dogs, thought Antony. *Now it's your turn to run.*

Suddenly, Pomponia felt a firm hand grip her shoulder. Quintus. "A priest can be flayed as well as any other man," she said. "Do not touch me."

"Priestess Pomponia, it is time to leave," he said. To Pomponia, it sounded too much like an order.

"Perhaps you need a lesson in religious protocol," said Pomponia. "A Vestal only answers to the Pontifex Maximus. And unless you have been promoted…"

A deafening crash. A rush of people climbing up onto the Rostra, heading toward the body of Caesar.

Marc Antony gave a silent order to his soldiers – stand down. Let it happen.

The impassioned mob tore the cloak off Caesar's body and more cries went up at the sight of his pierced body. Blood spotted through the toga, mapping the blade wounds. His eyes were closed.

In his mouth was a coin to pay the ferryman Charon for passage across the River Styx to the afterlife.

Pomponia stood and watched in bewilderment as the mob lifted the body of Caesar onto their shoulders and carried him off the Rostra, into the mayhem of the Forum.

She heard chairs fall around her and noticed that she had been pushed away from her seat. The high priestess and the priestesses Nona and Tuccia were nowhere to be seen. No doubt they had been swept back to the safety of the guarded litter and were being escorted back to the temple by Praetorians.

She spotted two remaining Praetorians calling for her, but in the madness she couldn't get to them. Pomponia didn't know what frightened her more: the idea of being at the mercy of the mob in the street or having to face Fabiana when and if she made it back to the temple. The Vestalis Maxima would be furious with her for not paying attention.

Quintus squeezed her shoulder. "Come with me," he said. "Now."

Pomponia hated to do it, but she obeyed.

They weaved for a long time through the riotous street and the frenzied crowd in the Forum, Pomponia's heart racing as she watched Caesar's body, limp arms and legs flailing, being set atop a makeshift funeral pyre not far from the Temple of Vesta. Men and women came from all directions and threw any kind of kindling they could find – baskets, wood pillars, shop-keepers stands – under the body.

A woman held up a torch, "Send him to Pluto in Vesta's fire," she shouted.

And then the flames went up, crackling sparks into the early evening air and licking Caesar's flesh with devouring heat. Women tore the jewelry off their necks and arms and threw it into the bonfire – the bone fire – of the funeral pyre. More gold to pay the greedy ferryman.

At last, Pomponia and Quintus reached the steps of the round temple. As before, soldiers and Praetorians stood guard to protect those who protected the sacred flame. Breathless, Pomponia put her foot on the first step and then turned around to say something to Quintus.

He stood several feet away, arguing with his frightened, disheveled young wife. “I knew you would be here!” she shrieked. He grabbed her by the arm and dragged her away.

Pomponia climbed the white marble steps of the temple, opened the bronze door and shuffled toward the roaring red hearth within the temple’s inner sanctum. Fabiana embraced her. The other Vestals made an offering of gratitude to the goddess.

Pomponia lowered herself and sat cross-legged on the white tile floor to catch her breath. How strange.

The dictator Julius Caesar was dead, now made *divus Julius*, the divine Julius, a god. The maniacal mob was burning his body just outside the temple door. A fearful omen hung in the sky. Antony had turned like a mad dog on those who thought they could leash him. Rome continued to convulse like a beast with no head.

And yet all she could think about was Quintus’s hand on her shoulder.

CHAPTER III

TIMEO DANAOS ET DONA FERENTES

(BEWARE GREEKS BEARING GIFTS)

GREECE 43 BCE

The only thing that fifteen-year-old Livia Drusilla hated more than a Roman man was a Greek man.

She reclined on the couch and swallowed the largest gulp of wine she could hold in her cheeks, not caring that it dribbled out the sides of her mouth and down her neck or that her midwife had warned her against excessive drink while pregnant.

An arm's length away, her husband Tiberius – forty-two years old, round and idiotic – chortled at a dirty joke told by his Greek friend Diodorus, owner of the villa they were visiting in Athens.

Livia drained her cup. What further damage could she do to her baby? With a father like Tiberius, the child was destined to be a fat, vapid *plumbeus* anyway. Not only was Tiberius an idiot, he was her cousin. Apollo often cursed the infants of such coupling with both dullness and deformity.

The baby kicked and she shifted uncomfortably on the couch, suddenly suffering an unwelcome flashback of her first night with Tiberius.

His weight had pushed the breath out of her and, when she had turned her head to avoid his sloppy lips, she had caught a glimpse of his wide ass in the polished-bronze mirror beside the bed.

The wine burned in her throat and she tossed her cup onto the floor. She knew what would happen next: a female slave bent down to pick it up and, when she did, Tiberius slid his hand between her legs and squeezed his fingers into her body. "There's room in here for both of us," he chortled at Diodorus. Another stupid, stinking old joke from a stupid, stinking jerk.

"I have to take a piss." Diodorus stumbled to his feet and shuffled past Livia, glancing down at her reclining form on the couch and raising his eyebrows in a silent *woo hoo!* as he stole a look down her dress at her breasts.

Feigning good sportsmanship, Livia grinned. She hated that she had to be nice to this hairy Greek pig; however, she and Tiberius were dependent on his hospitality. In fact – thanks to her husband's unbridled stupidity – their very lives depended on this Athenian refuge. She uttered a silent curse to Juno, goddess of marriage. Why had she been saddled with such a husband?

Wrapping her palla around her chest, Livia wondered what was happening back in Rome. It had all gone to Hades after Marc Antony's rousing speech on the Rostra during Caesar's funeral.

Rome had split in half as influential men and families were forced to pick a side: you were either a supporter of Caesar's assassins, led by Brutus and Cassius, or you were a supporter of Caesar's allies, led by the general Marc Antony and some upstart nephew of Caesar's named Octavian. The latter man – barely twenty years old – was Julius Caesar's sole heir and posthumously adopted son. Octavian had been a nameless nobody a year earlier: now he was the new Caesar.

Between the two factions, there really was no contest when it came to strength. Antony and Octavian had the support of the Roman army, commanding those mighty legions that had served

Julius Caesar for years and that now regarded him as *divus Julius*. A god.

On the other side, Caesar's assassins – a bunch of lily-handed senators – were friendly with some of the wealthiest patrician families in Rome. To put it simply, the anti-Caesar camp had money, and lots of it. The pro-Caesar camp had muscle, and lots of it.

Even at fifteen years old, Livia knew which side wielded the bigger sword. She was not surprised when her idiot husband Tiberius chose the wrong side.

And so here they were hiding out in Greece, eating bad fish and slumming in a villa that boasted all the style of a slave's latrine, all to avoid Antony's sword on their necks.

"Husband," she said to Tiberius, "any word from Rome?"

"Only that Antony's thugs have moved from slaying to stealing," he slurred. "Every day they add new names to their death list…men that are to be arrested and either executed or exiled, and whose fortunes are to be confiscated to fund their hunt for Caesar's killers…"

"What about our names? Are our names on the list? And our estate, is it protected?"

Tiberius burped and laid his head back on the couch. "*Tempus narrabo*." Time will tell.

In other words, the drunken idiot had no idea.

As Livia heard Diodorus's familiar shuffling behind her, she rested her face on her hands and closed her eyes. The ruse didn't work, however, since he stopped in front of her couch and reached down to tug at her hair.

"Tiberius," he said, "your wife knows how to go through the wine. I think she should start earning her keep around here, don't you?"

A snore from Tiberius's couch.

Swaying on unsteady legs, Diodorus lifted his toga. The stench made Livia cough and she opened her eyes to stare at the patch of coarse black hair between his legs, his manhood hanging limp at her forehead.

"Laocoon knew better than to trust the Greeks," he said, as he clutched a handful of Livia's hair and pulled her head between his legs. "Especially those bearing gifts."

CHAPTER IV

Annus Horribilis

(A YEAR OF HORRORS)

Rome 43 BCE

"Pomponia, this water doesn't smell right." High Priestess Fabiana stood tiredly by a fountain in the courtyard in the House of the Vestals. She sniffed a clay jug. "Put some in a glass jug and smell it. Have one of the slaves drink it. Let me know."

"Yes, Fabiana."

The last year had taken its toll on Fabiana. The political maneuverings of Rome's most ambitious and ruthless men, and their constant petitioning for favor from her as Vestalis Maxima, had made the lines around her eyes deepen and her normally light temperament grow heavy.

More and more duties – especially those that involved political or ceremonial duties during public festivals or rituals – were falling on the young Vestal Pomponia. The elder Vestal Nona was more senior than Pomponia and should have been the natural choice; however, it seemed to be Fabiana's wish that Pomponia take on more responsibilities and the high priestess had come to rely on her for duties small and large.

Nona didn't seem to mind. A deeply devout priestess of Vesta, she had always preferred the more private, even secret aspects of a Vestal's duties to those that involved public ritual or political ceremony. Many of her hours were spent in the temple's innermost sanctum that housed the sacred fire, offering prayers to the goddess of the home and hearth on behalf of Rome. If she wasn't there, she was instructing the novices in the study.

Nonetheless, even Nona was required to take on more public duties these days. In the aftermath of Caesar's assassination and the bloody power struggles that followed, the Vestal priestesses worked, by daylight and candlelight, to fulfill their sacred functions.

At any given moment, groups of Roman matrons knelt at the steps of the Temple of Vesta to request a priestess's blessing as well as embers from the divine fire which they would then burn in their own homes. It was tradition that each and every request had to be honored.

Long before Vesta had become a public religion complete with a state-funded priesthood and a gleaming white marble temple, it had been a private religion that blessed the homes of its faithful.

The presence of the sacred flame in the household hearth, oil lamp or candle made the home a sacred space – a domestic Temple of Vesta. In fact, the circular Temple of Vesta had been built in the style of the round huts that the earliest Romans called home.

Not only did the fire of Vesta provide a religious and political focus for the entire Roman world, it also continued to provide a spiritual focus for the Roman family unit. For that reason, the highest duty of a Vestal priestess – next to keeping the eternal flame alight – was to gift Vesta's sacred flame to any woman who requested it.

Other people arrived begging to receive a few consecrated holy cakes – the sacred wafers the Vestals prepared – to offer to the goddess for their own reasons: to heal a child's sickness, to protect a husband soldiering in foreign lands, to care for a wife in childbirth, to bless the home.

After arguing for too long with Medousa over how much more salt was needed for the next batch of sacred wafers – they would also be needed for countless public sacrifices in the coming months – Pomponia was about to review the curriculum of some novice Vestals when a temple slave approached.

"Priestess Pomponia," she said, "Lady Valeria humbly requests an audience."

Quintus's wife. Pomponia frowned. As if Quintus weren't self-important enough, his wife clearly had no problem assuming she could command an audience with a Vestal priestess. Still, it was unusual.

"Escort her in," said Pomponia. She ran her fingers down her veil, pushing it behind her shoulders, and then sat upright on a cushioned couch to await Quintus's wife.

A moment later, a distraught Lady Valeria burst into the courtyard, running ahead of the temple slave to collapse in an undignified heap at Pomponia's feet.

"Help us, Lady Pomponia. They've arrested him!"

"They've arrested who?" asked Pomponia, quickly standing.

"Quintus!" Valeria put her hands on her face. "His father, too! They came into our home yesterday…they dragged them both from the house! No one will tell me anything, Lady. I don't know where he is –"

"Who dragged them from the house?"

"A centurion," cried Valeria, "one of Octavian's men." She kissed Pomponia's sandaled foot – a serious breach in protocol – and then placed her forehead on the ground. "I beg you Priestess Pomponia, on the affection my husband has for you…" Her voice trailed off and then she began again. "On the *respect* my husband has for you as a fellow member of the religious collegia – "

Pomponia felt the blood drain from her face. She knew exactly where Quintus and his elderly father would be: in the Carcer, Rome's infamous prison that sat in the Comitium, not far from the Rostra.

"Go home," said Pomponia. "Let me think…"

Valeria looked up. "You are a priestess of Mother Vesta," she pleaded. "You have the authority to pardon any criminal, do you not?"

"Yes, but Vestals rarely invoke that power. We serve the goddess, not the condemned."

"Quintus is innocent. He is a priest of Mars. He served Julius Caesar and was injured in battle. He does not support the assassins, he does not sympathize with them, he has never given them a single *denarius*! What proof do they have of any wrongdoing? Why do they want his head?"

They don't want his head, thought Pomponia. *They want his money. They need to pay their soldiers somehow.*

Pomponia sensed Medousa at her shoulder. "Shall I see Lady Valeria out, Priestess?" Valeria's frantic state had attracted the attention of everyone in the normally serene gardens.

"Yes."

Valeria kissed Pomponia's sandal again and then allowed herself to be escorted out. She had done everything she could. It was in the shining hands of the goddess now.

A moment later, Medousa was back. She cast a warning eye at her mistress.

"You should consult the high priestess," she said.

"Fabiana had Caesar spared during Sulla's proscriptions," said Pomponia, "and that was before she was made Vestalis Maxima. I have the authority."

"Don't do anything impulsive."

"The high priestess is resting and should not be disturbed. Anyway, Medousa, there's a saying: *melius est veniam quam licentiam petere*." It is better to ask for forgiveness than permission. "Prepare my litter. No horses, but still on the showy side."

"Yes, Domina," said Medousa, "but it is not safe to travel through the Forum right now." She lowered her voice. "My Lady, I know you were fond of Senator Cicero – "

"What of it?"

"I have just received word that he was killed yesterday in Formia, executed by Antony's forces on the Appian Way." Medousa assessed her mistress's blanched face and then continued. "I am told that Antony ordered the senator's hands to be nailed to the doors of the Senate…crowds are gathering as we speak to look…"

"My litter," Pomponia repeated.

If what Medousa said was true, Rome was convulsing out of control. Cicero had been one of the most respected and influential men in Rome for decades, yet it was no secret that he and Marc Antony had been at each other's throats for years. Cicero, the scheming politician. Antony, the lawless soldier.

Cicero had often spoken against Antony in the Senate. His criticisms had been open and caustic, and – although he had not played a part in Caesar's assassination – he had nonetheless expressed the fanciful wish that Antony had been stabbed alongside his general. His hatred of Antony had led him to befriend and support Octavian; however, that clearly hadn't protected him from Antony's wrath.

Pomponia's thoughts turned to Quintus. If the untouchable Cicero could be executed with impunity, no one was safe. Especially not someone like Quintus, a man who possessed great wealth but little political importance.

As her litter was being prepared, Pomponia had Medousa quickly arrange her hair into the *seni crines*, the traditional multi-braided hairstyle of Vestal Virgins. The seni crines was also the traditional hairstyle of Roman brides; however, Vestals were considered brides of Rome and, for that reason, they also wore the style.

Next, Medousa placed an *infula* – the traditional red wool headband of Vestal priestesses – over Pomponia's head, and then fastened the long, flowing white *suffibulum* veil over that. Once finished the hair and headdress, she wrapped a long ceremonial palla over Pomponia's stola, the white drapery falling in a dignified fashion around the priestess's body.

"Such dress is for public rituals and festivals," muttered Medousa.

"Such dress is for commanding reverence," Pomponia corrected. "No matter the occasion."

Medousa smoothed the veil on her mistress's head and then placed her hands on either side of Pomponia's face, staring into her eyes with sudden severity. "Valeria is his wife."

Medousa felt the sting of Pomponia's hand against her cheek.

They climbed without speaking into the gold-gilded Vestal lectica, sitting opposite each other and shifting as the litter-bearers – four in the front and four in the rear – lifted it off the ground and began to make their way over the cobblestoned Via Sacra, toward the Carcer.

Medousa leaned forward to pull the red curtains of the lectica closed.

"Leave them open," said Pomponia. Medousa leaned back. *I should discipline her more often,* thought Pomponia. *It makes her more pleasant.* Still…they had known each other since they were both children, bound together as more than mistress and servant, but as friends.

"I'm just concerned," softened Pomponia.

"As am I, Domina." Her voice was still harder than Pomponia would have expected.

The procession along the Via Sacra rounded the corner to the massive and bustling Basilica Aemilia, its long expanse of two-tiered arches filling Pomponia's field of vision.

The wooden vendor's tables that lined the streets of the Forum were packed with fish, butchered pigs and dead birds still in their feathers. The smell wafted into Pomponia's nose. Baskets of fruit and bread, as well as sacks of grain and seeds, filled the spaces between tables. Carts, men, matrons, children, peddlers and animals moved everywhere.

The haggling of shoppers on the street and the loud, grumbling negotiations of merchants and bankers in the basilica died down a bit as those who saw the Vestal litter lowered their voices – and their heads – in respect to the priestess who passed.

The procession paused momentarily as a matted little dog nipped at the heel of one of the litter carriers. It took a slave in a torn tunic and two merchants in dazzling white togas to free the litter-bearer's sandal strap from the dog's mouth.

"Jupiter's ass," swore one of the merchants as he put a bloody finger to his lips. "That's the hellhound Cerberus, escaped from the underworld."

The litter hadn't cleared half of the basilica when Pomponia saw the chattering, ruminating crowd gathered in the open space in front of the Curia, the new and improved Senate House that Julius Caesar had commissioned only months before he had been assassinated.

This crowd had seen much in the last year. They had seen the body of the dictator Julius Caesar lying on the Rostra until Marc Antony's speech had incited them to rise up, claim it as their own, and burn it to ashes in the Forum, near the Temple of Vesta.

But this was different. Cicero was no dictator, no soldier. He was a politician. A civilian. And despite the stature and wealth he had acquired for himself, he was still a common Roman citizen. The sight of his hands nailed to the Senate doors – purplish, swollen and grotesquely caked with dried blood – was something they hadn't seen before.

It wasn't just the gory sight that gave people pause. Hardly. They had seen far worse during the wild beast hunts and gladiatorial fights of the games. Even a chariot race in the Circus Maximus couldn't be considered a success without a few severed limbs rolling onto the track or some broken bodies – whether charioteers or spectators – being tossed around.

The frightening thing about the sight of Cicero's hands nailed to the Senate doors was that it represented a total breakdown of Republican order. If Cicero could be murdered, and his murder so blatantly waved before Rome's collective face, there was no telling how far Antony and Octavian would go.

As the litter passed the Curia, Pomponia turned her head away from the Senate doors. She would not dishonor Cicero's life by gawking at his severed hands. *Surely this butchery does not please the gods.*

She thought of him that day so long ago, that day when the elephants were slaughtered at the games, and she was still a child who knew so little about Vesta's sacred fire.

But then they were through the crowd and the Carcer loomed in front of her, its unadorned stone face and utilitarian columns announcing itself as the most unfriendly, austere building in the Roman Forum.

"Set down near the entrance," Medousa instructed the litter-bearers.

As they did, she stepped out quickly and then turned to help Pomponia exit gracefully. A throng of onlookers had already gathered: a Vestal priestess coming to the prison? Why? Could she be pardoning someone? Murmurs of speculation and excitement filled the air.

Without a moment's pause, without stopping to think about what she would say or do, Pomponia wrapped her palla tightly around her body and strode past the dumbfounded guards that stood at the front entrance of the prison as if she were Vesta herself come to earth.

"My Lady," she heard one stupefied guard attempt, but he was quickly hushed by his colleagues. *Leave it to the prefect,* seemed to be the general consensus. *That's why he makes more money than us.*

Pomponia stood just inside the Carcer's portico as the prison's prefect – a tall, angular man caught with a mouthful of bread – stood up quickly from his desk, knocking over a cup of wine and trying to swallow his food whole.

"Priestess," he choked. And then more clearly, "Priestess, how may I be of service?"

"You may show me to the prisoner Quintus Vedius Tacitus without delay."

It was the *without delay* part that troubled the prefect. Shouldn't he check with someone? "Priestess," he stammered. "Perhaps I could just send a messenger to get General Antony or Caesar…they are just in the Tabularium so it would only take a moment…"

Caesar, mulled Pomponia. Of course. Julius Caesar hadn't just left his great-nephew Octavian his fortune in his will, he had also left him the powerful Caesar name.

Knowing the weight this name gave him, Octavian now insisted on being called Caesar at all times and by all people. And why not? His name made him *divi filius* – the son of a god.

Apparently the only one who wouldn't do it was Marc Antony. It was bad enough that Julius Caesar hadn't left him so much as a dirty toga in his will. There was no way in Hades he would call the suckling Octavian by Caesar's name.

"You can get them if you wish," said Pomponia, "but I will see the prisoner now."

Exploiting the prefect's uncertainty, Pomponia strode past him. She didn't want to give him time to think or stall or come up with an option.

The prefect rubbed his head. What were his choices? He certainly couldn't restrain her. If he laid a hand on her, he would quickly find himself a tenant inside the very prison he guarded. Sending a silent message to an open-mouthed guard – *Go get Caesar! Go get General Antony!* – he fell into step beside the Vestal.

"My Lady, it's this way."

"Thank you, Prefect."

Within four or five steps, the light of the world disappeared and Pomponia found herself swallowed by dank darkness. Cold radiated out from the square blocks of stone that confined her like a tomb and she pulled her palla around herself more tightly.

With each cautious step into the black, airless space she felt more disconnected from the living world. Her elbows brushed the hard rock walls. Instinctively, she began to take shallow breaths and lowered her head.

The heavy stone roof hung impossibly in the air above her. It felt as though it could collapse at any moment and crush her. Tiny shafts of light managed to snake through the small chinks between the thick blocks of stone, but other than that there was no light.

Why had the prefect not brought a torch along? A dry, hacking cough emanated from somewhere within the stony gloom.

He doesn't want me to see what's in here, she realized.

And then a few feet ahead, the underworld appeared.

It was a small hole in the stone floor – no larger than a man's body – from the depths of which flickered a faint orange flame. A low murmur reverberated out of the hole. The voice of Hades.

No. She knew the voice. It was Quintus, in prayer.

Pomponia felt lightheaded. She had heard about this hole. Prisoners who were to be executed were thrown down it – literally *thrown* down it – to squat twelve feet underground in filth and fear until the day of their death.

It wasn't that long ago that Julius Caesar had defeated the mighty Gaul warlord Vercingetorix, chieftain of the Arvernie tribe, and then had him thrown down this very hole where he had rotted for five whole years.

The next time Vercingetorix saw the light of day was when he was pulled out of the hole for Caesar's triumph. He was paraded in the Forum before a jeering Roman mob, ultimately needing to be dragged along the cobblestone by a horse when his legs gave out. Men and women swore and spat at him. Children threw food and feces at him.

Two executioners lugged him onto the Rostra, tore off his clothes, and strangled him to death.

Pomponia had watched the whole thing. It had been a great day. The warrior king of the Gauls – Roman's greatest enemy – was dead. Hail Caesar.

Swallowing her dread, Pomponia lowered herself with as much dignity as possible onto her knees. The cold instantly sank into her bones. The stench from the pit was unimaginable.

"Quintus Vedius Tacitus," she called down.

The murmuring stopped. Shuffling. Pomponia leaned forward, straining her eyes to peer into the dimly-lit tunnel to the underworld.

A voice rose up from below. "Priestess Pomponia?"

No pretense, no conceit. Just fear and desperation.

"Yes, are you – "

"My father," his voice was hoarse. "Have you seen my father?"

"*Fiducia in diva*," said Pomponia. Trust in the goddess.

Pomponia sensed someone else in the space around her. Still kneeling, she turned around to look behind her.

"Lady Pomponia," said Marc Antony. "To what do we owe the honor of a Vestal's presence in such a hateful place?" An edge of impertinence.

Pomponia stood up and faced him squarely. "In the sacred name of Vesta, I command the release of this prisoner, Quintus Vedius Tacitus, citizen of Rome, priest of Mars, *causarius* soldier of Julius Caesar." She paused and then met his impertinence with her own. "And his father."

"I see – "

Another voice. This one younger and sharper. "Free the prisoners immediately."

Pomponia looked past Antony and, even in the faint light, could see the glimmer in Octavian's cool grey eyes.

"Caesar," said Pomponia. "Thank you."

"No, thank you, Priestess," said Octavian, "for bringing the innocence of this man and his father to our attention. They will be released at once and any claims against their estates shall be removed. Chaos reigns in Rome right now and such mistakes are lamentable." He took a step back. "Now please Lady Pomponia, let me escort you out. This is no place for a priestess of Vesta."

The daylight bore painful holes into Pomponia's eyes and she squinted as Octavian led her to her litter and an astonished Medousa. Pomponia had the inopportune urge to laugh. With her startled expression – eyes wide, mouth hanging open – Medousa looked a little like the wild-eyed Gorgon depicted on her pendant.

"I shall send some extra guards to accompany you back to the temple," said Octavian. "You have my word that all I have said will be done." He smiled. "My divine father had great respect for the Vestals. As Caesar, I intend to continue our friendship."

"I am happy to hear so," said Pomponia.

Over Octavian's shoulder, Antony spat on the ground near the entrance to the Carcer. A look of restrained irritation crossed Octavian's face. As allies, he and Antony were united in their hunt for Caesar's assassins. As men, however, they were oil and water.

Pomponia stepped into the lectica, followed by Medousa.

The litter-bearers lifted it off the ground and turned back the way they had come, with the crowd of enthralled onlookers tripping over each other to clear a path for them along the Via Sacra.

"Perhaps this Caesar is not all bad," Pomponia whispered to Medousa.

But her slave only huffed. The memory of the rich red tapestry that hung from the ceiling of Julius Caesar's lectica filled her mind's eye.

"If you've seen one Caesar, you've seen them all," she sneered.

CHAPTER V

THE SERPENT OF THE NILE

EGYPT 42 – 41 BCE

"Apollonius, if you give me one more papyrus to sign, I shall have you ripped apart by crocodiles in the bathhouse."

Tiredly, Queen Cleopatra slouched back into the carved wooden chair that sat in the middle of her large study within the Royal Palace. She threw the stylus at Apollonius, making a half-hearted attempt to hit him as a sleek brown cat leapt noiselessly onto her lap.

"Majesty," bowed the slave. He collected the scrolls that were scattered across the expanse of the queen's ornate desk, the surface and legs of which were inlaid with gold and lapis lazuli. "I will speak to Vizier Amenhotep about this, I believe there is much here that he can handle – "

"I'm hungry." Cleopatra snapped her fingers and a female slave knelt before her. "Iras, bring me some wine cake."

"Yes, Majesty."

As Apollonius leaved over the desk to gather the last papyrus scrolls and pile them neatly into a basket, Cleopatra's languid gaze settled on him. "Any news?"

"Only that General Antony and Caesar – "

Cleopatra struck him on the head. The cat jumped off her lap.

"...General Antony and *Octavian* are in Macedonia. All sources say that Brutus and Cassius have fled there."

"One pair of Roman wolves hunting another pair of Roman wolves." She snorted. "Typical."

Iras returned with a platter of wine cake and set it before the queen. Cleopatra picked at it without taking a bite. An oil lamp on her desk sputtered and she passed her hand back and forth over the flame, lost in thought.

"Majesty," said Apollonius, "will you be attending the Royal Library today? The curator humbly requests your approval on a new wing dedicated to Majesty's writings. I have seen it myself and it is quite splendid. There is a central reading area with your works on mathematics and astronomy, and then another for philosophy –"

"Yes, Apollonius." She pushed the wine cake aside and took a sip of honey water. "It's just a matter of time until a Roman wolf is at our door. The Royal Library needs to be protected. Certain works must be hidden."

"Romans are not accustomed to educated women, Majesty. Nor to queens. Regardless of which wolf wins, they will try to destroy your books. A strong woman makes them look weak. And you did make enemies during your time in Rome..."

Cleopatra rubbed her temples. "I did my best Apollonius, but they were such vapid oafs!" She winced at the memory. "During supper, they would gorge themselves on baked dormice and ostrich brains and crows baked in feathers, all of it washed down with a drink made of fish innards. Then when their bellies were distended, the worst of the gluttons would vomit it all up so that they could start again, all the while tonguing the breast of someone else's wife. It was unbearable. And forget trying to elevate the conversation to something above the groin! Oh there were some bright lights. I did enjoy Senator Cicero's company in the beginning. He was fascinated by Ptolemaic Egypt but then he had the gall to accuse me of mocking him about some book. I still have no idea what he was going on about." She tapped a finger on her desk, thinking back. "I blame it on grief. He changed after his daughter died, you know."

The brown cat lifted a paw to claw at the queen's dress, but she brushed it aside, standing. "Are the prisoners ready?" she asked.

"Of course, Majesty. They have been brought to the courtyard and all is prepared."

She strolled regally across the large brown and green tiles of the palace floor, past a colonnade of thick columns painted to look like towering palm trees, past a long row of larger-than-life statues of Egyptian gods and goddesses.

Isis, all-powerful goddess of marriage and wisdom, wearing a scarlet red dress and holding a cobra. Osiris, god of the underworld and husband to Isis, his skin painted green to symbolize the cycle of death and re-birth. Horus, the sun god and son of Isis and Osiris, his falcon head painted brilliant blue with a red and white crown atop it.

She felt a pang of nostalgia. She had walked this corridor many times with Caesar. He had stopped in his tracks directly in front of the statue of Tawaret, goddess of pregnancy and childbirth. With the head of a hippopotamus, arms and legs of a lion, tail of a crocodile and stomach of a pregnant woman, it had made him laugh out loud.

Cleopatra, he had said, *when I am dead, I fear my Egyptian statue will have the limbs of a tortoise, the tail of a camel and the head of an ass.*

Ah yes, my love, she had replied, *but I will make sure it is dressed in full Roman armor. How better to outfit a god with an ass for a head?*

As the brown cat trailed behind her, playfully pawing the back of her dress and catching his claws in the fabric, she strode past the chamber room in which she had first met Caesar. She had been so desperate then.

Her brother Ptolemy – that fat-cheeked, back-stabbing little bastard – and his push for sole power had forced her into the desert, on the run for her life, while he ingratiated himself to Caesar in her palace.

But she had always been smarter than he was. She had arranged to have herself rolled into a carpet – oh the stifling heat in there! – and carried into the palace as a gift to Caesar, and all of it right under Ptolemy's little pig nose.

The guards had unrolled the carpet at Caesar's feet and, to his astonishment, out tumbled the exiled Queen of Egypt herself, her gold bangles jingling and her royal diadem perched in her messy hair. Caesar had jumped to his feet in surprise and amusement.

They had talked all night in the flickering light, the scent of the castor oil in the lamps perfuming the air. When his eyes fell on her breasts, she had pulled him down onto the carpet, on top of her and they had made love until morning. The virgin Queen of Egypt lying under the Roman General Julius Caesar. It was the way he wanted it. It was the way it always had to be.

Soon after, Ptolemy's bloated body had been found floating in the Nile.

For the most part, it was a good arrangement. Caesar was a reasonable lord and he trusted her judgment. She had shown him Egypt's mysteries, including the great pyramids, and they had sailed along the Nile not just as lovers and allies, but as true friends.

She had taken him to the tomb of his hero Alexander the Great. He had stood with bated breath while she pulled back the drapery of Alexander's sarcophagus to reveal the warrior's mummified body. Caesar had been moved to tears by the sight of the great general's soft wisps of hair, and she had kissed his face dry.

They had so many plans. If a Roman general and an Egyptian queen could be lovers, could not Rome and Egypt be friends? She thought of the great library they were to build together in the Roman Forum. Even the Romans had welcomed the idea: Cicero and the high priestess Fabiana had both expressed their support, as had many of Caesar's friends and enemies alike.

Ah, but Caesar was gone. And so was the certainty of her reign. So was the stability of Egypt. So was the safety of her life and the life of Caesarion, her child with Caesar. When it came to Caesarion, it didn't matter which wolf won. Both sides would tear out his throat.

Caesar's assassins would never let a son of Caesar rule Egypt. One day he would seek to avenge his father's death – they knew that – and he was too much of a risk. And Antony and Octavian? Perhaps Antony would not care. But Octavian, that opportunistic little runt who had the gall to call himself Caesar, he would definitely want Caesarion's head on a spike. Two Caesars was one Caesar too many.

As Cleopatra approached the doors to the courtyard, two slaves pushed open the heavy doors and an explosion of hot sunlight burst into the palace. She squinted but kept walking until the smooth tile under her sandaled feet turned to sand-covered tile and the courtyard surrounded her on all sides.

Five wooden chairs sat in a semi-circle on the sandy tile of the courtyard. Four men in loin cloths and one woman in a short dress were tied to the chairs. Two of the men were writhing in pain, mouths bubbling sputum and eyes rolling in their sockets.

The queen sat on a long couch that faced the chairs, tucking her feet under her body and casually scooping up a spoonful of cool pomegranate seeds from a large silver bowl on a nearby table.

"Proceed," she ordered to no one in particular as she crushed the seeds between her teeth.

A man with a bright orange scarf around his head bowed before the queen. “Thank you, Majesty.” His voice was as gravely as the sand under his feet.

He gestured showily toward the semi-circle of chairs. “The first prisoner is experiencing arsenic poisoning, while the second is demonstrating the effects of a hemlock tincture. Both were administered thirty minutes ago.”

The first prisoner emitted a guttural groan of agony and vomited on his loincloth. The second jerked and then began to convulse so violently that his chair fell over. Two male palace slaves rushed over to prop it back up, only to have it topple over again a moment later.

The slaves looked uncertainly at each other and then shrugged at the queen before leaving the prisoner to seizure, still tethered to the chair, on the ground. A pool of urine spread out across the sand as the prisoner lost control of his bladder.

Cleopatra’s handmaid Charmion arrived to stand at the queen’s shoulder. She turned up her nose at the twitching, drooling prisoners.

“An undignified way to meet Osiris,” she said. “Bloated, retching and contorted in pain. Majesty will not give her enemies the satisfaction of seeing her like this.”

“If it comes to that,” qualified the queen.

“If it comes to that,” agreed Charmion. “If Majesty must take her own life, there are ways that are more becoming a queen.” She snapped her fingers at the man with the bright orange scarf. “The snakes now.”

Obligingly, the man knelt before the queen and Charmion as his assistant placed a long rectangular tray, upon which sat two round covered baskets, on the ground in front of him. The man opened one basket and expertly pulled out a yellowish-brown snake with a horned head and prominent brown cross bands extending down its length.

Still clutching the snake, he rose to his feet and approached the third male prisoner who shrieked in wide-eyed panic, desperately struggling against his restraints and pleading to the queen and the gods for mercy. Cleopatra crushed another mouthful of pomegranate seeds between her teeth.

The two slaves who had tried unsuccessfully to right the convulsing prisoner's chair each grabbed hold of the prisoner's head and tilted it back to expose his neck. The snake handler clamped the snake's jaw on the prisoner's neck and a trickle of blood ran down it.

They all stood back to give the queen a clear line of sight.

Cleopatra stopped chewing and looked at the prisoner with interest. Almost immediately, the prisoner cried out in pain and the area around the snake bite swelled into a hard ball the size of a man's fist. The skin around it bruised into an ugly purplish hue.

The prisoner tensed and then fell into a paralytic state. His bowels emptied. The orange-scarfed man's assistant quickly covered the foulness with a large embroidered silk blanket, silently cursing himself for not bringing a cheaper papyrus one.

I'll take a beating for this later, he thought.

Cleopatra cast a sideways glance at Charmion. "That won't do," she said.

"This one may be more suitable for her Majesty," said the snake hander. He lifted the cover off the second basket and diligently grasped the snake inside, holding it up for the queen's inspection. "Cobra."

The snake handler carried the ribbon-like animal to the last male prisoner and, as before, the prisoner opened his eyes and mouth wide, pleading for mercy. He cast his frantic eyes at the other prisoners.

The three other men were dead – and unpleasantly so. The female prisoner was staring straight ahead and muttering a prayer in a language that he didn't know.

Again, the two palace slaves jerked the prisoner's head back and the snake handler clamped the cobra's jaw on the exposed neck. They all moved aside and stared expectantly at the prisoner who, like them, also waited to see what the effects of the snake venom would be.

At first, nothing. And then the prisoner inhaled deeply, as if caught off-guard by a sudden shortness of breath. His breathing became shallow, labored, and his head fell backwards.

And that was it.

"A fitting death for a queen," said Charmion. She nodded approvingly to the orange-scarfed snake handler. "Bring me two or three of your best specimens in the morning," she ordered. "And a handler as well. We shall keep them at the palace."

"Yes, Lady," he said. "I am honored to be of service to her Majesty."

As the queen began to stand, the female prisoner felt a swell of relief in her body. Tears ran down her cheeks and she silently praised the gods.

"Majesty," said the snake handler. "If I may be so bold, may I suggest that you witness the effect on the female body…I have selected a woman of a similar size and weight to your Majesty." He waved his hand toward the female slave.

"Oh," said the queen. "I suppose that's wise. Carry on." She took another spoonful of pomegranate seeds from the silver bowl.

* * * * * *

My Queen, her royal astrology had said, *the signs are clear. General Antony and Octavian will defeat the assassins. They will avenge the father of your son. Then Antony will come to you.*

And so it had come to pass.

Brutus and Cassius were dead. Caesar was once again a powerful name in Rome. The unstoppable General Marc Antony was on his way to Egypt to meet with Cleopatra.

Cleopatra descended the six marble steps into a giant oval bath and sank to her neck in the hot goat's milk. Iras poured a pot of melted honey into the bath and Cleopatra swam languidly to stir the luxurious mixture. Still, she couldn't quite relax.

Antony's messenger had stated the official purpose of his master's imminent visit to Egypt: a diplomatic meeting to ensure that Queen Cleopatra would continue to send grain shipments to Rome. After all, the new leaders of the Roman world needed to feed the bellies of the masses.

But Cleopatra knew there was more to it. Antony would want to know why she had delayed so long in sending coin or reinforcements to help him in the hunt for Caesar's assassins.

What could she tell him? The truth was, she could not risk taking sides in the Roman conflict. What if the side she chose ultimately lost? She would be seen as a conspirator by the victors and any chances she had for keeping her throne would be gone.

A large oil lamp fastened to the aqua and brown mosaic wall sputtered and then ran dry and the room dimmed. Iras quietly scolded a slave who just as quietly poured more olive oil into the basin. The lamp flickered back to life.

Submerged in the hot milk and honey bath, Cleopatra fiddled with the smooth lapis lazuli gems of her bracelet and then slipped it off and tossed it onto the steamy tile floor at Iras's feet.

She chewed her lip and thought back to the Marc Antony she had known during her time in Rome. He was loud and fleshy and carnal, but she knew little about his personal habits or vices. Now, she had to rely on her spies who still resided in the city, those who moved in Antony's circles.

She needed to know: What were his interests? What wine did he like best? What did he prefer to eat? What entertainment did he take? What did he find amusing? What were his weaknesses? Most important of all, what kind of woman was he attracted to?

Cleopatra sighed. Yet another artless Roman man to seduce.

CHAPTER VI

AETERNA FLAMMA VESTAE

(THE ETERNAL FLAME OF VESTA)

ROME 40 BCE

It was the kalends of March. The day upon which the most sacred ritual in the Roman world took place: the renewal of Vesta's eternal flame in the temple.

The *Aeterna Flamma Vestae*, the Eternal Flame of Vesta, was the flickering soul of Rome and her people. Goddess of the home and hearth, Vesta resided in the fire which was kept alight year-round by her priestesses, the Vestals, Rome's only full-time and state-funded priesthood.

As long as Vesta's sacred fire burned in the Temple of Vesta in the Forum, Rome would go on. As long as Vesta's sacred fire burned in the homes of her faithful, their families would go on.

Thousands of people – patricians, plebs, freedmen, slaves – had crowded into the Roman Forum to surround the Temple of Vesta and bear witness to the renewal of the sacred flame. Even people from foreign lands who had adopted Vesta as a goddess of their own stood reverent and silent in witness of Rome's most important annual public ritual.

Scarlet red celebratory banners had been raised along the Via Sacra. The statuary, fountains, colonnades and splendid facades of the many other temples near the Temple of Vesta had all been scrubbed clean for the occasion, and the cobblestone had been swept bare.

Nonetheless, by mid-day the cobblestone around the temple was covered in wild picked flowers, mementoes and plates of food, all offerings to the goddess from her faithful.

In years past, Fabiana had instructed temple slaves to remove these offerings as quickly as they were placed; however, the Vestalis Maxima – whose health continued to decline – was too ill to participate and Pomponia had inherited the sacred duties and rites. She left the offerings where they lay.

The Temple of Vesta itself had been adorned with long garlands of fresh laurel that hung from its high frieze and wound around each of the twenty fluted Corinthian columns that encircled the raised white-marble podium of its base. It had been meticulously dressed it in greenery and white flowers according to tradition and High Priestess Fabiana's exacting specifications.

Through an opening at the apex of the temple's domed roof, smoke from Vesta's sacred fire billowed out and then began to taper off as the Vestal priestesses inside allowed the fire to weaken. The crowd kept close watch on the temple's entrance. Any moment, the Vestals would appear.

The temple's bronze door – which faced east, toward the sun as a source of life – was usually closed to protect the sanctity of the inner hearth; however, it remained open today, letting in the sunlight and prompting people to crane their necks to catch a glimpse inside the normally cloistered temple.

At last, Pomponia descended the temple's stairs in solemn procession with the other Vestals behind her. In her arms, she carried a large bronze bowl within which were the last embers of Vesta's sacred fire taken from the hearth.

Behind her, the elder Vestal Nona carried a small terra cotta figurine of High Priestess Fabiana. Tuccia was next, followed by the younger Caecilia and Lucretia.

The sight of the Vestals – dressed in their pure white ceremonial robes and headdresses – ignited a collective exclamation of awe from the gathered masses. Men, women and children lowered themselves to their knees in reverence, many tossing fresh-picked flowers at the feet of the priestesses.

Pomponia led the Vestals to the marble dais adjacent to the temple, upon which already stood the Pontifex Maximus, a stately man by the name of Marcus Aemilius Lepidus. Carefully, she climbed the flower-lined stairs and strode across the platform to set the bronze bowl on a pedestal.

The two pontifices – the Pontifex Maximus and the *de facto* Vestalis Maxima – stood side by side as the other Vestals lined up behind them.

To the left of the dais – a smaller version of the Rostra – sat a who's who of Roman religious society and Pomponia took a moment to acknowledge them with a respectful nod. The Flamines Maiores, High Priests of Jupiter and Mars, sat in places of honor with their subordinate priests close by.

Pomponia avoided looking at Quintus. Their awkward friendship had been over as quickly as it had begun. A few days after she had secured his release from the Carcer, Quintus's wife Valeria had appeared at the temple with a beautiful gold bracelet and expressions of tearful gratitude.

The next time Pomponia saw her, her eyes were blackened from her husband's fists.

Since then, Pomponia had become as adept at ignoring Quintus as he was at ignoring her, regardless of whether they were at a public function or passing in the street. They hadn't exchanged so much as a courteous head nod in almost three years, although he still found occasion now and then to cast a scolding glance her way. She looked past him to acknowledge the Rex Sacrorum and the public augurs.

To the right of the dais sat just about everyone else of note in Rome, most notably Octavian with his sister Octavia, as well as Marcus Agrippa, Octavian's brilliant general and closest friend, and his political advisor Gaius Maecenas.

The rest of the chairs were taken up by senators, praetors, aediles and other magistrates, as well as visiting provincial governors and members of the wealthiest, most noble families in the city. Pomponia smiled inwardly to notice that Marc Antony was still absent; still in Egypt, talking grain with Queen Cleopatra. Although if the rumors were true, it wasn't all business.

Sprawling out before them all, stretching as far as the eye could see into the great Forum, was the rest of Rome standing shoulder to shoulder between the colossal, vibrantly-colored temples made variously of marble, brick and wood.

To make room for the crowds, Octavian had banned the presence of litters, livestock and market stands in the Forum until after the official renewal ceremony was over. A roaming squadron of eagle-eyed soldiers kept watch for transgressors.

A shout went up. "Bless us, Priestess Pomponia!" A swelling cheer.

"I bless you in the name of Mother Vesta," said Pomponia. She heard the authority, the commanding certainty, in her own voice. Fabiana was a meticulous teacher.

She had presided as acting Vestalis Maxima in several rituals and festivals over the past year: the Lupercalia, last year's renewal ceremony, the Fordicidia, even the opening of the penus Vestae – the annual opening of the inner sanctum of the temple to Roman matrons – during the Vestalia. With each festival, with each new responsibility, the natural ease with which she performed her duties and the Vestal rites increased.

The Pontifex Maximus bowed his head in respect to Pomponia and then put his hands out to address the crowd. They fell silent.

"Many generations ago," Lepidus began with a flourish, "our great ancestor the Trojan prince Aeneas fled the burning city of Troy with his family. From his royal bloodline sprang the kings of Alba Longa, including King Numitor, father of the Vestal priestess, Rhea Silvia. The priestess was beloved of the goddess Vesta, but another god also loved her – Mars, the god of war."

A thousand pairs of eyes were on her; yet Pomponia suddenly felt the weight of a hotter gaze. She looked at Quintus. He was staring at her.

The Pontifex spoke on. "One night as the priestess slumbered, the god Mars came to her, coupled with her, and put life in her belly."

Pomponia had heard the story – the story of Rome – a thousand times. This time seemed different. She looked away from Quintus and then back. His gaze hadn't let up.

"Rhea Silvia gave birth to twins, two boys whom she named Romulus and Remus. But her father's enemies learned of the children and, fearing the powerful men the boys would grow to be, they ripped the children from their mother's arms. They took the infants deep into the forest and left them there, exposed to nature's cruel elements, to die."

A snap from the sacred embers called Pomponia's attention away from Quintus's unrelenting stare and back to the bronze bowl in front of her. She placed her hands on the edges of the bowl as if protecting the last of the life within it.

"But Mars would not permit his sons by the priestess to perish. He sent a she-wolf to protect them. The she-wolf took the infants to her den where she warmed them, suckled them and let them grow into the image of their divine father. And when the boys were grown to men, they followed the she-wolf to a grassy hill – the place we now know as the Palatine Hill – where they desired to build a city of their own. But the brothers had the spirit of the war-god Mars within them and soon began to quarrel over who would lead the city. To end the conflict, Mars sent them an augur who divined that Romulus would build a city, an eternal city, a city that would rule the world. Jealous, Remus sought to slay his brother, but Romulus prevailed and his people named their city Rome in his honor."

Damn him to Hades, thought Pomponia. *He's still looking at me.* She kept her eyes fixed on the dying embers in the bowl.

"In honor of his mother, the Vestal priestess, Romulus built a hearth upon the ground within which burned the sacred fire of Vesta. Around this hearth he built Rome itself and from this hearth the earliest Romans took flame to burn the sacred fire in their homes. His successor King Numa built a temple around the hearth and appointed a priesthood of chaste women to tend it, night and day, so that Vesta's eternal flame would forever be the soul of eternal Rome."

The Pontifex pulled back a heavy red cloth that lay over a gold bowl and Pomponia reached into the bowl to pull out a smooth stone.

"Art thou on the watch, heaven-born Aeneas?" Pomponia called out the sacred rites. "Keep watch." As she spoke, she crushed the last embers in the bronze bowl with the stone, extinguishing the sacred fire.

"O Vesta," she called out. Thousands of palms turned upward in supplication and prayer to the goddess. She reached back into the gold bowl to pull out an iron striker and piece of stone flint. As she did, the Pontifex placed a new bronze bowl on the podium before her. Fresh tinder lay on the bottom.

"Great goddess," called out Pomponia. "First and last, your humble priestess begs you to breathe your sacred spirit into this flame as we renew your eternal fire."

As she had practiced countless times since she first took her vows to Vesta as a seven-year-old child, Pomponia lowered her hands into the bronze bowl and struck the flint against the iron striker once, twice, a third time. Sparks flew into the tinder and it began to smoke.

A moment later, an infant flame crackled to life. Its red embers spread through the tinder as its flickering orange flame reached out in search of more material to consume.

Lepidus put his hands in the air and a buoyant cheer of celebration washed through the crowd. For many people, the day's renewal ceremony wasn't just about renewing the sacred fire or keeping tradition alive. It was about renewing their own lives and commitment to their families.

Pomponia added more tinder to the bronze bowl and the fire crackled louder. A loud fire was a good sign. The cracks and snaps were the voice of the goddess speaking to her faithful. But what was the goddess saying to her?

She looked from the flames to Quintus and felt a hammer of emotion: he was still staring at her. She held his gaze for a moment – did his eyes soften? – but then his eyes took on that cold, condescending glare she remembered all too well and she turned away.

With all reverence, Pomponia lifted the bronze bowl and cradled it in her arms, leading the procession of Vestals back into the temple's inner sanctum to transfer the new fire into the ancient hearth. The bronze door closed behind them.

Moments later, plumes of smoke began to once again rise through the opening in the temple's domed roof.

The priests, politicians and dignitaries on either side of the dais stood up, stretched their legs and began to mix and mingle. The crowd broke apart and the celebrations spread noisily throughout the Forum, spilling into the streets and backstreets of Rome. Men shouted, women gossiped, children shrieked and dogs barked.

Vendors hastily set up tables to sell their wares and prostitutes lifted their dresses to do the same.

But Quintus Vedius Tacitus only stared at the closed bronze door of the Temple of Vesta.

* * * * * *

By mid-afternoon, the celebrations had spilled into the Campus Martius, the sprawling public land dedicated to Mars, where a hoard of Romans drank in the taverns and bathed in the public baths. Thousands packed into the amphitheatre to watch the wild animal hunts and gladiator matches. Some prayed in the temples, while those less pious visited the brothels.

In addition to marking the renewal of the sacred flame of Vesta, the kalends of March also marked the birthdate of Mars himself. Such an auspicious day presented political opportunities that Octavian, Rome's new Caesar, wasn't about to pass up.

Earlier that day, Octavian had made a massive donation to the Vestal order. Now, as he presided over a public sacrifice in the Temple of Mars in the Campus Martius, he was also promising to build two new temples in Rome.

Pomponia stood somberly beside the grand marble Altar of Mars as Octavian spoke. It had been a long day and she wished she could have stayed in the temple to tend the fire; however, a Vestal presence was required at all religious and civil ceremonies in the city.

At least she had help. Tuccia and Medousa were with her. In fact, it would've been impossible to keep Tuccia away. The day's events were to end with a much-anticipated chariot race between the Greens and the Blues in the Circus Maximus and Tuccia – who was obsessed with the races – would have sulked openly if she couldn't attend.

"At this moment, the foundation of a temple to the divine Julius is being laid on the very spot of his funeral pyre in the Roman Forum," Octavian's clear, commanding voice boomed outward. "It will stand only steps away from the sacred Temple of Vesta. In honor of the goddess's life-giving light, in honor of the star that shone over my divine father's funeral pyre, this temple shall be known as the Temple of the Comet Star."

A happy cheer – but it wasn't just for the temple. To the delight of the masses, Octavian's generosity extended beyond the construction of public buildings. The day's celebration included massive gifts of bread, wine and coin that were being distributed throughout the city.

And the more people ate, drank and put into their purses, the more they liked their new Caesar.

"As Romans, we all share in the victory over my divine father's assassins. Thanks must be given to Mars Ultor, Mars the Avenger! That is why, out of my own purse, I also pledge to build the Temple of Mars Ultor in the Forum of Caesar where the Priests of Mars shall daily make sacrifice to my victory at Philippi!"

Another happy, wine-fuelled cheer.

Shuffling and a loud bellow. Everyone turned their heads to see the sacrificial white bull being led to the temple. Its mighty head was topped with laurel and its muscular body was draped in strings of colorful flowers. A chorus of impressed murmurs ran through the crowd.

"*Favete linguis*," said Octavian, signifying the start of the sacrifice. He took a step back to make way for the magnificent beast and all fell silent.

Pomponia's stomach dropped to see that Quintus was at the animal's head, gripping the gold nose ring in its flared nostrils and pulling it toward the altar. He was dressed in a long white woolen robe that was belted at the waist and he wore a laurel wreath on his head; the ceremonial attire of a higher priest of Mars. He looked handsome.

She clutched the bowl of sacred wafers in her hands. *Why must he lead the beast?* But she knew it wasn't his choice. Like her, he was bound to the rites and rituals of his god. Like her, he performed the duties his High Priest put upon him. And guessing from his attire and position, he was being groomed as the next Flamen Martialis.

She met Quintus's eyes for a moment and then stared at the marble altar. On top, a bronze bowl burned with Vesta's fire and incense pots sent fragrant smoke to Mars. A gold cup held the priest's libation wine. In the center, a long silver blade waited to perform the killing stroke.

As Quintus grew nearer – they would be uncomfortably close during this ritual – her eyes dipped down to study the colorful relief carvings of battles and horses and legions that adorned the altar. Her eyes hesitated over one scene: the god Mars crouched over the sleeping Vestal Rhea Silvia.

In the carving, the priestess's robes had fallen off her shoulders to reveal her bare breasts and the mighty god gazed down passionately at them. He reached out one hand, about to touch her, while the other moved his cloak aside to expose his arousal.

When Pomponia next looked up, Quintus was standing only an arm's length away. One hand clutched the gold ring in the bull's nose and the other held a length of rope that attached to a loose halter around its giant white head. The animal was docile, having been hand-raised for this purpose, and contentedly chewed at whatever was in its mouth.

The Flamen Martialis approached the altar and laid his hand on it. "*Salutem divinus Janus, divina Vesta*," he said, beginning the ceremony with the traditional prayer to Janus and Vesta. "O Father Mars, we pray and beseech thee to be merciful and gracious. We pray and beseech thee to fill the hearts of our sons with courage. We pray and beseech thee to bless our land and strengthen our households. To you, *Mars pater*, we offer this pure beast as testimony of our will and devotion."

Pomponia took two large salt wafers from her bronze bowl and then set the bowl on the altar. Quintus pulled downward on the bull's nose ring, compelling it to lower its head, so that she could more easily lift the wafers over the tall beast's head.

As he did, Pomponia noticed his hands. They were large and strong and the muscles of his forearms rippled under his robe as he clung to the nose-ring and rope. Wide gold cuffs encircled his wrists and he wore a single gold intaglio ring. She squinted at the image of the god on the carnelian stone. Not Mars. Vesta.

"*Vesta purificat vos,*" she said. Vesta purifies you. She crumbled the mola salsa wafers over the bull's head.

"*Ad deos,*" said the Flamen Martialis. To the gods. He took the wine-filled gold cup from the altar and took a sip from it, then passed it to Pomponia who did the same.

According to custom, she then offered the cup out to Quintus – and then immediately realized that he could not let go of the animal. She held the cup to his lips. Pomponia watched his throat move as he swallowed the wine and she felt her skin flush. She had performed this custom many times with priests; however, this time it felt strangely…intimate. She set the cup on the altar.

"*Victimarius*," the Flamen Martialis called out. At that, a man in a black robe approached the altar and gripped the handle of the silver dagger upon it.

"Step up, Priestess," Quintus commanded under his breath. The same brash, reproaching tone.

She cursed herself. Why was she so distracted? Lifting her stola, she stepped onto the two-stair marble elevation alongside the altar. As she did, Quintus raised the bull's head and the victimarius – the sacrificial servant – opened its neck in one deep, skilled stroke.

Without so much as a groan, the bull fell onto its front knees and then collapsed onto its side, its breath heaving for a moment before stopping altogether. Blood pooled out over the marble and around Pomponia's step. Much of it was absorbed by the sand that had been liberally sprinkled around the altar, but rivers of red still ran outward over the marble to soil the priests' sandals and spill over the edge of the platform onto the soft earth.

"*Gratias divinus Janus, divina Vesta*," said the Flamen Martialis. The ceremony was over.

Thank the goddess, thought Pomponia.

As the haruspices approached the dead animal to open it up and inspect its entrails for omens good or bad, Pomponia lifted her stola to her ankles and stepped down onto the salt-and-blood covered marble floor. She felt like her own insides had been exposed for the world to see; however, no one seemed to have noticed the tension between her and the priest of Mars.

But in fact, someone had. Quintus's wife.

It didn't take long for the crowd that had gathered in front of the temple to thin out. Most people were scrambling to catch the rest of the day's chariot races at the Circus Maximus. Others were scattering into other areas of the Campus Martius where Caesar's bread, wine and coin were calling. Pomponia would have liked to leave as well; however, Tuccia was busy laughing with a number of senators and priests, all of them arguing about the races, laying bets and insulting each other's favorite horses and charioteers.

Distractedly, Pomponia clutched the heavy white woolen palla that Medousa – when had she appeared? – wrapped around her shoulders.

"You're shivering, Domina."

"It's chilly."

"It's warm enough." Medousa's beautiful face was stone.

Pomponia pulled the palla tight around herself. Her slave didn't miss a thing. They stepped silently into the Vestal's ornate golden litter, the gold and red colored curtains pulled back to wait for Tuccia who finally dove in, glowing and grinning, to sit opposite Pomponia.

"I have five hundred *sesterce* riding on the Blues," said Tuccia, "and I'll have Persephone herself toss that twit charioteer Flavius's balls into the underworld if he wraps himself around the spina in the first lap again."

"Flavius has more curses on his head than a poxed whore," said Medousa. They laughed at their own flippant bawdiness. It was a release from the day's strict rituals and solemn religiousness.

Enjoying the sense of relief that was finally washing over her, Pomponia tiredly reached down to pull on a sandal strap. "My feet hurt."

"Oh stop complaining," said Tuccia. "At least it isn't raining. It's been good signs all day."

"Give me your foot, Domina," said Medousa. She began to loosen Pomponia's sandal straps, but Pomponia slapped her hands away.

"Leave it. It'll just hurt worse when you tie them back up." She leaned back on the cushions inside the lectica, wishing it were her own bed, and closed her eyes.

* * * * * *

When Pomponia next opened her eyes, Tuccia was slipping out of the litter with a determined look on her face. They had arrived at the Circus Maximus. The races had already been underway for hours and she didn't want to miss another lap.

Pomponia exhaled and wondered how Tuccia still had so much energy. They had been up since well before dawn. An energizing thought occurred to her: perhaps Quintus would be at the races as well. She felt a sudden longing – a hope to see him again – and she swore at herself. She could sense it was happening. Despite their cool interactions and his typical unpleasantness, she was finding it more difficult to ignore the flush that came over her in his presence.

She would have to talk to Fabiana about it. Vesta's priestesses served the goddess during those years that the body's desire was at its strongest and at twenty-two years old Pomponia knew that her body's instincts would work against her sacred duty.

It was expected that natural feelings would arise in a Vestal; however, it was also expected that they would be suppressed through a strict regimen of prayer and medicinal remedies. Fabiana had already prescribed such a regimen to Tuccia and even the younger Vestal Lucretia. Both applied camphor oil to their breasts twice daily, using the scent to quell desire. They also ate the berries from the Chaste Tree at every meal to resist the passions that Venus placed in their hearts.

While sexual indulgence was strictly forbidden – every Vestal knew the horrific punishment for incestum – Vestal priestesses nonetheless enjoyed the distraction of other physical indulgences. The House of the Vestals was as luxurious as any palace or upper-class estate in Rome, with private rooms and the finest of baths, libraries and gardens. Vestals ate the most sumptuous of foods and their every need was tended to by slaves.

Still, the sight of Quintus's strong hands gripping the bull's rope lingered in Pomponia's thoughts. She heard his whisper, deep and masculine, in her ear. *Step up, Priestess.*

Forcing the memory from her mind, she slid out of the litter after Tuccia. Medousa followed on her heels.

Even before they entered the stadium, their eardrums throbbed from the sounds of the races.

The thunderous sound of hooves pounding the sand. The loud roar of wooden chariot wheels shaking and straining under high-speed pressure. The slap of the charioteers' whips on the backs of the sweating horses. The constant, deafening din of the crowd as over one hundred thousand spectators cheered for their favorites and jeered at their foes.

Vendors lined the entrance to the Circus Maximus, selling wine and fresh sausage, and the smell made Pomponia's stomach rumble. She tried not to think about food as the guards escorted her, Tuccia and Medousa to Caesar's private seats. Normally, they would sit in the area reserved for Vestals; however, with most of the priestesses busy at the temple, Octavian had invited them to join his family and friends.

"Ah, Priestess Pomponia," said Octavian, rising to greet her. "Welcome. And welcome to you, Priestess Tuccia."

"Thank you, Caesar," said Pomponia. "I hope we haven't missed the final race between the Greens and the Blues. Tuccia has a small fortune riding on it."

Octavian grinned widely at Tuccia. "As do I, Lady. Greens or Blues?"

"The Blues," said Tuccia. She turned to him coyly. "And I am certain that Caesar would never bet against a Vestal."

"*Numquam mille annos*," Octavian replied lightly. Never in a thousand years. "Ladies, please sit." Graciously, he seated Pomponia and Tuccia on either side of his sister Octavia. She wore a white stola – not unlike a Vestal – although it boasted rich purple embroidery that complemented the deep purple stripe on her brother's toga.

Octavian returned to sit next to his general Agrippa as a row of Praetorian guards stood behind them all, keeping vigilant watch over their master while their crested helmets and gleaming armor advertised Caesar's power to the citizens of Rome.

The massive oval of the Circus Maximus, the oldest and largest racetrack in Rome, spread out in the long valley below Pomponia. Waving, shouting fans lined its mile-long circumference as four teams of four-horse chariots thundered down the track, shaking the ground and taking the turn around the spina at breakneck speed.

"Priestess Pomponia," said Octavia, "forget the chariot races. Let's bet on which one of us most wishes she were home right now sitting in a hot bath."

Pomponia laughed. She had always liked Octavia. And despite Octavian's obvious efforts to nourish a friendship between the two women – such an alliance could only benefit his position – the truth was that their friendship needed no encouragement from him.

Octavia leaned toward her discreetly. "It hasn't been officially announced yet," she said, "but it looks like I'm to be married."

"Oh? To whom?" asked Pomponia.

"To Marc Antony. It's no secret that he and my brother have had strained relations. Caesar believes such a marriage will strengthen their alliance."

"Oh..."

"You don't approve, Pomponia?"

"It's not that..."

"I've heard the rumors about him and Cleopatra," said Octavia.

"Are they only rumors?"

Octavia looked sideways at Pomponia. "Of course not. Everyone knows they've been having an affair. Although I cannot blame Antony. He's only a man and you remember what Cleopatra was like. Every man in Rome was fascinated by her."

"Men are always fascinated by novelty," said Pomponia. "Roman men are accustomed to Roman women. Cleopatra was something different. She wasn't ruled by a man, she ruled over men. She didn't whisper with other women in the garden, but rather dominated conversation with men in the *triclinium*. She didn't wrap her palla around her shoulders in modesty, but rather let her gown cling to her breasts as tightly as a senator clings to his purse."

Octavia grinned. "Well, Antony will have to make due with a wife who wears looser-fitting clothing, I'm afraid. My brother believes that women should be virtuous in all things, including dress. He'd have me outfitted as a Vestal priestess if custom allowed it."

"This Caesar, like the one before him, is a great friend to the Vestal order." She smiled warmly at Octavia. "And I am certain the affection Caesar and Antony have for you will be a bond between them. It will strengthen their alliance and maintain the peace. All of Rome will have you to thank for that."

The crowd erupted into a sudden roar and Pomponia and Octavia stood up, along with tens of thousands of other spectators, just in time to catch a glimpse of a green and silver chariot bounce into the air, flip over and land hard on the track, flying apart into wooden splinters.

"Where's the charioteer?" asked Pomponia.

"There he is," said Octavia, pointing at a pair of legs – one of them bent at an impossible angle – lying under the pile of large wooden fragments. "Oh, and there's the rest of him." The charioteer's head and torso lay on the sand a few meters away. His body had been severed in half from the force of the impact and from the reins that he had wrapped tightly around his waist.

The crowd erupted into an even louder roar as another chariot approached the wreck at full speed. It was too late to maneuver and the driver had no choice but to trample the body of his competitor, mashing what was left of him into the sand.

"Normally I prefer the races to the games," said Octavia," but not today."

"I remember watching an elephant hunt once when I was a child, and Senator Cicero said – " Pomponia bit her lip. What a stupid thing to say.

"I am sorry, Pomponia," said Octavia. "My brother deeply regrets the loss of Cicero. He was a shrewd politician and a true Roman, and would have been a valuable advisor to Caesar." She folded her hands in her lap and spoke more privately. "Octavian bartered tirelessly for Cicero's life, but Antony was immovable. It threatened to undermine their alliance, so Octavian finally conceded."

"Let's hope a softer voice can temper Antony's nature," said Pomponia.

Octavia nodded. "Yes, let's hope." She opened her mouth to say something else, thought twice, and smiled pleasantly instead. "Bad luck for that driver," she said airily. "I don't know if you follow the races, but he drove as a slave for ten years and was just granted his freedom a month ago. In fact, I think this might have been his first race as a freedman."

"Tuccia is the race fanatic," said Pomponia. "I cheer for whomever she's cheering for. I've found she's easier to live with that way."

A female slave with a platter bowed before Octavia and the Vestals. "Mint water, Dominas?"

They all took a glass and Pomponia had to stop herself from draining the cool, refreshing liquid in one swallow. To her delight, the slave returned moments later with a selection of pears, oysters and cold pork cuts. Gold cups filled with good wine followed.

Pomponia's stomach had just settled when a familiar deep voice made it flip.

"…yes, it took longer than expected, Caesar. The haruspices think the more time it takes them to study the entrails, the more impressed we are at their divinations. They mistake our relief for awe."

"Do you know the old haruspex Longinus?" asked Agrippa. "May the gods either help you or slay you if you put a pig liver in front of that man! He'll poke it and interpret for hours, and then say the signs are unclear and start over with a different pig. And all to hear his own shrill voice prophesize. He could talk the ears off a donkey and the donkey would be grateful for the silence."

"Thank merciful Fortuna he retired last year, General, but there's always another. *Semper idem.* It's always the same thing with haruspices."

Pomponia willed herself to make small talk with Octavia, doing her best to ignore the sound of Quintus's voice and the looming presence of his body standing next to her. But it wasn't to be.

"Ah, Lady Pomponia, your colleague Quintus is here," said Octavian. "What good fortune to have the both of you here today. With Vesta and Mars on the side of Caesar, what need have we of haruspices? The signs can only be good."

Pomponia offered Quintus an obligatory formal smile. Her blood quickened in anger as he turned back to Caesar without so much as acknowledging her presence.

"Caesar, rumor has it that you will be the next Pontifex Maximus. Has Lepidus tired of ceremony so soon?"

"Lepidus tires of anything that requires work," said Octavian. "But I expect he will keep his office as long as possible. Still, I look forward to the appointment. My divine father performed his solemn duty as chief pontiff, and I desire to someday do the same."

A clamor rose from the track and Pomponia blinked to see fresh chariots charge out of the starting gate. She had been so distracted by Quintus's arrival that she hadn't even noticed one race had ended and another begun.

As the horses charged down the track, their hooves kicking sand into the air, the chattering ceased and everyone took their seats to watch. Pomponia's chest tightened as Quintus sat in the empty seat next to her.

She watched him out of the corner of her eye, careful to appear as though captivated by the race below. He sat rigidly in his chair, setting his hands on his lap and then awkwardly placing them on the armrests. He cleared his throat.

"There's a lot of money riding on the heads of these drivers," he said, making a clumsy attempt at small talk. "Which man do you favor, Priestess?"

"I favor no man in particular." The words had a more bitter edge than she had intended.

He said nothing. Then softly, almost intimately, "Pomponia..." but he caught himself and stopped.

The unexpected softness of his voice struck Pomponia harder than she could have imagined. She hadn't heard a man say her name plainly, without an honorific before it, since she was a child. She felt a flutter deep in her stomach and her throat tightened as if tears would follow.

Quintus had exposed himself simply by the way he had uttered her name. And in that one moment, he had shattered years of pretense between them.

CHAPTER VII

THE ALTAR OF JUNO

ROME 40 BCE

"The augers are good for a wedding. Too bad the groom is already drunk as Bacchus on the Liberalia."

The Vestalis Maxima Fabiana laughed under her breath at her own joke. Pomponia smiled mischievously at her. It was wonderful to see the high priestess feeling well enough to leave her bed, and even better to see glimmers of her usual audaciousness shine through the sickness that had plagued her for months.

Marc Antony and Octavia Minor stood under a sky-blue canopy before the Altar of Juno, goddess of marriage, as a robed and hooded priest said incantations to Jupiter.

Upon the altar was an oil lamp that burned with the sacred flame of Vesta, a gold cup of wine, the wedding cake and the marriage contract. Wedding torches burned on either side of the altar.

The bride looked beautiful. Fresh, duteous and the living image of Roman tradition, although many of the wedding guests privately suspected this was to please her powerful brother more than her new husband.

She wore a pretty white tunica tied at the waist with the nodus Herculaneum, the knot of Hercules, a symbol of her fidelity to her husband. The knot was believed to be so strong that only the demi-god Hercules or a loving husband could unfasten it to enjoy the pleasures it protected. A vivid orange veil covered her face, and upon her head was a wreath of flowers and fragrant herbs.

Her hair was arranged in the seni crines, the ancient and customary hairstyle of Roman brides and Vestal Virgins. Following strict custom, it had been parted with the tip of a spear. Not only was the spear sacred to Juno, it hearkened back to the earliest marriages in Rome when the first generation of Roman men abducted – at the point of their spears – women from the neighboring Sabine tribe.

The groom looked resigned. He wore a royal-blue tunic, gathered at his thick waist with a gold belt. The wide gold cuffs around his forearms looked like manacles. He was blinking just a little too slowly, obviously feeling the effects of his pre-marital reveling.

Bona Dea, thought Pomponia. *It's like Europa and the bull! May Juno protect her.*

The priest said a final prayer to Juno as Octavia stood regally and Antony rocked on his heels. Octavian stood behind his sister with his palms up to the gods. He watched, like an all-powerful overseer, as the priest poured wine over the wedding cake on the altar as a libation to the gods and then placed the right hands of the bride and groom together.

The hooded priest wound a white band of cloth around the forearms of Antony and Octavia, "binding" them together as husband and wife. Stepping forward, Octavian lifted the corolla of flowers and herbs from Octavia's head and raised the veil off her face so she and Antony could exchange the traditional vows said at every Roman wedding.

"*Ubi tu Gaius, ego Gaia,*" said Octavia. As you are Gaius, I am Gaia.

"*Ubi tu Gaia, ego Gaius,*" said Antony. As you are Gaia, I am Gaius.

Two people becoming one person.

Or at least that's the idea, thought Pomponia. *There's no way in Hades that Antony really loves her. But then again, marriage is business, not pleasure.*

Antony took Octavia's left hand and slipped a gold ring onto the third finger, around the *vena amoris* – the vein of love – that traveled from the third finger directly to the heart. She did the same, although with more difficulty. Antony's thick, battle-scarred fingers seemed to resist the shackle, but he shoved the ring on with a grunt and then smirked.

Next, the priest held out his arm to Octavian, indicating it was time for him as the *pater familias*, the male head of the household, to give his sister to her husband's care. Bending over the altar, Octavian pressed the wax red seal of Caesar onto the marriage contract.

The priest uncovered his head to show that the ceremony was complete and the wedding guests erupted into applause. If this marriage lasted, so too would peace in Rome. Many stood and threw grain onto the new couple to promote their fertility.

"If the grain sprouts, it will only be a burden to her," Fabiana whispered to Pomponia. "Take me to the litter, my dear. I will rest on the way to Caesar's house and we will offer our sympathies" she winked playfully "I mean our *congratulations* there."

"It warms my heart to see you well," said Pomponia.

She linked her arm through Fabiana's arm and escorted her toward the waiting Vestal litter, noticing just how frail the chief Vestal had become in recent months.

A sudden crash behind them made them both spin around just in time to see Antony clutching the side of a table to regain balance as two slaves hurriedly mopped up the shattered wine jug at his feet. Octavia was apologizing to those whose togas and gowns were splattered with wine.

Bona Dea, thought Pomponia again. *She hasn't been married long enough to boil asparagus and she's already making excuses for her husband.*

As she helped Fabiana into the lectica and then stepped in after her, Pomponia thanked the goddess for making her a priestess and freeing her from the obligation to marry. As a Vestal, she would step down from the order – if she so wished – with wealth, property and privilege.

As a Vestal, even a retired one, she would never be forced to marry a man she didn't want to marry, nor would she ever be subordinate to a husband's will or whims. She would never be forced to bear children for him, again and again, until her body wore out in the quest to give him the perfect son he could parade around as his legacy.

She had seen countless women endure the rigors and risks of pregnancy, only to have Pluto drag them to the underworld in the midst of their fear and screaming agony, with or without the child inside them. And as often as not, the grieving husband had a new wife in his bed before his old wife's ashes had even cooled.

Talk about a thankless job.

Pomponia arranged her stola and glanced at Fabiana. The high priestess was resting her head against the cushioned side of the lectica, her eyelids already struggling to stay open.

"Sleep, Fabiana," said Pomponia.

Quietly, she instructed the litter-bearers to wait so the high priestess could rest. There was plenty of time. Judging by how freely the wine and conversation were flowing, it would be a while before the wedding guests all made their way to Caesar's house. She sighed contentedly, sat back, and watched it all from the comfort of the lectica.

With a raucous laugh, Antony extinguished one of the wedding torches and passed it to Octavia who jovially tossed it high into the air. Male and female guests scrambled at once to retrieve it. It was good luck to catch the wedding torch. And for those who were still single, it portended imminent marriage.

Pomponia wrinkled her nose.

Hercules couldn't force that wretched thing into my hands, she thought, *even if it does burn with Vesta's flame.*

* * * * * *

The first thing that always stood out to Pomponia about Octavian's home was the fact that nothing stood out about it.

Located on the Palatine Hill, Caesar's home was strategically close to the ancient *casa Romuli* – the hut of Romulus, Rome's legendary founder. The casa Romuli had been damaged and restored more times than anyone could remember, but still it stood as it had for centuries: a small, round, single-room peasant house that Romulus himself had once called home.

While Caesar's palatial home was definitely an improvement on the rough walls and thatched roof of the casa Romuli, it was nonetheless far more modest than many of the homes owned by senators and families of patrician or even equestrian rank. His comparably simple living reflected his personal desire for purity in all things.

Yet Pomponia knew that Octavian's penchant for modesty was as much about propaganda as it was about personal preference. He led by example, promising the Roman people that his rule would usher in a return of Rome's most honored virtues.

Pietas: sacred loyalty to one's family, past and present. *Gravitas*: the development of a dignified, thoughtful and strong character.

After the violent uncertainty that had infected Rome following the assassination of Julius Caesar and during the bloody years of the proscriptions – for a while, it had been every man for himself – Romans of all classes were once again aspiring to these traditions and holding them up as the virtues that brought glory to the eternal city. Rome had come out of the darkness, back into the light.

And Octavian was carrying the torch. He wore the traditional toga and insisted that all male citizens do the same. He required the female members of his family, especially his sister Octavia, to dress in the traditional stola and encouraged all Roman women to have more children. More Romans!

He sang the praises of the traditional Roman matron while simultaneously proposing laws and policies that advanced the rights of women, finding precedent in the old Republic and citing Cato the Elder: "A man who strikes his wife or child lays violent hands on the holiest of holy things."

To Octavian, Rome was a mixture of tradition, virtue and family. And by the gods, he was determined to make sure his vision of Rome was realized.

Not that anyone was offering a contrary vision. It had been a long time since Rome had been so united and hopeful. Octavian had been a merciless butcher during his rise to power. Once established as Caesar, however, he had become remarkably beneficent, even good-humored.

Like the two-faced god Janus, thought Pomponia. *Let's just hope his benign face isn't a mask.*

No doubt others had similar hopes. Despite the unified front and political alliance between he and Antony, Octavian was clearly becoming the lead wolf in the pack. Pomponia had always known that was inevitable. The name "Caesar" had a commanding, king-like ring to it. And most kings shared a similar character trait: a strong preference to rule alone.

Nonetheless, there were high hopes that the union between Antony and Octavian's sister would forge a genuine bond between two men who were as different as wine and water. It would take the blessing of Juno and the luck of Fortuna, but perhaps this marriage could serve as sweet balm to Rome's wounds. Perhaps Octavia would be the one to finally leash Antony. Perhaps she would be able to break the spell that senators and gossips alike believed Queen Cleopatra had placed on him.

But how long would the proud general be content to play second man to the upstart Octavian who, brother-in-law or not, was twenty years his junior? How long before one wolf lunged at the throat of the other and Rome once again convulsed like a beast with its head cut off?

Despite herself, Pomponia smirked as she remembered Medousa's typically plain and churlish assessment of it all: *Semper in faecibus sumum, sole profundum variat.* We are always in shit, it's just the depth of it that varies.

The Vestal litter slowed as it approached Caesar's home. As it stopped before the short colonnade of columns that adorned the front of Caesar's home, Pomponia heard the buoyant festivities of the wedding party within. The mouth-watering smells of the banquet and the happy sounds of music wafted into the street.

She instructed the litter-bearers to set down closer to the portico that would normally be proper. The high priestess, just now rousing from her nap, was easily winded. Pomponia stepped out of the lectica to greet Medousa who had been duteously waiting for them at Caesar's house. Her long auburn hair was blowing in the breeze and she was trying to brush it off her face.

"*Salve*, Domina," said Medousa. "Was the wedding ceremony a tear-jerker? Or was it only the bride who wept?"

"The bride didn't have time to weep," said Pomponia. "She was too busy mopping her drunken husband's wine off her sandals." She stepped out of the lectica and then held back the curtains for the high priestess who also slipped out.

"You should beat your slave for that mouth of hers," said Fabiana, knowing that Pomponia would never do it. "Now mind yourselves. Here comes Lady Octavia."

Octavia glided to greet High Priestess Fabiana with all the grace expected of Caesar's sister. She had changed out of her wedding gown and wore a pale orange stola made of linen rather than the more luxurious silk, widely belted around her waist, her only jewelry a rather unimpressive set of gold earrings and a bracelet. Her make-up was equally subdued, with the shades of color that had brightened her cheeks and lips during the wedding ceremony largely wiped away.

"Vestalis Maxima," said Octavia, bowing deeply to Fabiana. "I have prayed to the goddess that you would be well enough to visit today." Her words were utterly sincere. "I am so happy you could come."

"I'm sorry we are late, my dear," Fabiana replied. "I would like to say it is out of fashion, but alas, I fell asleep in the lectica and Pomponia wouldn't wake me."

"She cares for you as a mother," said Octavia.

"And fusses over me as a child," Fabiana replied. She took Octavia's hands in her own. "Congratulations on your marriage and the success of your family, Lady Octavia. You have married one of Rome's great men and your brother is Caesar. Fortuna smiles on your family."

"May she continue to do so," said Octavia. "The gods can be fickle. Now let's go inside. It's a hot day for October, nay? And

Lady Fabiana, I know there is someone special here who will be delighted to see you."

They strolled past the columns of the portico into the atrium of the house, enjoying the coolness given off by the rainwater in the *impluvium* – the sunken pool in the marble floor – and the lush greenery that surrounded it.

A pair of sparrows quarrelled noisily over some seeds that lay scattered under a rose bush until one of them flew up and out of the opening in the ceiling through which sunlight filtered into the home and rain fell into the impluvium below.

The *lararium* – the household shrine that graced every Roman home no matter how prosperous or poor – stood just inside the atrium as a symbol of pietas and faith. Located here, near the entrance to the home, it served to bless the comings and goings of family members.

In its center stood a statue of Vesta, goddess of the home and hearth, beside which a white terracotta oil lamp burned with the sacred flame. Mementoes of family members living and dead adorned the lararium, as did a guardian snake made of ivory. The diamonds that lined its long back twinkled as they reflected the flame from the oil lamp.

On the scarlet wall behind the lararium hung several death masks of Octavian's great ancestors. Naturally, the most prominent of these was the death mask of Octavian's adopted father, *divus Julius*, the divine Julius Caesar.

Although Caesar's face had suffered stab wounds during his assassination, the mask-maker had done a remarkable job of capturing the dictator's solemn facial characteristics in wax and then overlaying it with gold. His slender face with its sharp nose and strong chin, his piercing eyes and his receding hairline, it was all there, no different in death than it was in life.

The effect was masterful. Visitors were greeted by the omnipotent, god-like face of the revered Julius Caesar, a man whose name had taken on an almost mythical quality in the few short years since his death. His great presence was palpable and sent an unmistakable message to all who entered the new Caesar's home: you are within the walls of the most important house in Rome.

And those walls were something to see. As Pomponia and Medousa trailed respectfully behind Octavia and the Vestalis Maxima to join the wedding guests already mingling in the boisterous atmosphere of the dining room, Pomponia gazed at the colorful frescos that animated every wall in Octavian's home with vivid images of theater scenes, garden landscapes and exotic animals. Images of birds, flowers and dazzling geometric designs adorned the high arched ceilings.

What Octavian's house lacked in size or marble statuary, it made up for in the grandeur of its frescos. With every step, the eye was treated to a rich feast of blue, red, yellow and turquoise illustrations, framed by ornate painted columns and brought to moving life by the flickering oil lamps that illuminated them and the lively sound of music that washed over them.

Octavian – a vocal patron of the arts – often boasted that he had hired the best artists in the Roman world. For a man who rarely boasted, that meant something. His love of art and his willingness to invest in it wasn't limited to his own property, either. From temples and fountains to basilicas and bathhouses, Rome was slowly enjoying a much-needed facelift. And all of it on Octavian's denarius.

At his sister's request, the new Caesar had readily gifted a monumental sum to update and expand the House of the Vestals, adding new rooms, painting frescos in the triclinium and having elaborate mosaics lain on the floor of the atrium, all of which had been done at the speed of Mercury.

Once that was done, he had privately commissioned ten more marble statues of Vestal priestesses for the courtyard and personally hired contractors to restore the temple itself with white marble from the mountains of Carrara. He had even proposed motions in the Senate that markedly increased the already generous pensions and land that Vestal priestesses received for their service to the goddess.

As she accepted a ruby-rimmed gold cup of red wine from a slave, Pomponia had a sudden flashback to a conversation she had had with Octavian years ago. A conversation in the black, dank depths of a stone prison. *My divine father had great respect for the Vestals. As Caesar, I intend to continue our friendship.*

She sipped the sweet wine and took inventory of the wedding celebrants in the dining room. As with all Octavian's functions, the guest list was a social register of Rome's most influential people, all of whom were well-known to her. Octavian's general Agrippa, his advisor Maecenas and his ally Lepidus, who also served as Pontifex Maximus, were in a heated discussion about a treasury matter.

Close by, three prominent senators, the Rex Sacrorum and chief priests of the Mars and Jupiter collegia were laughing and draining their wine as Marc Antony lifted the tunica of a very pretty slave woman, pointing between her legs and nodding in approval. Pomponia could hear Medousa's low groan of sympathy.

In the center of the dining room, lavishly-dressed Roman matrons mixed, mingled and gossiped their way to a good time. To Pomponia, they looked like a moving rainbow in their elegant stolas of blue, green, saffron, gold and violet. Even through their chatter – which increased with each cup of wine consumed – she could hear the soft clinks and chimes of the gold jewelry that hung like ornaments from their limbs and waved with every motion they made.

"Ah, here comes your special friend, Lady Fabiana," said Octavia. "He has missed you terribly."

Fabiana cried out in delight and Pomponia swallowed her irritation as a small, white, fluffy dog came bounding around a column to scramble gracelessly toward the high priestess, its nails scratching the floor and its tongue lolling out of its mouth. It shoved its pointed nose into the folds of Fabiana's stola and whimpered with joy as she reached down to tug gently on its ears.

"Perseus!" exclaimed Fabiana. "Oh, my little friend! Octavia, I have not seen him since your mother died."

"I know, Lady Fabiana. He was my mother's favorite but she knew his heart belonged to you."

Fabiana laughed and the sound of it dissolved Pomponia's annoyance at the little dog's ceaseless hopping and the sharp, high-strung whining that pierced her ears. She turned to Medousa. "Perseus, hey? The hero who slayed Medusa. Better keep your distance."

"How clever, Domina."

The wife of the high priest of Mars, a dignified woman by the name of Cornelia, noticed the arrival of the Vestalis Maxima and before Pomponia knew it, Fabiana was surrounded by a throng of matrons asking about her health and giggling at the antics of the little dog Perseus.

Hungrily eyeing the several dining tables stacked end to end with cooked meat, dormice and other delicacies – she had missed lunch thanks to Fabiana's extended nap in the litter – Pomponia discreetly excused herself to stack a plate with what she knew was more food than was becoming a lady, never mind a Vestal.

Medousa stood a few paces behind her. Pomponia would have liked to offer her something as well; however, it was bad enough she was stuffing her face with all the decorum of a toothless peasant. She couldn't be seen letting her slave eat off Octavian's table on top of it.

"You can gorge yourself like the Cyclops when we get home," she whispered to Medousa who raised her eyebrows as if to say, "Oh, I will."

Pomponia had just pushed a piece of oil-soaked bread in her mouth – the whole thing at once – when she suddenly felt an uneasy presence beside her. Holding a cloth to her lips and praying to the goddess that her cheeks didn't look as stuffed as they felt, she found herself looking into the lovely young face of Lady Valeria. Quintus's wife.

She wore a pink sleeveless stola, richly embroidered with tiny flowers, with a long violet veil that was fastened to the back of her head to hang down her back. Gold bracelets wound around her bare upper arms and long gold earrings brushed her shoulders. Small pink flowers peeked out from between the black locks of her hair, and black kohl lined her eyes in the almond-shaped style that immediately reminded Pomponia of Queen Cleopatra.

She caressed the soft mound of her belly in the exaggerated manner that too many pregnant women seemed to display when in the company of those believed to be barren.

"Priestess Pomponia," said Valeria. She raised her eyebrows at the oil on Pomponia's lips. "My, you're looking healthy."

Pomponia wiped the oil off her mouth, taken aback by Valeria's thinly veiled cattiness. Quintus's wife had clearly indulged in too much wine. Before she could think of what to say in response, Valeria let out a furtive sigh and rubbed her fruitful belly again.

"Oh, I wish I could eat like that," she said. "But I always lose my appetite in early pregnancy. I don't know what it is about Quintus's children. They are as hard on my body as their father is." She smiled widely, goadingly, at the Vestal.

Pomponia sensed Medousa's body tense in anger behind her.

The priestess smiled back. "Congratulations on being with child yet again," she said. "Perhaps this time Juno will bless your belly with the son your husband is praying for. Third time's a charm, nay?"

The smile melted off Valeria's face. She bowed to the Vestal. "I am feeling unwell. With your permission, Priestess, I shall take my leave of you and find some fresh air in the courtyard."

"Why of course," Pomponia replied. "You always have my permission to leave, Lady Valeria."

Medousa watched Valeria slink away into the gardens and then turned to her mistress. "What a meager little trollop," she said through clenched teeth. "You could have her thrown off the Tarpeian Rock, Domina."

"Medousa, I can hear your teeth grinding in your skull. It is no matter."

"I could launch her off the edge with my own foot."

"You're a harpy when your stomach's empty, Medousa. Here, I don't care who sees it…eat this dormouse."

"Did you see the way she was rubbing her belly? Gods! She acts like she's carrying a demi-god son of Zeus!" Medousa swallowed a mouthful of meat and her shoulders relaxed. "If not the Tarpeian Rock, Priestess, at least order a public beating? I shall speak with the magistrate – "

"You will do no such thing," said Pomponia.

"Are you sparing her the punishment or are you sparing her husband the embarrassment?"

"It would be a debasement to respond to the sad trilling of a common housewife, Medousa. Her life is punishment enough. Think of it! Always subordinate, always doing what you're told."

"Yes, how awful," quipped Medousa.

"You could have it worse. Now come help me find this new fresco Lady Octavia was telling me to look at…some garden scene with blue birds...she said I'd know it when I saw it. We aren't staying long. I told Tuccia and Caecilia I would be back in time for them to attend the races."

Pomponia wandered through Octavian's house, easily greeting friends, engaging in snippets of small talk with senators and their wives, and accepting pious head nods and smiles from those few people she didn't personally know.

As always, Medousa walked several paces behind, seeming to disappear when Pomponia was in conversation and then reappearing to once again trail duteously behind her mistress.

The Vestal liked occasions like this. She was free to socialize with friends old and new, without having to preside over some rigid ceremony. It was pleasantly refreshing to be a guest rather than having to fret and fuss over every detail of a public ritual, all the while trying to ignore the itch of the wool infula under her ceremonial headdress and the stifling heat of her robes. A simple white veil and stola, like the ones she wore tonight, were much more liberating.

"Ah, this must be it." Pomponia laughed out loud as she found the fresco she sought, suitably situated in a serene, private alcove of Octavian's house. The fresco depicted the gardens in the Vestal courtyard.

In the painting, white and pink rosebushes surrounded one of the courtyard's rectangular pools, in the center of which stood a marble statue of Vesta. The goddess tipped a bowl of flames and they cascaded down to magically transform into the water that filled the pool. Inside the vivid turquoise reflections of the pool, ten or twelve blue birds splashed in the warm water.

Pomponia's nose almost touched the wall as she inspected the intricate details of the fresco. "It's beautiful," she said to Medousa, who stood at her shoulder.

"If such things please you." A man's voice. It wasn't Medousa who stood beside her, it was Quintus.

Her stomach dropped and she quickly looked at him. As ever, his expression was impossible to read. Anger? Disapproval? Her brow furrowed in confusion and the discomfort of his closeness.

His toga was snow white, with a broad purple stripe along its border to symbolize his upper-class status. He was freshly shaven and smelled slightly of oil – no doubt having just come from the baths that morning – and Pomponia's eyes once again fell on the gold ring he wore, the one with the Vesta intaglio.

"You and I once saw another creature splashing in that pool," he said.

"What creature was that?"

"The groom."

Pomponia bit her lip to stifle a laugh. Quintus cocked his head and looked at her curiously, and it occurred to Pomponia for the first time that perhaps she was as much a mystery to him as he was to her.

"I hear that Caesar has granted you the quaestorship," she said. "Congratulations, Magistrate."

"He did so when my father retired."

"Well, I'm sure you deserved the posting."

Quintus turned to her coolly, eyebrows raised. "I never thought otherwise."

Pomponia stiffened. "Well, no man can think of everything."

An awkward silence.

"I've been watching your temple, Priestess," Quintus said cautiously, "the improvements that Caesar has made are…acceptable."

"Acceptable?" said Pomponia. "Yes, Magistrate. The improvements are acceptable. But tell me, what about the construction of the new Temple of Mars? I regret that my duties have kept me from visiting the Forum of Caesar in the last while. Do you find the construction to be…acceptable?"

Quintus looked at her and Pomponia held his gaze. *Bona Dea,* she thought, *I cannot tell if he wants to smile at me or strike me.*

The Priest of Mars and the Priestess of Vesta stared at each other in the quiet alcove. Although they had known each other since they were no more than children, this was the first time they had shared a truly private moment, a moment where no other eyes were upon them.

Pomponia felt the familiar flutter in her stomach, the flutter she always seemed to feel when Quintus was near. In a nervous gesture, she raised a hand to smooth the side of her veil and, when she did, the sleeve of her stola fell down to reveal the gold bracelet Quintus's wife had given her years earlier when she had demanded his release from the Carcer.

Quintus's eyes fell on the bracelet and before Pomponia could react, he reached out his hand and grasped her wrist tightly. Pomponia heard herself gasp and pulled her hand back, but Quintus held it firmly, his grip so tight that it hurt.

"You will let go of me at once," she spat. "Or I'll have you thrown you down the same black hole I had you pulled out of."

His grip around her wrist loosened, but then his hand slipped up under the sleeve of her stola to clutch the bare skin of her upper arm. His face wore an angry, almost pained expression that betrayed the struggle he was having with his own restraint – wanting to hold her but knowing he should let go – and his nostrils flared with every deep, deliberate breath.

"Quintus, you're hurting me."

In an instant his face softened and he pulled her toward him, his one hand still clutching her upper arm and his other hand moving up to hold the back of her neck. Pomponia felt the fullness of his warm lips press against hers. His fingers clutched the fabric of the veil behind her neck and he brought her lips even closer to his. His tongue slipped into her mouth, his hot breath mixing with hers.

The wave of her body's reaction flooded over her, washing away the sense of outrage, of violent indignation, that she had felt only moments earlier. Instead, her heart pounded and she surrendered herself to his mouth, his tongue, his force.

"Pomponia," he said breathily. "What do you think of me?"

She swallowed. "I think you're an ill-tempered brute who has to be in control of everything and who delights in telling me what to do."

He smiled and his face opened up as Pomponia had never seen it. "You have me there," he said. "Tell me that I'm the only man you'll ever love. Swear it on the Altar of Juno."

Was this *love?* Pomponia opened her mouth but nothing came out.

Quintus moved his hand under her veil to feel her hair. His fingers slid up the back of her neck, caressing her scalp, and a shudder ran through her.

And then they were apart. From out of nowhere, Medousa stepped between them. She turned to Quintus and pushed him with both her hands, causing him to stumble backwards. Her beautiful face showed none of its usual sarcasm or removed amusement; rather, sheer terror filled her eyes.

At the same moment, a shout echoed off the marble walls of the alcove.

"Damn you to Hades!" Quintus's wife was standing at the entrance to the alcove, her lips quivering with rage and her eyes wildly glaring with shock and spite. She pointed at her husband and the Vestal. "*Incestum!*"

* * * * * *

Although they were in a private alcove of Octavian's expansive house, three or four wedding guests heard the shout and quickly came to investigate. An outburst like that could only mean one thing: some very good gossip was about to be had.

The first to arrive was Caesar himself. "Are you well, Lady Valeria?" he asked Quintus's wife. His eyes were cool, but his face grimaced as he regarded her intoxicated state. Octavian was not a man who approved of such indecorous behavior on the part of a well-bred Roman matron.

Valeria dropped her jaw open and shook her head, still pointing to her husband and the Vestal. Her whole body wobbled. "My husband," she slurred, "and that…that *woman*…."

She muttered something inaudible, pointed her chin at Pomponia and then shouted directly at Quintus. "I knew it! You told me I was mad, but I knew it! Every time there is a crisis, where are you? Certainly not at home protecting your wife and daughters! Oh no, you're at the Temple of Vesta, rushing to *her* rescue. You have a sickness, Quintus, a sickness and a perversion in your heart. Every day you pass by the temple, every day you stand outside the House of the Vestals and stare at the portico as if Venus herself stood there naked for you!" She swallowed hard as the wine came up her throat. "I tell you, it's a sickness and a perversion! And you are a faithless husband!"

"Oh let off, you drunken fool," said Marc Antony, himself slopping wine from his cup and slurring his words. The hypocrisy wasn't lost on those around him and they burst into laughter, as did he. "Jupiter only knows what your dog of a husband has been sniffing after, but there's no way he's wolf enough to catch a Vestal."

Valeria swallowed hard again. "You are wrong, he – "

"It is *you* who is wrong," said Medousa. "*I'm* the one he loves and has loved for years." She bore her eyes into Valeria with the fury of a gorgon. "And who can blame him, with a wife like you? It is no wonder he thinks of me first. It is no wonder he comes to me every day. What husband would want to come home to you?"

Valeria blinked stupidly. "No, you're not…" She shook her head feebly.

"Ah, the smoke clears," said Antony. He pursed his lips and looked at Medousa, nodding in approval. "Quintus, I commend you on your choice of bed slaves. This one's hot as Hades. You are a true connoisseur, sir." He took a stumbling step toward her, hand outstretched to touch her hair. "But how did such a creature escape my notice?" Suddenly, he turned to Octavian and slapped him hard on the chest. "*Futuo*! Jupiter's cock, my boy, you're right! I do have to be more aware of things!"

At that, he let out a good-natured guffaw and turned on his heel, heading back toward the party in the music-filled triclinium. The few guests who had gathered to watch the scene unfold followed him. The gossip wasn't that good after all: just a drunken wife driven mad with jealousy over the beauty of her husband's bed slave. Amusing. Not scandalous.

Only Octavian remained in the alcove. Medousa looked at him and then turned to the dumb-struck Pomponia. "I submit myself to your mercy, Domina," she said. "My indiscretion is unforgiveable."

"Caesar, the fault is mine," said Quintus, "for allowing my wife to attend today. The physician says her humors are unbalanced and I should be keeping her confined. Her behavior will be punished. I apologize for the disruption."

"Not at all," Octavian replied with his usual coolness. It took a lot more than an unbalanced or jealous wife to perturb Caesar. "It would not be a wedding party without some kind of scuffle. Send her home and stay, Quintus. There will be more dramatic tussles to come as the evening proceeds."

Quintus smiled graciously. "Thank you Caesar, I will do that." He turned to Pomponia. "Lady Pomponia, I am truly sorry that you had to witness this. Please excuse me."

Without another word, without another glance at Pomponia or Medousa, Quintus placed his hand on his stricken wife's back and escorted her away.

"Priestess," said Octavian. "Would you like me to have the Lady Valeria executed? It would be an appropriate response to her behavior. It could be done quietly, if you prefer. We could dispense with the public scourging and just have her killed – "

"No," interrupted Pomponia, struggling to keep her composure and marvelling that no one seemed to hear the thumping of her heart in her chest. "It is already forgotten and Quintus and I have been friends and colleagues for too long. His wife is quite unwell…and I am not blameless…"

"Forgive me, Domina," interrupted Medousa. Her eyes were moist with emotion and fear. "I should never have put you in this position. I begged you to let me see him and you allowed it out of your love for me. I am sorry."

Pomponia took Medousa's hands in her own. There was so much she wanted to say. *It is I who am sorry, Medousa. I am sorry that my weakness and my foolishness forced you to do this. You are the best friend I have in the world.*

But there was nothing she could say. For the sake of her own life, the life of Quintus and the esteem of the Vestal order itself, she had to go along with the fiction Medousa had created.

Octavian tugged absently at his toga, straightening a fold. "Your slave has exploited the affection you have for her," he said to the Vestal. "It's always bad business to give them too long a chain. I have made the mistake myself, Priestess, especially with those slaves I've known since I was a child. However, I can always use educated Greek slaves in my household. You can leave her here. She will be treated well enough."

"Yes," said Pomponia. There was no other way. She was lucky enough to have dodged Valeria's arrow of accusation once. Suspicion was bound to follow if she, a priestess of Vesta, kept a slave who had engaged in such lascivious behavior. The Temple of Vesta and the House of the Vestals were enduring symbols of purity. Medousa could no longer be associated with them. "Thank you for accommodating us, Caesar. I am certain she will serve you well."

"I have no doubt."

Before she could say good-bye to Medousa, before she could speak with her in private about what had just happened or how the slave's life now belonged to Caesar, one of Octavian's house slaves quietly ushered Medousa away. Caesar was not known for his sentimentality. And slaves were not people. They were property.

Pomponia regained her poise. She had never felt such a flood of conflicting emotions before. The arousal from Quintus's closeness and her desire to be close to him again. The shock and terror of Valeria's accusation, followed by the quick relief that no one had taken her seriously. The guilt over Medousa's sacrifice and the sadness of losing her lifelong friend and companion.

All of these feelings swirled in the pit of her stomach. Yet she calmed them, calling upon the grace of Vesta and her years of Vestal training, years spent learning how to remain dignified and clear-headed in all situations, from banquets to barbarian invasions.

A familiar voice, although one that she hadn't heard for a long time, filtered into her ears.

"*Bona Dea!* Julius had a new slave girl in his bed every market day. You didn't see me making a scene of it on the Rostra, did you? I swear, Priestess Pomponia, the Roman matron just isn't what she used to be."

It was Lady Calpurnia, Julius Caesar's widow. She had watched the drama unfold from the safety of the shadows: always seeing, but never being seen. Such was her talent. More than that, it was how she had survived life with the dictator.

"My divine father had his vices," Octavian said to her, "how fortunate for him that his wife conducted herself with decorum and dignity. I wish my wife Scribonia would follow your lead, Calpurnia."

"She serves her purpose, Caesar. She is with child."

"Yes, I thank Juno for that," said Octavian, "but I will divorce her today if you will have me, Calpurnia."

Calpurnia laughed. "I have had enough Caesars. But wouldn't the scandal be divine?"

"And useful," grinned Octavian. "It would distract the people from blaming me for the grain shortage."

Pomponia compelled herself to join the conversation. "Is Queen Cleopatra not sending her shipments?" she asked Octavian.

"Not regularly," he said. "Not reliably. There is nothing reliable about that woman."

"You can rely on one thing," said Calpurnia. "She will not be pleased to hear of Antony's marriage to Octavia. Pray to the gods the marriage will strengthen your alliance with Antony. But it won't fill Roman bellies with Egyptian grain anytime soon."

"Stability in Rome is a priority," said Octavian. "A hungry Roman is better than a dead Roman."

He was about to say something else when Agrippa approached, nodded politely at Calpurnia and Pomponia, and then discreetly whispered in Octavian's ear.

Octavian rolled his eyes. "Please excuse me, ladies. It appears a couple senators are coming to fisticuffs over some disbursements I made in the Subura.

"Of course, Caesar," said Pomponia.

"Fisticuffs," Calpurnia sniffed. "May blessed Concordia protect you, Caesar. Senators may show their fists, but they hide their daggers."

Octavian kissed her on the cheek. "You and I know that all too well," he said as he parted.

Now alone, Pomponia and Calpurnia fell into easy conversation, slowly making their way back to the crowd of wedding guests in the main part of the house.

In the large, frescoed triclinium, Antony lay on a couch chatting loudly but idly with Octavia and Maecenas. He openly eyed his new bride, looking up and down her body in obvious anticipation of the wedding night.

"Do you think there is any affection at all between them?" Pomponia asked Calpurnia.

"No," Calpurnia replied, "but in time, there may be. Antony has not had a wife like Octavia. His other wives were shrews, especially that Fulvia. Not one was a proper Roman matron. They were ambitious and wanton. One of Antony's house slaves once told me that Fulvia used to dress in a toga! Gods, can you imagine such a thing? Octavia is different. Modest, virtuous, subordinate to her husband – those are qualities Antony may grow to admire." She took a sip of wine. "If he can forget that painted whore-queen of the Nile, that is."

"May the gods make it so," said Pomponia. "Oh, Lady Calpurnia, look – there is Priestess Fabiana with that vicious little dog again. She will not part with it. It dirties her stola and causes the most foolish cooing sounds to come out of her mouth, yet she doesn't notice any of it, not even the smell that comes from its yellow teeth."

"*Amare et sapere vix deo conceditur,*" Calpurnia replied with a forgiving smile. Even the gods cannot love and be wise at the same time.

Pomponia felt a sudden heaviness in her heart. "Perhaps." She touched Calpurnia's shoulder. "You have been kind to accompany me, Lady Calpurnia. Now go visit the High Priestess and her little white Cerberus. She would like that. I have duties at the temple and must leave soon."

Once Calpurnia had taken her leave, Pomponia exhaled deeply for the first time since the episode with Quintus's wife. She mingled duteously with friends and colleagues, relieved that Lady Valeria was nowhere to be seen. Her husband had sent her home.

But Quintus remained. He stood by a fountain, deep in animated conversation with Agrippa, two or three of Caesar's other advisors and the high priest of Mars. He was smiling and drinking as if nothing had happened. Detached. Cold.

She glanced his way and he met her eyes for a moment, but only smirked with that all-too familiar edge of superiority and indifference before ignoring her utterly and laughing with his companions.

Pomponia put her hands on her stomach as if to quell the storm of confusion she felt going on inside her. Lady Valeria's words filled her mind. *You have a sickness, Quintus, a sickness and a perversion in your heart.*

Perhaps he did. Pomponia knew that many men found sport in the conquest of an unattainable woman. To such men, seducing a woman was a roguish diversion that bolstered their ego.

And there was no doubt that Quintus had the ego of Hercules himself. She had seen it many times. Every scowl, every criticism, every chastening and condescending rebuke she had endured from him over the years, they all came back to her with renewed clarity.

Perhaps his wife was not as mad as she appeared. Pomponia though back to Valeria's blackened eyes and submissive disposition, to the way she cowered and quickly retreated into obedience when her husband so much as looked at her.

Slowly, the confusion in Pomponia's stomach gave way to indignation and she cursed her own womanish imprudence. It hadn't just stripped her of her dignity. It had cost her the lifelong companionship of Medousa.

It wasn't fitting for a priestess to weep over the loss of a mere slave; however, Pomponia had a sudden memory of the day she had been taken as a Vestal, the same day Julius Caesar had appointed Medousa as her slave.

As her hair was being cropped for the Vestal veil, as was the custom, she had started to cry at the sight of the dark locks falling onto the white marble floor. Medousa – herself only a child of twelve or thirteen at the time – had picked them up and held them to her face, making herself into a bearded man and shouting mock orders at the other slaves.

The memory was too much. Knowing the tears would soon come, Pomponia said a brief round of good-byes and ordered for one of Caesar's litters to take her back to the temple. Fabiana was enjoying herself and could follow later in the Vestal litter.

Fabiana. Pomponia knew exactly what she'd say when she heard about Medousa. *Good riddance. That woman doesn't just look like Helen of Troy, she causes that much trouble, too.* The Vestalis Maxima had never liked Medousa. If only she could know the truth.

Pomponia passed into the relative quiet of the sunlit atrium. In the corner adjacent to the family lararium, a bronze bowl burned with the sacred fire of Vesta. The priestess took a sprinkling of salted flour from the gold tray beside it and tossed it into the flame as offering to the goddess.

Divina Vesta, protect Medousa in her new household.

And then the priestess walked out of Caesar's house and into the waiting litter, feeling more alone than she had ever felt in her entire life.

* * * * * *

Somewhere in the dimly-lit room an oil lamp sputtered noisily. Other oil lamps burned with more strength, their tall orange flames casting flickering shadows onto the frescoed walls.

In one painted scene, Cupid lay on top of his beautiful lover Psyche, his wings caressing her bare skin and his hands exploring her body.

Another fresco brought to life the erotic myth of Leda and the Swan. Zeus, in the form of a swan, rested his long neck between the bare breasts of Leda. He makes love to her in her sleep, creating life inside her – the child will be Helen of Troy, the most beautiful woman in the world. Helen, the Greek queen whose love affair with a Trojan prince sparked the Trojan War with the Greeks. Helen, the woman with the face that launched a thousand war ships.

But one fresco was more prominent than the others. It was painted on the wall opposite the large, luxurious bed. In it, the god Mars lay on a long couch with the Vestal Virgin Rhea Silvia. One of his muscled hands held her down in the frenzy of his passion, while the other hand tore at the fabric of her white stola.

Medousa knew the story well.

Caesar's chief female house slave, a middle-aged Greek woman named Despina, sat beside Medousa on the bed. "Are you a virgin?" she asked.

"No."

"Who has had you?"

"Julius Caesar took me for the first time. He had me several times. He was the only one."

"I see." A pause. "You will find this Caesar to be a less reciprocal lover. More aggressive, too. You will remain still at all times. Say nothing. Do nothing. It will not last too long and you will be cared for afterward." The slave's words were blunt but kind.

A cosmetic slave entered the bedchamber carrying a tray of grooming tools. She instructed Medousa to sit on a chair and then brought a pair of shears to her scalp. Long locks of auburn hair fell to the marble floor. Another slave quickly swept them up.

Medousa's head felt strangely light and airy without her mane of thick hair. She clenched her jaw. She would not cry. It was pointless to cry. It wouldn't change a thing.

"Stand up and remove your clothing," said Despina.

Without a sound, Medousa stood up and stripped out of her fine tunica. As she stood naked in the room, the cosmetic slave brought the blade to her pubic hair and removed every trace of it. She instructed Medousa to raise her arms, and then removed the hair from under her arms as well.

"Let's get you dressed, shall we?" Despina snapped her fingers and a young servant girl approached carrying a pure white stola. Medousa stood silently, holding out her arms as the slaves worked together to wrap the stola around her body. A white veil followed. It covered Medousa's short hair and fell down to her waist.

"Caesar will treat you more favorably if he believes you are a virgin," said Despina. "He is Mars, you see, and you are Rhea Silvia. That is how it will happen." She held an outstretched hand to Medousa. In it was a small sponge, the center of which was soaked in blood.

"Put this inside," she said. "When he penetrates you, the blood will come out. When it does, you must pretend to feel pain. He will finish quickly and it will be over."

"Thank you for your kindness," said Medousa. She spread her legs and put the sponge inside her body. The house slave wiped away the blood that dotted her fingers.

A creak of a door and a slant of light pierced the room. Octavian entered the bedchamber with the same stately presence with which he entered every room, strolling to the bed with confident purpose and natural supremacy. The slaves and servants scattered subserviently and disappeared.

Medousa bowed her head but said nothing. She heard the sound of Octavian's toga falling to the floor. He muttered something as he struggled with a sandal strap, but a moment later he was standing in front of her, naked and already fully erect. His eyes moved up and down her body.

He pushed her gently toward the bed and then roughly threw her onto her back, quickly mounting her and tearing at the stola and veil. He inhaled sharply at the sight of her close-cropped hair and smooth pubic area and entered her, fast and hard, all at once.

Medousa cried out in pain, not having to pretend at all.

CHAPTER VIII

Fortuna

Rome 39 BCE

Livia Drusilla grabbed her young son's arm and yanked him up into the lectica. The little brat was pissing on the litter-bearers' sandals again. She'd be smelling urine until they reached the next milestone. What evil spirit had charged her with such a child? What debt to Dis, unhappy god of discontent, was she fulfilling by enduring such an utterly horrible son?

His name was Tiberius – so-called after his father – but the similarities didn't stop there. He had the same dull-wittedness, the same brainless humor and the same square block of a head.

A priest of Diana had once told her that a child's capacity was always superior to that of its parents. Livia vowed to herself that if her path ever crossed that charlatan priest again, she would strip him of his robes on the street and beat him to death with the first piss pot she could find.

Still, things were looking up. The proscriptions in Rome were over and Caesar had announced a general amnesty for those Romans who had fled during them. For the time being at least, Rome was at peace, thanks to the marriage between Caesar's sister Octavia and the general Marc Antony.

Athens was behind her and so was that stinking, sticky Greek pig Diodorus. No more would she have to suffer his ribald jokes or feign illness to avoid his vile fondling. The smell of his unwashed genitals still lingered in her nostrils. The taste of his bad wine and salty olives still stuck in her throat.

She glared at her dozing husband on the other side of the lectica. Tiberius, a dreadful husband at the best of times, had been an absolutely atrocious husband during their years of exile in Greece. He should have been outraged every time Diodorus stumbled into her bedchamber to pound into her with all the finesse of a battering ram.

Instead, he had turned a blind eye. The coward. Not only had he fled from Rome like a bawling catamite, he had been too chicken-hearted to speak against his hairy beast of a benefactor.

Then again, life hadn't been as intolerable for him as it had been for her. The wine was waste water and the food was excrement, but there were plenty of both. There were plenty of slave girls, too. Livia – a woman not inclined to sympathy for anyone, never mind slaves – had nonetheless felt sorry for them.

She had seen them scramble out of Tiberius's bedchamber night after night, sometimes three or four of them at a time, and the expressions of disgust they wore on their faces were all too familiar to her.

She had seen the same expression stare back at her from her own mirror. The gods only knew what he had made them do to him, to each other and to themselves.

The lead litter-bearer shouted an order and the litter began to move again. Livia held back the curtain inside the lectica and looked out. She sighed contentedly at the sight of the tall cypress trees that lined the long cobblestone road. Little Tiberius kicked her shin as he clambered to sit beside his snoring father, but Livia took no notice. She was going home.

Home. Her brow furrowed. What condition would their home be in? After years of their absence, what valuables would remain? The letters from the house slave had stopped coming months ago. It was likely that at least some household treasures had been looted, perhaps by the slave himself. Either that, or he had been killed or stolen trying to defend his master's house.

She offered a silent prayer to Vesta. *I don't give a fig for Tiberius's wretched marble statues and gold dinnerware – but my jewelry! My good gowns! May they still be where I hid them.*

She smiled as she remembered her favorite – a yellow gown with red and orange embroidered birds along the border – but her smile quickly melted into a scowl of worry.

Her blood hadn't come this month or the last. If she was with child, it would be ages before she'd be able to slink into that dress. But her waistline wasn't the worst of her worries.

Would the child have Tiberius's block head or Diodorus's hairy back? Pray Juno it would be another boy. Pray the gods would be merciful and not burden a girl with the attributes of either man. It would take a dowry the size of Olympus to marry off such a creature.

The pace of the litter slowed and Livia cranked her head out of the lectica to see the massive stone blocks of the Servian Wall ahead. It reached ten meters into the sky and surrounded Rome, protecting the eternal city from the barbarians and invaders that always seemed to be at her door.

The Porta Collina – the major gate that led into the City of Rome – was visible in the distance, although a bottleneck of congestion forced the litter-bearers to set down once again as a throng of people, animals, wagons, litters and vendor carts of all kinds slowly filtered past the inspectors, through the gate and into the great city.

Normally, such a delay would have angered Livia. But not today. She had waited years to return to Rome. Another hour or two to pass through the gate was nothing to be upset about.

A small, dirty child managed to slip past the litter-bearers and stick his grimy hand into the lectica, begging for coin. Livia was about to stab his hand with a hairpin when she noticed the temple that stood not far from the Porta Collina – the Temple of Fortuna. It would be bad luck to stab a child, even a peasant one, so close to the temple. The goddess would not like it.

Instead, she reached for a small sack of coins on the floor of the lectica and sprinkled a couple denarii into her palm. The peasant boy's eyes opened wide and she tossed them outside, watching him dive to the muddy ground and roughly shoulder two other children aside to retrieve them.

A snort and a cough. "Juno's tight ass, woman! Are you throwing money away?"

"How remarkable," Livia said to her husband. "You manage to sleep through a brawl of drunken Dacians rushing the litter and shouting war cries, but you awaken at the soft chink of coin."

Tiberius huffed and Livia curled up on her cushioned seat as the litter slowly moved forward in stops and starts, making its way through the clattering, clamoring gridlock of congestion at the gate.

The journey is so much more pleasant when he's asleep, she thought.

Eventually, they passed through the Porta Collina. Just inside the walls of Rome, a newsreader stood on a pedestal shouting the latest news that would be relevant to returning citizens or visitors to the city: upcoming market days, the latest laws passed by the Senate, current games and chariot races, Caesar's building projects, road closures and so on.

Tiberius elbowed his son and pointed at the field beyond the road. "That is the Campus Sceleratus," he said. "The evil field." The block-headed toddler squealed with excitement. "Do you know what they do there?" he asked the child, who blinked stupidly back at his father, opening and closing his mouth like a carp. "They bury Vestal priestesses alive!" Tiberius made a spooky look and the child squealed again. The sound pierced Livia's ears.

"Well," she groaned to herself. "That's one way to get some peace."

* * * * * *

"*Ave, Caesar! Nos morituri te salutamus!*" Hail Caesar! We who are about to die salute you!

Octavian stood to acknowledge the two gladiators who saluted him from the arena below. "*Avete vos.*" Fare you well. He sat back down and smiled at his well-dressed companion, a man by the name of Titus Statilius Taurus, the wealthy senator who had commissioned construction of the new amphitheater the games were being held in.

It was the first permanent amphitheater of its kind in Rome. Located in the Campus Martius, its perfectly circular shape, massive size and stone construction made it a spectacular improvement on the temporary wooden, semi-circular structures that were normally erected in the Campus Martius to house the games.

Although construction wasn't yet complete, the amphitheater was nonetheless functional enough to comfortably seat many thousands of spectators. The fighting arena was covered in sand to prevent the gladiators from slipping on their or their opponent's spilled blood. The sand also made clean-up easier by absorbing the blood of the brave (as well as the urine and feces of the not-so-brave).

"The structure is most impressive, Taurus," said Octavian. "Rome rejoices in your generosity."

"I would have built a temple, but you've snatched up all of those," Taurus grinned, "and with great speed, I might add. Perhaps you should build a temple to swift-footed Mercury? I think he's the only god you've missed."

"I shall think on it, Taurus. I admit that I prefer religion to sport. You know I'm no lover of the games, but I am well aware how popular they are with the people. And when the people are entertained, they are easier to govern."

"Such has always been the purpose of sport, Caesar." He sighed happily and admired the half-finished amphitheater around them. "My architects modeled this building after an amphitheater in Pompeii. Of course, this one is much bigger and more modern. Rome is the head of the world, after all. The *caput mundi* deserves the best. You will see that the drainage is superior to any structure in Rome, and the framework for the private box seating – see, there and over there – is already up for your family and the Vestal priestesses. There will be all manner of hidden traps doors for wild beasts and the re-enactment of famous battles. And when it rains, a great canopy will stretch over the stands and – ah, look, Caesar. They're finally finished tiptoeing around each other and are ready to fight."

The *summa rudis* – the referee – barked his final rules and warnings to the gladiators, and then retreated quickly as the two warriors faced off.

The crowd erupted. Noblemen and freedmen, patricians and peasants, matrons and children, all cheered the name of one gladiator in fervent unison – Flamma! Flamma! Flamma!

Flamma. The Flame. A gladiator of celebrity proportions, he was idolized throughout the Roman world for having the longest winning streak in recent history: he had won every one of his last twenty-one games, each one a bloodier and more dramatic victory than the last. And Taurus was the man of the hour for having managed to snag him for today's headline match.

In response to the crowd's applause and cheers, Flamma thrust his *gladius* – the gladiator's sword – into the air and bellowed a deep, murderous roar. The crowd descended into unbridled frenzy.

"Gods, he sounds like the Nemean lion!" said Taurus.

"From what I hear, it will take Hercules to kill him." Octavian replied.

"Hercules couldn't get close enough," said Taurus. "I think only Medusa could kill him. She could turn him to stone and then chisel him to Hades one strike at a time."

"We shall test your theory, Taurus." Octavian raised his hand. "Medousa, come." She was at his side in an instant, her head down and her hands folded submissively in front of her pure white stola. A white veil hid the short hair underneath.

"Medousa? What a terrifying name for a slave, Caesar," Taurus laughed. "You'd better watch yourself." The friends laughed, but the sound of their laughter was soon consumed by the clamor of blood-thirsty spectators.

The great gladiator Flamma was a *secutor* fighter: he was naked except for a loincloth, and his body armor consisted of nothing more than a metal greave on his lower left leg, a leather manica over his over his right arm, and a smooth, close-fitting helmet. He carried a heavy curved shield called a *scutum* along with his gladius.

As always, the secutor's opponent was a *retiarius* – a net-fighter. Agile and quick in comparison to his opponent, the retiarius carried a long three-pronged spear called a trident, as well as a net.

The fight was as simple as it was brutal. The secutor would chase the retiarius around the arena trying to kill him with his gladius. The retiarius would evade his opponent while at the same time trying to cast a net over him. If the retiarius managed to entangle the secutor in the net, he would proceed to stab him to death with the trident.

The Flame charged at his opponent, bursting with sudden violence, like some kind of fiery Vulcan belched from the mouth of an erupting volcano. The net-fighter twisted his body to barely avoid the advancing gladius. He sprinted a few steps away, the sand flying under his feet and the crowd screaming in his ears, before stumbling and falling to the ground.

The roar of the crowd was deafening. The scent of imminent death was in the air and, like wild animals, they fell back on brutal instinct – kill him! Make it gory! Let us see it!

A flare of rage ran through the net-fighter. To die this soon was a disgrace.

He saw the gleam of Flamma's polished gladius over him. Although he rolled in the sand, the point of the sword came down hard at his throat. He leapt to his feet and placed his hand on his neck – no blood! Flamma's lunge had missed its mark by a hair's breadth.

But Flamma didn't know that. He had his back to his opponent. After his lunge, he had advanced toward the stands, strutting like a peacock toward a group of young women shouting his name and promising him favors after the match. In a show of overconfident bravado, he hadn't bothered to look back at the fallen retiarius whom he believed to be lying dead in the sand.

The Flame held up his arms to Victory as the crowd jumped to its feet. Shouts echoed off the stone walls of the amphitheater and thousands of arms waved in the air to celebrate his twenty-second consecutive win…but wait…what were they shouting? It didn't sound like a victory cheer…

The net fell over his head as if dropped from the heavens by Jupiter himself. The rope was heavier than it looked and the weights fastened to the corners did a surprisingly effective job of securing it down. He struggled to find a loose spot, an opening, which he could pull over his head, but one of his feet became entangled in the mesh and he fell to the ground.

Unlike Flamma, the net-fighter cared nothing for showmanship. Survival was all that mattered and Fortuna had granted him a split-second of opportunity.

In an act that seemed surreal even to him, he thrust the points of his trident into the net again and again. Blood spurted out of the net as the Roman world's most famous gladiator thrashed about inside. From the most distant seats in the amphitheatre, it could have been a net full of fish flopping on the shore.

And then the thrashing stopped. The crowd fell silent for a moment – had they really seen a no-name retiarius defeat The Flame? – and then burst into a maniacal cheer. They had come to watch Flamma extend his winning streak. His victory had been certain. Instead, the Fates had cut a thread that no one imagined could be severed.

"Ah," said Octavian, more to himself than anyone else. "There's a lesson here."

Flowers and palm leaves littered the sand of the arena as the ecstatic spectators celebrated the underdog's victory. The retiarius's *lanista* burst into the arena and threw his arms around his star gladiator's shoulders, hugging him tightly and promising rewards of coin, food, drink, women, boys, whatever he wanted.

Meanwhile, several slaves busied themselves at the body of The Flame. They untangled him from the net and rolled his huge, bloody corpse on a stretcher. A horn sounded loudly as the giant doors to the arena opened wide. The crowd fell suddenly silent and somber.

Slowly, a frightening figure strode toward the body of Flamma. He was dressed in torn black robes and carried a double-headed hammer. It was Charon, the lifeless ferryman who carried the souls of mortals to Hades by ferrying them across the River Styx: the river that separated the living world from the afterlife.

The slaves lifted the stretcher and moved forward as the dark, sober figure of Charon escorted the fallen gladiator out of the arena for the last time. In the silence of the amphitheatre, a low death chant arose from the stands and a few sobs echoed off the stone walls.

"I must commend you, Taurus," said Octavian, "your people certainly know how to put on a good show."

"Thank you, Caesar," Taurus replied, "but a little Greek drama goes a long way. I will have to talk to them about overt sentimentality." He shook his finger at Flamma's corpse as it was carried from the arena. "Did you know that Flamma was offered the *rudius* four times? Yet each time he turned it down and chose to fight again. Imagine that! He could have retired a rich man, could have been coupling with his wife right now, but instead he's crossing the black river." He clucked his tongue. "Why would a man make such a choice?"

"It was not his choice to fight," said Octavian. "It was his nature to fight."

"But for such a magnificent fighter to be brought down by such a scrawny cipher! I've seen chickens with bigger bones than that retiarius."

"The retiarius didn't bring him down." Octavian squeezed Medousa's buttocks. "Medousa did."

Taurus laughed out loud. "Don't say your dear friend Taurus didn't warn you, Caesar. You shan't sleep well until that one's head is in a sack. And what a shame, for such a pretty head it is, too. Ah, but there is always another pretty head about. Here comes one now."

Octavian and Taurus stood to greet the smiling couple. "Caesar, may I introduce you to Tiberius Claudius Nero and his lovely young wife Livia. They are recently returned to Rome after an extended...*vacation* in Greece."

Octavian regarded Tiberius. "We are no strangers. I trust you are well, Tiberius. I know you served my father well as quaestor, even though you are an optimate at heart. I am certain you will find Rome a more peaceful place than when you left her."

"Of course, Caesar." Tiberius swallowed his pride. Both men knew that Rome's "peace" and Tiberius's return to Rome came at a price: Octavian had annexed massive amounts of money and property from those nobles who had not supported him in his hunt for the assassins, or who had not supported him with enough enthusiasm. Both men also knew that Tiberius's former appointment as quaestor had less to do with his skill and more to do with his connections.

"What an exquisite creature you have on your arm, Tiberius," Octavian said as his eyes moved to Livia. "You are the daughter of Livius Drusus Claudianus, are you not, my dear?"

"I was while he was alive," said Livia. "My father killed himself in his tent at Philippi."

Octavian held her gaze. He knew that her father had fought alongside the assassins Brutus and Cassius. What's more, he knew that the man had chosen to fall on his sword after their defeat rather than live to see Octavian and Marc Antony rule Rome.

"Your father was a man of principle," he said coolly. "If only all men were so."

"He was a wise father, but a foolish man," Livia said. "You must forgive me, Caesar. I mean no disrespect to my great family, but my father had no mind for strategy. If in any given situation he had the choice of using his head or his heart, he would invariably choose to use the wrong one." She glanced sideways at her husband. "It runs in the family."

Tiberius clenched his jaw. His little trollop of a wife was ingratiating herself to Caesar by clawing over his own back. He managed to hold his temper only by imagining the ways he would beat her once they got home.

"Such sagacity in a woman is a rare thing," admired Octavian, "and of more value than the Golden Fleece." He looked at her pregnant belly. "Pray Juno your child will be as politic."

"Pray Juno," said Livia. She studied Octavian. So this was the *divi filius*? The son of the god Julius Caesar?

Because of his ambition, she had been forced to flee to Greece and spread her legs for Diodorus. Because of his ambition, her father had committed suicide. Because of his ambition, half of her fortune – and all of her dowry – were gone.

But Livia Drusilla had ambitions of her own. As Caesar took his leave of her and Tiberius, she summoned her courage and let her eyes move over him. At the same time, she stroked her pregnant belly, letting the back of her hand caress the area under her full breasts.

Caesar was unreadable; however, Tiberius was as conspicuous and inelegant as always. The moment Caesar was out of sight, he grabbed his wife's arm and dragged her unceremoniously out of the amphitheater, toward the litter that was waiting for them in the street.

"You're a backbiting little harlot," he said as she shoved her inside the lectica.

"Give me a reason to not be so," she shot back.

They didn't exchange so much as a look on the way home, but as soon as the portico of their house was in sight, Tiberius jumped out of the moving litter and stormed inside.

"Lock the doors," he shouted to his slaves. "Let the bitch sleep outside like the rest of Rome's she-wolves."

Livia reclined against the cushions in the lectica. She wouldn't give him the satisfaction of banging on the doors or begging entry to the house. She'd sleep outside all night long if it came to that.

But as it happened, it didn't come to that.

For when night fell and Tiberius finally opened the doors and shouted for his wife to come inside, he found that – to his great surprise – she wasn't sleeping in the lectica after all.

"Where is she?" he asked a blanched-faced slave.

"Dominus," the slave dropped to his knees. "A litter came for her. It was Caesar's litter. We were ordered to say nothing." The slave braced for his master's fist, but it never came.

Quietly, Tiberius turned and went back inside. Despite his aching rage and the heat of his humiliation, he couldn't stop himself from marveling at his young wife's audacity. *It is true what they say,* he thought to himself. *Fortuna audaces iuvat.* Fortuna favors the bold.

* * * * * *

The Vestal Virgins were judging her. She knew it. She could tell by the way their eyes moved from her belly – still distended from giving birth only days earlier – to her saffron wedding veil.

They're just jealous, she told herself. *They're jealous that Caesar divorced his wife Scribonia to marry me. They know they're just a bunch of dried-up old crones that no man would want.*

The problem was, they didn't look old or dried-up. Well, not all of them. The Vestalis Maxima Fabiana and Priestess Nona were old as Rome itself, but the four priestesses whom her new husband Caesar had invited to their wedding – Pomponia, Tuccia, Caecilia and Lucretia – were too attractive for Livia's liking.

She couldn't even mock their barrenness to feel better about herself. While Livia had given birth twice, both children were by her first husband Tiberius, not her new husband Caesar. And having children by an oaf like Tiberius was barely better than having no children at all.

Still, Fortuna had always fought on Livia's side. Even her pregnant belly hadn't dissuaded Caesar from wanting her. He had ordered Tiberius to divorce her and had continued to take her until the last days of her pregnancy.

The moment she had pushed the baby out of her, before the blood was even wiped from its wrinkled face, Caesar had had it whisked off to live with Tiberius and their first son, the blockhead. She had only learned later that the child was a boy. Tiberius had named him Drusus.

Of course, that was all fine by Livia. She was marrying up. Yet she had her share of problems. First, there was the irritating fact that Caesar's child by his ex-wife was disgustingly cute. Caesar insisted that baby Julia live with him and Livia, and he doted on his daughter as though she was born to be Empress of Rome.

Her second problem was that she could no longer claim the respected status of the *univira*: the virtuous "one-man woman" who had only married, coupled with and borne children by one man. As if a woman had any say over such matters.

Personally, Livia snubbed her nose at such ridiculous notions of modesty. Wasn't a cunning mind and a beautiful face and body, especially when matched with a noble family name, to be more desired in a woman than some outdated idea of virtue? If so, then why were so many men tripping over their togas to speak with the Vestals?

Her elder sister Claudia – who now always dressed in royal purple to assert her new status – seemed to read her thoughts.

"You forget yourself, Livia. You are now the wife of Caesar. We are standing in his courtyard, *your* courtyard. There is your grand husband, consulting with the greatest men in Rome – the generals Antony and Agrippa, the pontiffs of the religious collegia, the noblest of senators and magistrates. Think on it! Only months ago you were squatting in a gruesome Greek villa and our family was forsaken. Whatever injustices you suffered there, you have redeemed your honor and the honor of our family name."

"Let's hope the redemption lasts," said Livia. "Caesar is a capricious lover, sister. He plays games but bores of them quickly."

"Then you must find a way to make the game last," Claudia replied, "or to at least come out the winner."

A chorus of shrill barks suddenly sounded in the courtyard and both sisters jumped. Perseus the little white dog was yipping wildly in the arms of Caesar's sister Octavia while the Vestal Pomponia regarded the animal with obvious disdain.

Octavia called out to her new sister-in-law. "Livia, come meet Perseus," she said. "You can say hello and good-bye at once."

"Why is that, dear sister?" Livia asked sweetly.

"Because Perseus is moving out of my brother's house on the same day that you are moving in," she said. "I am sending him to live at the House of the Vestals. And look, Lady Pomponia, he is already dressed in white to serve the goddess." Octavia laughed at Pomponia's curled lip.

"He will lift the spirits of the high priestess," said the Vestal, "and for that I give thanks. But as you know, Octavia, a Vestal has her hair cropped when she enters service. We shall see how Perseus likes temple life when he is pink to the bone."

Tuccia took the little dog from Octavia's arms. "Oh, Pomponia," she said, "we all know your heart is as soft as a lamb. You will be cutting up Perseus's food for him by the Lupercalia."

Livia laughed along, all the while assessing the company she now found herself in.

Her sister-in-law Octavia was the quintessential Roman matron: well-mannered, pious and devoted to her husband Marc Antony. In fact, she was already pregnant with their first child together. No surprises there. She knew what her powerful brother needed her to do, and she was doing it.

The Vestal Tuccia was also what one might expect. She looked to be the same age as Livia and was certainly the prettiest of the priestesses, although she appeared utterly guileless and oblivious to anything other than the ugly little dog that squirmed in her arms and talk of the chariot races.

The Vestal Pomponia was more interesting. When Livia had left Rome for Greece some four years ago, the Lady Pomponia had been a subordinate Vestal; however, it was clear that the priestess's status had grown while she was away. From Caesar to the house slaves, everyone seemed to regard her with particular reverence.

Pomponia scratched the little dog's head and her sneer broke into a smile. "Excuse me ladies," she said. "You know that my former slave Medousa now serves Caesar. I wish to speak with her before I leave."

As the Vestal walked away, Claudia whispered in her sister's ear. "You must befriend that priestess," she said. "You will gain a virtuous reputation by mere association. The people are easily swayed. They will see you with a Vestal and forget your past life."

Livia nodded and watched the Vestal cross the courtyard to speak privately with Medousa, who greeted her former master with more familiarity than Livia thought appropriate. Then again, there was much about the slave named Medousa that Livia didn't approve of. That included Caesar's preference for her.

"Domina, you are looking well."

"Medousa," Pomponia began. She looked worriedly at the slave's dress – the white stola and the head-covering veil – and pursed her lips in concern. "Why are you – "

"All is well, Priestess." She ran her palm over the white veil on her head. "It is not as it seems. Do not worry about me. I made an oath to you as a child, remember? It was an oath to the goddess, as well. I honor that oath still, even from Caesar's home."

"Now I know something is not right," Pomponia said flatly. "It's not like you to be so sacrificial."

"Then repay me for my sacrifice," Medousa said, her voice taking on a harder tone. "Stay away from Quintus Vedius Tacitus."

"I have petitioned the goddess to forgive me," said Pomponia. "He played me like lyre and I was too womanish to stop the music. Fear not, Medousa, I shall not let him play me again."

"It's not him I fear," said Medousa. "Have you seen the Lady Valeria lately? She looks like she swallowed the Trojan Horse. She's a wreck at the best of times, but this pregnancy has made her even more mad. Give her no reason to speak against you."

"I will not live in fear of a common woman, Medousa."

"It's not fear, Domina. It's prudence."

"Enough, Medousa. Now tell me, how is life under Caesar?"

Medousa huffed. "You hit the mark. I live *under* Caesar. Life is very different than it is at the temple, but the food and wine is just as good, and he is not a vicious master." She pointed her chin at Livia. "It has been better since he took up with that one. He is tiring of me, but she is still new."

"I am sorry he has dishonored you, Medousa."

"A Caesar cannot dishonor a slave, Priestess." Medousa laughed and Pomponia saw a flicker of her former impishness. "Anyway, Spes looks over me. Caesar says that I remain your property. Once your thirty-years of service to the goddess are over, you can reclaim me. If you choose to stay with the Vestal order, I can at least live in one of your villas in the country."

"It will be so." Pomponia took Medousa's hands. "Only fourteen years to go until you and I walk through the green fields of Tivoli together."

The slave squeezed her mistress's hands. "Stay away from him, Domina," she repeated, "or we shall be walking through the green fields of Elysium together instead."

CHAPTER IX

Hoc Nomen Dare Infernum

(This name I give to Hades)

Rome 39 BCE

Valeria felt the familiar cramp of pain deep in her belly. Blood trickled down the inside of her legs, but she didn't stop. She gripped the stick more tightly and struck the slave again on her exposed back.

Good. Now she wasn't the only one bleeding.

Quintus walked into the room and casually bit into a pear. "Why are you beating her?" he asked his wife. "It wasn't her fault."

"The sheets look worse than they did before she washed them!" howled Valeria. "They're ruined. She didn't get any of the blood out!"

"Jupiter gives a shit about the sheets," Quintus replied. He turned to leave, but Valeria threw down her stick and scurried after him.

"Where are you going?"

"Not that it's any of your business, but I'm going to the tabularium."

"Let me guess, husband. You're going to pass by the Temple of Vesta on your way."

Quintus threw his pear on the floor and the slave with the bleeding back gathered her tunica around her before crawling over to dispose of it. He wiped his mouth with the back of his hand and then pointed to a blanket-covered basket in the corner of the room.

"If that thing isn't gone when I get home, I'll throw it in the Tiber myself. And you with it, gods help me."

"Throw it in the river, father!" Their seven-year-old daughter, Quintina, shuffled into the room, half carrying and half dragging her little sister along the mosaicked floor.

Valeria pointed at Quintus. "Do you see, daughters, how little your father cares for his children?" Her hand trembled as she wagged her finger at him. "We shall have to find you husbands soon so that you may leave his house."

"I don't want a husband," said the older girl. "I want to be a priestess instead, like my great aunt Tacita. I want to guard the sacred fire and go to parties."

"Do not talk to me of the sacred fire!" Valeria stomped across the room and spat into the flame of an oil lamp.

Quintus barked at the slave. "Mind the children," he said. "Don't let her see them today."

"Yes, Dominus." The slave ushered the girls away.

"You cannot keep me from my children, Quintus. You may not care whether they live or die, but I do!"

Quintus shrugged and walked away. Only the crash of the oil lamp breaking against the wall made him stop and turn around.

"I piss on the sacred flame," said Valeria.

A moment later, she found herself on the floor. Her jaw ached and her eyes streamed with tears. She blinked to clear the blurriness from her eyes and tried to get up, but the room was spinning so she sat back down.

"Get rid of that wretched thing today," he said, pointing angrily at the basket. "It's been dead for a week. The rats will be at it soon."

"That *thing* is your son!" screamed Valeria. "Come back here!" But it was too late. His back was already to her, and he was gone from the house before she could get to her feet. She moved across the floor on her hands and knees until she reached the basket.

Slowly, she pulled back the blanket.

The baby was grey now and his face was sunken, although his neck and body were bloated. The smell made her stomach rise. She touched his hair and recoiled as the soft skin of his scalp sloughed off under her fingers. She couldn't wait any longer. She had to send him to Pluto.

Gently, she placed the blanket back over his small body and tucked the corners into the edges of the basket. She looked at the broken oil lamp on the floor.

This was the fault of Priestess Pomponia. She knew it. The priestess had cursed her child. She had called upon Vesta to destroy Valeria's home because of the lust she had for Quintus.

She had sacrificed to the goddess and Vesta had answered by keeping the child, the son Quintus so desperately wanted, too long inside Valeria's womb. When the child did not come at the right time, Quintus had grown suspicious. He claimed it was not his.

He also blamed Valeria for its death. The midwife had told him that excessive drink had caused the child to wither and weaken, and he foolishly believed her. Valeria had tried to tell him that it was Pomponia – she had killed their son by some black magic! – but her only answer from him had been yet another blackened eye.

His perversion for the priestess ruled his mind. Something had to be done.

She looked around the room. The slave, the one she knew Quintus regularly bedded and ordered to spy on her, was elsewhere in the house with the children.

Quickly, she wrapped herself in a hooded palla, gathered the basket in her arms, and slipped unseen from the house. Quintus had left on foot for the Forum. He would be easy enough to follow.

Well, on a normal day he would be easy enough to follow. Today, however, her belly cramped and the dried blood on the inside of her legs pinched her skin as she trailed behind him along the cobblestone streets, darting in and out of porticos, ducking behind vendor's carts and hiding behind the laundry that hung down from apartment windows above, all while clutching the death basket in her arms.

Valeria followed him, growing more exhausted and confused by the moment. Quintus wasn't headed for the Roman Forum. That meant he wasn't going to the tabularium, although she knew he went there almost daily since being granted the quaestorship.

He had lied; however, it wasn't all bad. If he wasn't headed for the Forum, that meant he wasn't going to the Temple of Vesta, either.

Unless he was meeting his lover somewhere else. Somewhere secret, perhaps a brothel or a rented apartment. Many men of class carried on illicit affairs in such places.

Soon, she found herself tracking him through the newer streets of the Forum of Caesar: the forum that the dictator had started to build a few years before his assassination. Construction was underway on a number of basilicas and temples, the largest of which was the Temple of Mars Ultor, commissioned by the new Caesar to honor his victory over Brutus and Cassius.

Quintus weaved through the scaffolding, dodged falling hammers and stepped carefully to avoid the nails that littered the construction-filled streets.

Valeria limped behind at a safe distance and then retreated into a portico when Quintus stopped in front of the staircase of the Temple of Venus Genetrix.

He looked up thoughtfully at the statues that stood on either side of the temple's entrance. One was of Venus blessing a child. The other was of Julius Caesar.

Valeria's heart leapt up. Venus Genetrix, goddess of motherhood and domesticity: Quintus was there to pray for the health of his wife and the soul of his son.

Yet instead of climbing the staircase to enter the temple, Quintus turned to walk down a side street where a number of wooden shrines to Venus had been erected against the marble exterior of the massive temple.

He stopped before one of them. Valeria hid behind a shoddy scaffolding from which some workers had hung their dusty cloaks. She was closer to Quintus than was probably prudent, but she needed to see what he was doing. She needed to hear what he was saying.

The shrine was modest and makeshift, with bunches of dried myrtle and roses hanging on the marble wall against which it leaned. A lifeless swan had been affixed to the wall in front of the shrine as well, a sacrifice to the goddess. The taxidermist had placed ocean-blue beads in the place of its eyes to symbolize Venus's birth from the sea. Several large scallop sea-shells adorned the top of the altar and a tall candle burned within each one.

A man dressed in a white toga with a blue cloak bowed deeply to Quintus as he approached the shrine. They exchanged a few words before Quintus passed the man some coin.

Quintus knelt before the altar. He placed his hands upon it and looked into the ocean-blue eyes of the lifeless swan.

"Venus, changer of hearts," he said. "I am Quintus Vedius Tacitus, former soldier of Julius Caesar, priest of Mars, quaestor of Rome. Hear me now, Venus. I make this sacrifice so that the priestess Pomponia will love me."

Quintus took hold of a dagger that lay on top of the altar.

As he did, the man in the blue cloak reached into a cage that sat on the ground and pulled out a plump white dove. With his head lowered in solemn respect to the ritual, he passed the dove to Quintus.

"Venus, I make this sacrifice so that our love will burn as embers in the sacred fire until we can be together. It is many years hence goddess, but I ask that it be made so."

Quintus drew the blade across the dove's throat in one move and the animal's head collapsed between his fingers. Its blood trickled down his arm to form a small pool of red on the cobblestone.

Valeria gripped the scaffolding beside her. In all her years of marriage to Quintus, she had never seen him humble himself so. She had never known him to show any softness, and certainly never anything resembling love. Not to her and not to their daughters. She took a final look at him – his head lowered in prayer and blood running down his arm – before she turned and walked away.

She walked for a long time. She walked until the cobblestone streets of the Forum Julius became the cobblestone streets of the Forum Romanum. She walked, drained of emotion but full of purpose, until she reached the Temple of Pluto, god of the underworld.

A thin woman with blood painted on her cheeks and a black palla wrapped around her shoulders eyed Valeria and the basket she carried.

"Domina," she called out. "Come."

Valeria obediently followed the woman to a row of wooden shop-fronts adjacent to the temple and into one which was heavily draped in purple and black cloth.

As she entered it, the light of day faded into a space that was dimly lit with oil lamps and that smelled strongly of incense.

Without a word, the thin woman took the basket from Valeria's arms and set it on a table.

She lifted the blanket and looked at the dead baby underneath it without any discernable reaction – or rather, with the reaction of someone who was accustomed to looking at dead babies.

Valeria reached into the basket to remove a small purse of coins buried under the blanket. She pressed a few pieces of silver into the palm of the woman, and then placed one – a gold aureus – into the baby's gummy mouth to pay the ferryman for his passage to Hades.

"It won't take long, Domina," said the thin woman as she gently removed the baby's body from the basket. "And of course, all is done with the utmost respect."

She carried the baby away, waiting until she had safely passed behind a black curtain to remove the gold coin from the child's mouth and replace it with a bronze one. Surely Charon didn't charge that much for something so small.

Feeling detached from reality, Valeria sat down on a chair to wait for her child's ashes. As she stared into the flame of an oil lamp, her thoughts wandered to her life with Quintus Vedius Tacitus.

She had been given to him as a bride of fourteen. It had taken him months to couple with her: even then he had preferred his slaves to his wife, although she had never understood why. Everyone said she was the most beautiful woman to be born to her family in generations.

She performed her duties as his wife with devotion and diligence. She bore him two perfect daughters. Yet when she dared ask why he felt no love for them, his answer had come in the form of his fist.

But now all was clear as glass. His obsession with the Vestal had taken hold of him before they had even married, when he and Pomponia were still children. He had fallen in love with her inside Rome's marble temples as they learned to perform their sacred duties to Mars and Vesta.

Yet Quintus, more than anyone, knew it was impossible. The priestess was bound to the Vestal order and a life of chastity for thirty years. They could never have a life together; however, every time he saw her the fantasy of that life flickered before his eyes.

How could Valeria compete with that? How could the reality of his all too familiar wife, whose body was his to take or leave as he pleased, compete with the fantasy of a woman he could never know in that way? It was not fair.

It was not fair that his first thought in times of danger or public discord was of the priestess. It was not fair that he rushed off to protect her, leaving his wife and children at the mercy of whatever mob might surround them or break through their doors.

Spite tightened her chest. How she longed to see Priestess Pomponia climb down the ladder into the black pit in the evil field. How she longed to see her husband whipped in the Forum not just for his sacrilege, but for the years of cruelty and indifference he had inflicted upon her.

Her chest ached with growing anger. She could not accuse the priestess of breaking her vows to the goddess. There was no proof the Vestal and Quintus had coupled – in fact, Valeria doubted they had – and the priestess had powerful friends. Caesar himself doted on her. Plus, most of Rome already thought Valeria was mad on account of her outburst at the Lady Octavia's wedding reception.

And although she hated to admit it, she did not want Quintus dead. She just wanted him to love her as his wife and to regard his children as blessings rather than burdens.

There was only one path left open to her.

"Bring me a lead sheet and a stylus," she said to no one in particular.

A boy, perhaps ten or eleven years old, quickly collected a tray and set it on the table before the distressed woman. Her request was nothing unusual. Those who found themselves drawn to the Temple of Pluto often had reason to use a curse tablet.

Valeria smoothed the thin sheet of lead and clutched the stylus in her hand. She pressed the tip into the lead and drew a stick figure of a woman, and around it the swirl of a Vestal's stola.

"I call upon black and shaded Pluto," she whispered, "I call upon dark and hidden Persephone. *Hoc nomen dare infernum:* the Vestal Virgin Pomponia, white-robed harpy. I curse her food, her drink, her face, her laughter, her virginity..."

As she spoke, Valeria dragged the stylus over the lead sheet, creating deep criss-crossing lines over the stick figure of the Vestal. "...I curse her watch over the sacred fire and her service to the goddess. I divorce her as a bride of Rome and marry her to Pluto."

Quietly, the thin woman reappeared and placed a terracotta urn on the table beside the curse tablet. Valeria removed the lid and dipped her fingers inside, scooping out a wet pile of grey ashes. She smeared the ashes over the lead tablet and then rolled it up as though it were a scroll.

She sat back in her chair as the young boy leaned over the table: he held a thin nail over the curse scroll and then tapped it with a small hammer, nailing it closed.

Valeria stood. She held the urn in one hand and clutched the lead scroll in the other.

"You can do what you like with the curse tablet," said the thin woman, "but I recommend throwing it in the Lacus Curtius or burying it near the Temple of Pluto. The dark gods will read it faster."

"*Gratias tibi ago*," said Valeria, "but I know precisely which temple to bury it by."

CHAPTER X

VIRGO VESTALIS

ROME 38 – 37 BCE

"*Salve*, Caesar and Lady Octavia," Pomponia welcomed Octavian and his sister into the courtyard at the House of the Vestals. "I had not been informed you were coming. I will have some minted honey water brought out.

"It's already on the way," said Fabiana, emerging from under an archway. "Thank you both for coming." She gestured to the cushioned benches beside one of the pools. "Please sit."

As they did, Fabiana leaned forward and put her hand on Pomponia's knee. "You will let me speak and not interrupt."

Pomponia was taken aback. "Of course, Fabiana."

"I am eighty-three years old," said the high priestess, "and I have served Vesta for seventy-seven of those years."

"No," Pomponia stood up. "It is not proper." She caught herself and sat back down.

Instead of chiding the Vestal, Fabiana's voice took a forgiving tone. "It is time, Pomponia. The goddess wants me to rest."

"It is not proper for the Vestalis Maxima to – "

"There is precedent for the chief Vestal to step down," said Fabiana. "You know that. I shall remain active within the order, but you shall lead us. Our duty is to the goddess. It is to sustain her sacred fire and perform her rituals. It is to preserve and honor the Vestal order, and in so doing to protect Rome and her people."

She took Pomponia's hands. "That is no small duty. The Vestal order cannot be guided by a weak and frail priestess. It needs – it *deserves* – a strong and vibrant Vestalis Maxima. That must be you. As the sacred fire is rekindled, so must our order be rekindled."

Pomponia furrowed her brow. "I am too young. Priestess Nona is next in – "

"Priestess Nona would rather boil her hands in a pot of oil than be Vestalis Maxima. She has never enjoyed public worship or spectacle. If she could do it, I suspect she would close the temple and return to the days when Vesta was only honored in the home. Nona supports my decision and will be an invaluable resource to you. Priestess Alba would have been next, but alas, Charon's boat came for her too soon. I have spoken privately with Tuccia, Caecilia and Lucretia as well, and we are all agreed. You have served as the *de facto* chief Vestal for years and always with grace and diligence. Your fellow priestesses and the priests of the other collegia respect you. The people love you and the Senate trusts you. It shall be you."

Octavian cleared his throat.

"Great Lady, we are all indebted to your lifetime of service to the temple and to Rome," he said to Fabiana. "You've sustained the sacred flame with all reverence and skill." A wide smile. "But you've always had a certain wit and that has sustained the people's spirit over the years as much as any fire. I am happy you will remain with the order."

"It has been a good life," said Fabiana. "I thank you for your kind words, Caesar. Now if you will excuse me, I think I shall go sit in the shade."

She ribbed Pomponia. "See? I have learned to shirk my duties already. I must read some letters that arrived for me this morning. My great-niece has married again – fourth time, *Bona Dea!* – and she is either asking for advice or money. I suspect I know which one."

As Fabiana rose to leave, a slave appeared with a tray of minted honey water. "It's about time," Fabiana rebuked as she took a glass and walked off.

Octavia giggled. "High Priestess Pomponia," she said, "you look like you've seen the basilisk."

"I feel that way," replied Pomponia. "She is not so old, is she?"

"Priestess Fabiana will be with us for many years," assured Octavia. "Do not look so sad."

Octavian drained a cup of the sweet water and set the empty glass back on the tray. "She would strike Charon with his own hammer if he came for her. Take heart, High Priestess Pomponia. All is as the goddess wants it to be. My sister and I congratulate you on your good fortune." He held out his hand a slave slapped a scroll into it. "I have here your first task as Vestalis Maxima. It is a list of girls who I think have potential to join the Vestal order."

"Oh good," said Pomponia, brightening as she focused on the task at hand. "We are of one mind, Caesar. I have been thinking that we need one more."

"I have compiled the names from some of the best families in Rome," Octavian continued, "and I have seen the girls myself. They are all of high intellect and free of defect." He handed Pomponia the scroll.

"I will interview each girl and her family and make my choice by the kalends," said Pomponia.

"Excellent," Octavian replied.

"Brother," said Octavia, "if temple business is finished, I think I should like to visit with my friend a while longer. I will borrow a Vestal litter to take me home."

"As you wish, sister." He smiled at Pomponia. "I shall have the newsreader announce your appointment as Vestalis Maxima and also have the bulletin nailed to the Senate door. We shall publically celebrate next week. Rome rejoices in your exaltation. As Caesar and as your friend, I rejoice also. I am confident we will work together for a better Rome."

"I have no doubt, Caesar. Thank you."

Pomponia regarded Octavia: her brother had no sooner exited the courtyard than she burst into tears.

"Oh Lady Pomponia," she wept, "your appointment isn't the only thing the newsreader will be shouting from the Rostra today."

"What else? What is the matter?"

Octavia spoke through soft sobs. "You know that Antony has been in Egypt...my brother sent him back there to attend to the grain shipments. He promised me he would not take up with her again. But he has. He has even claimed his children by her – twins!" She caught her breath. "A boy and a girl. Cleopatra Selene and Alexander Helios. Their names mean moon and sun." Her fingers tightened around the glass of water in her hands. "Isn't that sweet?"

"Sweet as poison, Octavia. What will Caesar do?"

"He will do nothing. There's nothing he can do right now. Rome needs grain." Octavia regained some of her composure. "Antony has proven a faithless husband to me, but for now he is honoring his agreement with Caesar. The grain arrives. It isn't always on time, but at least it comes. That is Caesar's only concern. Antony's fidelity to his wife is of little significance."

"The Roman people will think no less of you because of Antony's carousing," said Pomponia. "You are a kind and virtuous woman and they adore you. It is only Antony who stands to lose the people's respect."

"That's what my brother said. To be honest, I think the news pleases him. The worse Antony looks to the people and the Senate, the better he looks to them."

"He is a politician and a Caesar. He will take such news as a duck takes to water. That is to be expected. Never doubt his love for you, though."

Octavia passed her glass to the slave and folded her hands on her lap. For the first time, Pomponia noticed something – Octavia almost always wore a simple white stola. It seemed a curious choice for the sister of Caesar and a woman with more gold than Midas. Perhaps Octavia couldn't choose her attire any more than she could choose her husband.

"I must stop raining tears on your big day," said Octavia, wiping her eyes with her palla. "Let's look at that list. Who will be Rome's newest Vestal novice?"

Pomponia opened the scroll and swallowed hard at the first name on the list: Quintina Tacita Major. Quintus's eldest daughter.

Octavia peered over the Vestal's shoulder to read the scroll.

"Quintina Tacita," she mused. "A good candidate, to be sure. Her father is a quaestor and priest of Mars, and her family has a history of serving the goddess."

"Yes," Pomponia's mouth felt dry and she took a sip of the sweetened water. "Her great-aunt was the Vestal Tacita." She smirked. "She beat a Gaul to death with an iron stoker when he broke into the temple and tried to extinguish the sacred fire."

"I have heard that story many times," laughed Octavia. "A true Vestal and a true Roman. There is good blood in that girl, Pomponia."

"I know it," Pomponia said more throatily than she had intended. "I suppose that I shall have to meet with her."

* * * * * *

A temple slave escorted Quintus and his wide-eyed daughter into the office of the Vestalis Maxima inside the House of the Vestals.

The girl gripped her father's hand tightly, partly in worry and partly in excitement, as she absorbed the beauty of the palace: nature frescos on the walls, Corinthian columns with strings of flowers wrapped around them, gold-gilded furnishings and painted statuary. The sound of water from an indoor fountain echoed off the marble walls.

The Vestalis Maxima sat at a large ornate desk surrounded by blue frescoed walls upon which were painted all the gods and goddesses of the Roman pantheon. Her head was down as one hand busily scribbled something on a scroll and the other hand absently tucked a loose lock of hair behind her ear.

"Domina," said the slave, "Quintus Vedius Tacitus and his daughter Quintina are here."

Pomponia rose. She saw Quintus's eyes move over her and it occurred to her that he had never seen her dressed in anything other than a stola, palla and veil. All their interactions to date had been at formal or semi-formal public events. Today, however, no real formality was required and she was dressed casually in a close-fitting, long white dress with a high-belted waist that revealed her figure. Her dark hair was pinned up in a bun, but she wore no veil.

"*Salve,* Quintus," she said as plainly as possible before smiling down at his daughter. "I am happy to meet you, Quintina. My name is Pomponia."

The girl bowed deeply. "Priestess Pomponia," she said, "I wish to join the Vestal order."

Quintus gave her arm a tug. "What did I tell you? Answer the questions put to you."

Pomponia took Quintina's hand from her father. "Speak as freely as you like," she said to the girl, whose eyes widened even more. She had never seen anyone challenge her father's authority, never mind a woman. Even more shocking, her father conceded.

"I want to show you something that I think will interest you," Pomponia said to Quintina. "Come." She looked up at Quintus. "You may stay here or accompany us. It is your choice."

"I will come."

Pomponia led them out of the palatial House of the Vestals, along the peristyle and into the courtyard, passing by the white and pink rosebushes and two large rectangular pools. In the center of one pool stood a marble statue of Vesta tipping a bowl of flames which magically transformed into the water that filled the pool. Several blue birds splashed in the turquoise water.

It was the exact scene depicted in the fresco on Octavian's wall – the same fresco Pomponia had been admiring when Quintus had grabbed her arm and kissed her. When he had spoken of love. It had been almost two years, but her body stirred at the memory of his closeness.

"That is a pretty statue of Vesta," said Quintina.

"If such things please you," Quintus replied.

"They do, father." The slightest hint of impertinence.

Pomponia suppressed a smile. The girl had a spark of her great-aunt in her. No doubt she had a streak of her father's strong will as well, although with the right training that could be a good thing. But what of her mother?

For a moment, Pomponia wondered how Valeria would be coping with the possibility of her daughter joining the Vestal order. Of course, it didn't matter.

The *patria potestas* gave Roman fathers ultimate control over their children. When a female child married, control then passed to her husband under the *pater familias*.

There were exceptions, of course, where Roman women were emancipated and enjoyed legal independence. Vestal priestesses were the top ranks of such women.

If Quintina was chosen to serve the goddess and the Temple, Quintus would lose all power over her. If she chose to marry after her years of service, she would retain her legal independence and her wealth. The idea of her life being controlled by a man would be as alien and distasteful to Quintina as it was to Pomponia.

They reached the far end of the courtyard where several life-sized statues of Vestal priestesses were being cut from massive marble blocks by dust-covered sculptors. Chisels, hammers, drills and various scrapers and grinders lay scattered on the grass as the sculptors chattered and shook their heads at imperfections in their work.

One of them noticed the Vestal's approach. "Priestess," he said, "We are working diligently. You will be pleased with our finished work." He wiped dust out of his eyes.

"I know that, Agesander," Pomponia replied lightly. "Lady Fabiana makes me sneak into the courtyard at night with her and inspect your work. Carry on."

The sculptor laughed and returned to his marbles. Caesar may have commissioned the statues, but it was Priestess Fabiana who had insisted they be constructed in the courtyard so that she could follow their progress.

Pomponia pointed to one of the statues. "That is the Priestess Tacita," she said to Quintina. "Your great-aunt."

The girl's face swelled with so much emotion that Pomponia herself could feel it. Without asking permission, she picked a flower from the garden and placed it at the statue's feet.

Quintus's body tensed at his daughter's boldness; however, it seemed to him that her assuming nature – one Quintus had tried to suppress – was being encouraged by the priestess.

"Do you know the story of Tacita and the Gaul?" asked Pomponia.

"Oh yes," she said proudly to the Vestal. "Father says it is one of the greatest stories in our family history."

It was the way Quintina looked up at her father. With such familiarity. A sudden image of Quintus formed in Pomponia's mind: he was in his home, chatting idly with Valeria and playing with his children. The children he had created with her in the dark of night and in the warmth of their bed. She could imagine him gripping Valeria's arm the same way he had once gripped her own.

It was a world and life she had never known, and it roused within her a mixture of emotions. Sadness. Curiosity. Envy. A longing to know Quintus in a way that was free of the protocol and custom that separated them. In the private, familiar way that Valeria knew him.

Quintina brought her back into the moment. "If I am accepted into the order will I still be able to see my father and mother?"

"Yes of course. You will be able to visit your home quite often, and we have regular visiting days here for parents and families."

"Do your parents visit you?"

"Sadly, no longer. They died when I was very young."

"How?"

"My mother died in childbirth with my brother. My father was killed on campaign for Pompey."

"How long have you been a Vestal?"

"I was chosen when I was seven years old and I have been a Vestal for seventeen years, so..." Pomponia pretended to count on her fingers. "...I have thirteen years of official service left."

Quintina giggled. “Do you want to get married when you’re done or stay a priestess?”

Pomponia could feel Quintus’s eyes on her. “The Fates have not spun that thread yet.”

“How many priestesses live here?”

“There are six Vestal priestesses who are dedicated to tending the sacred flame in the temple and performing public rites and rituals,” said Pomponia, “as well as three older Vestals who are retired from active service but remain with the order. They help us teach the novices, younger girls like you, how to perform their duties. If you are accepted, you will be one of several girls who are in training.”

Quintina nodded, as if in approval. “Do the priestesses who train here go to other temples? What about the Temple of Vesta in Tivoli or Capua? Or the ones in Africa?”

“Yes, our priestesses are sent to oversee temples in other towns and provinces,” Pomponia explained. “They are responsible for everything. That includes the selection and training of novices, managing the temple and bakery mills for sacrificial wafers, the storage of wills and other official documents, consulting with Caesar and the senate, performing public rites and rituals and – what have I forgotten? – oh yes, making sure the sacred fire doesn’t go out!”

Quintina giggled again as the Vestal looked over her shoulder at a young girl in a white tunica who was waiting patiently to speak.

“What is it, Sabina?” asked Pomponia.

“Priestess, can I show her inside the temple?”

“By all means. But find Nona and have her take you.”

Quintus watched his daughter excitedly run off with the other girl. “She is too bold for a girl,” he said. “She will be difficult to rule.”

“Some women wish to rule themselves,” said Pomponia. “Is that really so hard for a man to understand?”

"And what about you, Lady Pomponia? Do you rule yourself?" Quintus took a step closer and lowered his voice. "The Regia is empty after dark," he said. "If I asked you to meet me there tonight, would you?"

Her face flushed. "No."

Quintus offered her a patronizing smile. "Then you do not rule yourself at all, High Priestess."

* * * * * *

Her eyes were dilated and her words were slurred. Her movements were slow, deliberate, clumsy. But at least she was quiet. At least her fury and her outbursts had subsided. At least she left him alone most of the time.

Quintus watched his wife recline on the couch and drain the last of her wine. He knew the physician's tonic that he had stirred into her drink would soon usher her to sleep.

But for the moment, she was resisting it. "Did they cut her hair?" she asked him.

"Yes."

"Who cut it?"

"The Vestalis Maxima." He didn't tell her that Pomponia was now the chief Vestal. Valeria assumed it was still Fabiana. She hadn't been out of the house in weeks to learn otherwise and there was no point in telling her. It would only be a fight.

"Did she cry?"

"No."

"What did she do?"

"She was happy." He let out an irritated sigh. "She hung her locks on the Capillata tree herself."

"What else?"

"She was clothed in white and said her vows. The Pontifex Maximus, Lepidus, claimed her as a bride of Rome."

Valeria tried to take another sip of wine, but realized her cup was empty. She let it drop to the floor. "What else?"

"I don't know. They took her into the temple after that. Obviously I couldn't go inside." He drained his own cup of wine in one swallow. "She'll be happier there."

"You couldn't care less for your daughter's happiness," slurred Valeria. "All you care about is your own advancement and having a good excuse to visit the House of the Vestals." She jabbed an angry finger at him. "You are sickeningly transparent, Quintus, but do you know what? I am thankful Quintina is at the temple. I am thankful that she will never have to submit to a husband like you. I am thankful...I am..."

Her head bobbed and then fell back onto the couch.

Quintus sat heavily on the couch beside her. Valeria was right: he was transparent. And if he didn't find a way to force Pomponia from his thoughts, it was only a matter of time until his feelings for her were seen by all.

He had already withdrawn from many of his religious functions to limit his contact with her, and had instead immersed himself in his civic duties. That would have to continue. He couldn't risk having so many eyes on him when he was in her presence.

A female slave slipped quietly into the room. "Dominus, should I take Lady Valeria to bed?"

"No," said Quintus. "Leave her here."

He glanced up at the slave and she obediently nodded her head in understanding. "Of course, Dominus. I will prepare myself and wait for you in your chambers."

There is always one way to forget, Quintus thought to himself.

CHAPTER XI

Militiae Species Amor Est

(Love is a kind of war)

Rome 36 - 33 BCE

"Juno's tits," Livia swore under her breath. Her blood had come yet again. Every month, her cycle was as certain and predictable as the moon's.

She had been trying to conceive a child with Octavian for nearly three years: after all, Caesar needed a male heir. It used to be that her husband would ask every month, "Are you with child?" But no more. Now he didn't even bother to ask. Now he knew that his wife's womb was as barren as salted Carthage.

The slave named Medousa handed her the menstrual wool to absorb her flow and she pushed it between her legs. The cramps were coming so she allowed the slave to wind a heated wrap around her middle before falling back on her bed with a pained groan.

"Medousa, tell me something."

"Yes, Domina?"

"Has Caesar been taking you more lately?"

"Yes, Domina."

"Oh. I thought as much."

Medousa placed a pillow under Livia's head. The two of them had developed a somewhat unique dynamic over the past couple of years, largely due to the fact that Medousa was still considered the property of the Vestalis Maxima Pomponia.

The ownership issue didn't really affect day to day life: Medousa was a slave in the house of Caesar and was expected to do anything asked of her, which included satisfying Caesar's sexual needs; however, it did mean that she often escaped the harsher treatment Livia doled out to other house slaves.

Medousa had discovered early on that Livia was the type of mistress who would beat her slaves halfway to Hades just for the exercise; however, Caesar frowned on such behavior. He often spoke publically against the unnecessary or excessive abuse of slaves.

Nonetheless, Livia was known to shred a back or two when he was away.

Livia yanked a blanket over her legs. "When you are coupling with him," she asked Medousa, "what does he have you do? Is there anything...unusual? Anything that might surprise me to know about?"

Medousa sat on the edge of the bed. It was an informality that would have had another slave whipped in the courtyard.

"The first time he took me, he believed I was a virgin," she began. "He had a fantasy that I was Rhea Silvia and he was Mars. Lately, he has been having that fantasy again. I use a blood-soaked sponge and when he penetrates me. I act like it hurts and the blood comes. It seems to give him much pleasure, Domina."

Livia furrowed her brow, but she wasn't angry. She was thinking.

"Is it just me, Medousa, or does Caesar at times look at his sister with desire?"

"I have not noticed that, Domina. But he does seem to be drawn to purity and virtue. I think that is why he asks Lady Octavia to dress the way she does. She has so many white stolas in her wardrobe that I sometimes think I'm back at the temple."

Livia snorted. The slave had a mouth on her, but at least it was a useful mouth. "Get your cloak, Medousa. I have an errand for you to run."

* * * * * *

The last time Medousa had been to a slave market, she had been the merchandise. This time she was purchasing merchandise. The memories came back all the same.

The bustle of bodies and the shouts of competing bids. The wooden cages with dirt-covered men, women and children crouching inside. Some of them stared vacantly past the bars. These were the ones who had been bought and sold before. They knew what was happening. It was just life. All they could do was wait and see what master they'd be serving tonight.

Others wept, prayed or trembled with fear. These were the ones who had been torn from their homes in other lands – the spoils of war or piracy – and taken to Rome to be sold as slaves. Families clung to each other as if their embrace could prevent the slave-traders from tearing them apart and removing all hope that they would ever see each other again in this life.

They called out in a chorus of foreign languages, but they all said the same thing: *Don't take my child! I want my mother! Stop! I am not a slave! Please have mercy!*

In her mind, Medousa heard a voice from long-ago. *I love you, Penelope. Mother loves you, never forget. No matter what happens, never forget.*

The voice felt like a wound opening. She tried to picture her mother's face but nothing formed except the vision of the Medusa pendant she always wore around her neck and a vague image of thick, auburn hair.

She could still see her father's face, though. Dark, bearded and strong. He had held himself with dignity and courage until he had seen his wife stripped naked on the auction block, and then he had raged against the chains that bound him like a wild animal in the arena.

Only Hera knew what had become of them.

"Medousa, is that you?"

The voice brought her back. She turned her head at the sound of it and found herself staring into the face of Quintus Vedius Tacitus. He wore a rugged brown tunic and had a bunch of scrolls tucked under his arm. He held a much-used wax tablet in one hand and a stylus in the other.

"Yes, it's me," she said flatly. "I didn't know you were in the slave business."

"I'm not. I'm here on official business," he pointed his chin at the scrolls under his arm. "Tax audits of slave-traders."

"Oh." She stared at him frostily. "Is there anything else?"

He shifted his eyes uncomfortably and then looked back at her. For a moment, Medousa thought he might offer an apology or at least some kind of acknowledgement of how his sacrilege had separated her from Pomponia. But of course he didn't. The beastly man had no capacity to think of anyone but himself.

He shifted uneasily on one foot and Medousa grinned. She knew he wanted to ask about the high priestess, but she wouldn't give him the chance.

"If you'll excuse me," she said, and walked past him without looking back. She was on official business too.

Medousa craned her neck above the crowd until she finally saw what she was looking for: a large wooden sign that advertised *Virgo* and boasted a rough drawing of a naked woman. A raised platform had been erected under the sign, upon which stood a naked girl perhaps fifteen years old.

She tried to cross her arms to cover her bare breasts, but the slave-trader poked her with a stick and she lowered them to her sides. He barked something and pointed the stick at her again, and she turned around slowly to show her backside to the bidders.

"That's ten thousand denarii," the slave-trader shouted. "Eleven thousand? It should be eleven thousand! Look at this girl, such a beauty. And so docile! Just like a little lamb. Speaks Latin well enough. Guaranteed intact." He jabbed her with the stick and she turned back around.

"Prove it," yelled a toothless man from the crowd, "open her legs!"

The slave-trader threw a rock and hit him on the head. "Get out of here you sack of shit or I'll call the guards. Serious buyers only! Go to the Subura if you want a free look."

"Eleven thousand denarii," shouted Medousa.

"Where is your man, honey?" asked the slave-trader.

"Private buyer," she replied, and held up the heavy purse Livia had given her.

"Eleven thousand," he announced. "Twelve? Did I mention that this one can read a little?" But the crowd was already breaking up and moving on to cheaper fare. The slave-trader shrugged his shoulders – eleven was two better than he had expected anyway – and tossed the girl a stained tunica which she quickly pulled over her head.

Medousa set a few more coins onto the slave-trader's rickety desk to expedite the transaction and soon the slave girl was obediently trailing behind her down the cobblestone street to Caesar's house on the Palatine Hill.

By the time they arrived, night was falling and both of them were dripping sweat. Medousa led the girl – who said her name was Maia – into the slaves' bathhouse where the chief house slave Despina was already waiting, along with the cosmetic slave who stood ready with her tray of grooming tools.

She cropped the girl's hair, removed her body hair and scrubbed her clean in the water before dressing her in a white tunica and veil.

"A man is going to penetrate you," Medousa said to the wide-eyed girl.

A nod.

"It will be painful, but do not try to hide your pain. Let him see it. It will not last long and afterwards you will be cared for and fed. Do you have any questions?"

The girl shook her head just as Livia strode purposefully into the room. She looked the girl up and down as though she were a side of beef: inspection was necessary, but not necessarily pleasant.

"Intact?" she asked Medousa.

"Yes, Domina. The physician at the market confirmed it."

"Good." She lifted the slave's tunic to look beneath it, dropped it, and then said, "Come with me."

With the girl in tow, Livia marched through the dimly-lit house directly to her and Octavian's bedchambers, forcing her sober expression to transform into a flirtatious smile before opening the door a crack and peeking around the corner like a mischievous child playing a game.

"Hello, dear," said Octavian. He was lying on top of their luxurious four-post bed. The red silk canopy that was draped over it was blowing lightly in the breeze of an open window. When he noticed her expression, he set down the scroll he was reading and looked sideways at her impish grin. "What are you up to, you little minx? You look like Eris about to strike."

"I have a gift for you, husband."

He folded his hands across his chest and clucked his tongue. "And what might that be?"

Livia opened the door wider and led the slave girl to the foot of the bed. "Husband, this gift is wrapped in pure white," she lovingly smoothed the veil that fell down the girl's back, "and for a reason that you will soon discover."

"Oh?" Octavian tried to maintain a passionless expression, but Livia could see evidence of his arousal already forming beneath his tunic. "Tell me, wife, are you going to share this gift with me?"

"I think not," Livia said naughtily, "but I will share a cup of wine with my husband when he is finished with it." She put her hands on the slave girl's shoulders to urge her onto the bed, and then glided giddily back to the door, winking at her husband as she closed it. "Hail Caesar," she said.

As the door clicked shut behind her, Livia exhaled and leaned against it. Medousa was already waiting in the hall.

"It will be over in less time than it takes to boil an egg, Domina."

"When it's over, take the girl to the slave quarters for the night. Bring her back to the market first thing in the morning and sell her."

"She won't be worth as much now."

"I don't care about that," said Livia. "And next time, Medousa, choose one that isn't quite so pretty."

"Yes, Domina."

"Have some fresh linen ready," Livia ordered. "I want the sheets changed as soon as it's over. And bring a washing bowl for Caesar, too."

"Yes, Domina."

"And then come back with some refreshments. Wine. Perhaps some pears or figs, and a little cold meat. I will eat with Caesar."

"All will be done, Domina."

Livia watched Medousa disappear down the hall. She pressed her ear to the door. A grunt. A cry of pain. *Less time than it takes to boil an egg.*

Livia knew that she had failed to fulfill her primary purpose as the wife of Caesar: to provide her powerful husband with a son and heir.

As a divorced woman with children from another man, neither could she exploit the univira virtue that Caesar loved to preach about. Although she had a good family name, her personal past lent little weight to his public persona as a man who upheld traditional Roman morals and sexual values.

Yet there were other ways to be useful to Caesar. And as long as she kept bringing those ways to his bedside – dressed all in white and pure as Alps snow – her status as Rome's first lady would be secure.

* * * * * *

"Argh," Pomponia lifted her tunica above her ankles as she navigated her way through a patch of sticky mud in the Vestal stables. She glared at several stable slaves who were hurrying toward her. "Why is this not cleaned?"

"Deepest apologies, High Priestess, it rained last night."

"It rains every night in October," she scolded, "hardly a supernatural event." Then she bit her lip. She was sounding more like Fabiana every day.

As she sat on a bench, a female slave rushed toward her with a washing basin. She untied the priestess's sandals and placed her dirty feet in the warm water. With her feet soaking in the water, Pomponia waved her hand in irritation at the slave.

"Move," she said, "I can't see."

She looked toward the riding arena where Quintina was cantering a white horse in wide circles. The girl caught on quickly to everything and learning to ride a horse was no exception.

Every Vestal was trained to tack and ride a horse in the event that a hasty exit from Rome – whether on account of fire, flood or invasion – was required, and the Vestal order had its own stables for such training.

Riding for pleasure was also one of the many privileges that Vestal priestesses enjoyed. Priestess Tuccia could be found quite often at the stables; however, Pomponia rarely had the time. Or the inclination. She had always preferred scrolls to saddles.

The stable's manager – a tall, muscly freedman named Laurentius – waved politely to Pomponia as he approached. Quintus followed behind him.

"High Priestess," he said, "Quintus Vedius Tacitus is here to see Miss Quintina."

"Thank you, Laurentius. You may leave us."

"As you wish, Domina."

The stable's manager left and Quintus scraped the bottom of his sandal on the low rung of a fence, leaving a lump of mud on it.

"You should beat your slaves," he growled.

"Perhaps I should let you do it," said Pomponia. "It might put you in a better mood."

Quintus stopped scraping his sandals and looked squarely at her. "This is my normal mood."

Pomponia rolled her eyes. "I know."

She rubbed her bare feet together in the water to scrape off the last of the dirt as Quintus sat down beside her – albeit at a respectable distance. He leaned forward with his hands on his knees.

It was the way Quintus always sat when he was beside her. Still awkward. Still slightly uncertain, even though Quintina was nearing her fourth year of training with the Vestal order and he had on many occasions spent his visits chatting idly with Pomponia.

In fact, those visits had been growing more frequent these last months. They had also been growing more personal. Their shared interest in Quintina had cleared common ground upon which an uneasy but evolving friendship had, after so many years of knowing each other, finally taken root.

It was a much different dynamic than it had been during those days they had performed their religious duties together, always stiff and in the public eye.

"How is Lady Fabiana?" asked Quintus.

Pomponia shrugged. "Good days and bad. She is starting to forget things."

"And how is Perseus?"

"Perseus is a wretched little hell-hound who digs up the flowers and chews my sandals. That dog must be a hundred years old by now. He is an immortal."

Quintus smiled widely.

Pomponia hated when he did that. His face opened up in that rare way and for a passing moment the normally detached, choleric Quintus became accessible, even inviting. She found it hard to look away. It reminded her of that day years ago: in Caesar's house, by the fresco of the Vestal courtyard.

Pomponia, what do you think of me?

I think you're an ill-tempered brute who has to be in control of everything and who delights in telling me what to do.

You have me there. Tell me that I'm the only man you'll ever love. Swear it on the Altar of Juno.

Of course, they had not spoken of that day since. Nor had they spoken of the day years ago when Quintus had first brought his daughter to visit the temple: the day he had abandoned all pretense by daring Pomponia to meet him at the empty Regia after nightfall.

They never spoke of these things, yet the memories were part of every conversation, every glance and every interaction between them. From the words they chose to the way they sat next to each other, the tension was always there. The unspoken past was ever-present.

"Your wife and younger daughter are well, I trust," said Pomponia. She splashed her feet in the water to emphasize how carefree the question was.

Quintus's smile suddenly turned into a snigger. That was nothing new. One moment he would be pleasant enough, the next moment he would snap back into his usual churlish, sullen self. There was no predicting it.

Even at his most tolerant, he was always a breath away from flashing Pomponia a scolding glance or chastising her for some real or imagined misstep. She had learned to live with it.

He shook his head in irritation for a moment, and then turned to her. "Why must you ask questions you know the answers to?"

"Why must you be so changeable?"

He fumed quietly for a moment and then said, "My younger daughter is well enough. My wife is..." He shook his head again. "Irrelevant."

"I'm sure she would be delighted to hear so."

Fully expecting Quintus to stand up and storm off, Pomponia forced herself to casually take her feet out of the basin as if she didn't care one way or the other what he did. She reached for the towel beside her, but Quintus wrested it out of her hand.

To her utter shock, he knelt on the ground before her. He spread the towel over his legs and then set Pomponia's bare feet on top, lifting the edges of the towel to softly, almost reverently, dry her feet.

The act was forbidden in a thousand ways.

"Quintus..." She told herself to pull her feet away from him, but for some reason they felt like they were too heavy to lift off his legs. The soles of her bare feet tingled with the warmth and sensation of his body beneath them. The sight and feel of his hands moving over the top of her feet quickened her breath.

"I saw Medousa in the market again," he said, as if nothing unusual was happening.

Pomponia caught her breath. "What was she doing?"

"Just buying more slaves for Caesar's house, I assume." He held the towel in one hand and moved it above her ankle to absorb the moisture there.

At the same time, his other hand caressed her lower leg, moving slowly upwards, until his fingers slipped behind the bend in her knee to stroke the soft, sensitive skin.

"Quintus, stop."

He didn't stop, of course. He never did what she told him; however, this time he wasn't being defiant. He was simply lost in the feel of her. But then he stopped stroking and gripped her leg more tightly.

"Caesar is sending me to Egypt," he said abruptly. "Queen Cleopatra has stopped her debt payments to Rome. Worse, the grain shipments are getting smaller, and that's providing they come at all. I am to meet with Marc Antony and assess the situation." He loosened his grip and again caressed her more gently. "A war is mounting between Caesar and Antony. It will happen soon. General Agrippa is already planning his campaign."

"I knew it was bad," said Pomponia. "I didn't know it was that bad." She pressed her feet into his legs. He responded by wrapping his strong hands around her ankles. "When do you leave?" she asked breathily.

"Tomorrow."

"Tomorrow? Why didn't you tell me earlier?"

"I only found out this morning."

"How can he send you so soon? With no warning?"

"He is Caesar. He can do as he likes."

She bit her lip. "How long must you stay there?"

"Indefinitely."

Pomponia put her hands to her face. “Then you will be there when the war between Egypt and Rome begins?”

“Without doubt,” he said, “but I have seen battle before.”

“Not like this. Caesar will be relentless and Antony will fight like a cornered animal.”

“That is like any battle, Pomponia.” He realized he had said her name without the honorific “priestess,” but did not apologize.

Instead, he got up and stood in front of her so that she had to look up to meet his eyes. “You will meet me at the Regia tonight after dark,” he said. It wasn’t a request. It was an order. “We will say our good-byes then.”

And then he was gone, picking his way through the mud toward the riding arena and the waving form of his daughter on horseback.

A female slave returned carrying Pomponia’s washed and dried sandals. She knelt down to tie them, but Pomponia waved her away. “I’ll do it myself.”

She tied them quickly and then marched toward the stable house where Laurentius was busily repairing some tack on an outdoor workbench. The faster she could get away from Quintus, the better.

“I must leave now,” she said to the stable manager. “Have two slaves and an armed escort bring Quintina back to the temple when she is finished her day’s lesson.”

“An armed escort? Is anything wrong, Domina?”

“No, Laurentius. I am just feeling a bit jumpy today.”

“Always wise to heed such feelings, High Priestess. It is how the gods speak to us. I shall accompany Miss Quintina back myself.”

“Thank you.”

She stepped into the lectica and let her body collapse back onto the cushions before the litter-bearers had even taken up their positions.

There was no way she would meet Quintus in the way he had said. His words and his presumptuousness were grossly insulting to her and, worse, were a sacrilegious affront to the great goddess and the Vestal order itself.

If that weren't enough to condemn him – and it was – there was his barbaric lack of judgment and total disregard for the danger he was putting them both in. Her reluctance to see him flayed alive in the Forum was matched only by her reluctance to see herself buried alive in the Campus Sceleratus.

But now Quintus was leaving for Egypt, possibly to never return.

Keenly aware of each passing hour, she moved through the rest of the day's duties. Taking inventory of corn, salt and coal. Inspecting the bakery. Writing letters and signing documents. Accounting. Overseeing new curricula for the girls and approving the image of Vesta's temple that Caesar wished to mint on his coins. Watching the construction that was going on within various areas of the House of the Vestals. Scheduling Tuccia, Caecilia and Lucretia for upcoming festivals and public events.

Yet no matter the task, she found her mind wandering back to the stables and to Quintus.

To the feel of his strong hands wrapped around her ankles. To the sound of his voice. To the thought that he would be walking out of her life soon and crossing the *mare nostrum* to whatever the Fates had in store.

It was one of those long days when her Vestal duties didn't bring her anywhere near the temple's fiery hearth. It was one of those days when she longed for simpler times, when she would spend quiet hours in the temple tending to Vesta's sacred fire with her own hands.

Life was simpler before Fabiana had taken ill. Life was simpler before Quintus, too.

She told herself she would meet him tonight – but only to say good-bye. Only to say that, despite his vulgar insolence and her sacred vows, she hoped in her heart that would be safe. She would pray daily to the goddess to make it so.

Finally, the sunset descended on Rome like a vibrant orange blanket, putting the city to bed. Pomponia wandered through the still House of the Vestals. Except for a handful of slaves – their work was never finished – she alone was awake. Or so she thought.

Perseus came trotting down a corridor to greet her, his nails clicking on the marble floor and his tongue hanging out.

She bent down to scratch his ears. "I am afraid to go alone, Perseus," she whispered. "You can come with me."

Pomponia slipped out of the portico and onto the cobblestone street of the Via Appia. The setting sun had cast a vivid orange glow onto the white marble of the circular Temple of Vesta. It looked even more beautiful than it usually did. She watched the smoke from the sacred hearth bloom out of the opening in the temple's tiled roof and spiral upwards into the evening sky, up toward the goddess.

She could hear the six guards laughing and chatting on the other side of the Temple of Vesta, almost closer to the Temple of Castor and Pollux. *I'll have to speak to them,* she thought irritably, but for the moment their laxity served her purpose. They could not see her.

She hesitated for a moment, but then Perseus tugged on his leash as if daring her to go through with it and she walked toward the Regia with renewed purpose.

She knew the Regia – which was located only steps from the Temple of Vesta – would be empty. As the office of the Pontifex Maximus, it was only used during the day and then only when Lepidus was in Rome, which he currently wasn't. These days, he was off in the provinces on triumvirate business more than he was in the city on religious business.

As she approached the portico of the Regia, her eyes wandered up the tall columns of the nearby Temple of the Comet Star. This was the temple that Octavian had dedicated to Julius Caesar several years earlier. It stood on the exact spot where the frenzied mob had erected a makeshift funeral pyre and burned the dictator with fire taken from the Temple of Vesta.

Pomponia remembered that night well. As the crowd – roused to action by Antony's funeral speech – had pushed forward to carry Caesar's body off the Rostra, Quintus had appeared at her side. He had seen her through the chaotic streets of the Forum to the safety of the temple's steps.

But Valeria was already there: she had gripped her husband's cloak in anger: *I knew you would be here!*

A pang of guilt stabbed at Pomponia. She wasn't just betraying her own sacred vows by meeting Quintus. She was also showing impiety toward the marriage vows Valeria had exchanged with him. She wound Perseus's leash around her hand in thought.

I am losing my way, she said to herself. *I am losing sight of who I am. I must commune with the goddess.*

She gripped the leash tighter and turned to walk back to the House of the Vestals, but Quintus suddenly opened the doors to the Regia from inside.

"Come," he said.

Instinctively, Pomponia looked nervously over her shoulder; however, this part of the Forum was still. Other than the preoccupied temple guards and the few street-cleaners who swept and washed the streets and collected trash by the light of their torches, she and Quintus seemed to be the only souls still awake.

Not that it really mattered if she was seen. She often had business in the Regia and it would not have aroused anyone's suspicion to see her enter it, whether day or night.

She climbed the steps of the Regia and stepped inside. Quintus closed the heavy doors behind her and she strained to see by the light of the single torch that was fixed to one of the blood-red walls.

By its flickering flame, a painted image of the warrior god Mars seemed to come to life, ready to kill and eager for the excitement of war.

Pomponia had been in this somber space many times. It held a particularly imposing and sacred shrine to Mars on account of the ancient relics that lay heavily across the marble altar: a massive shield and spear.

It was said that these had belonged to Mars himself, and that the god had thrown them down from the heavens to protect the people of Rome. Past priests of Mars had said that the spear trembled, as if demanding to be picked up, whenever Rome was threatened.

Perseus whimpered and then sat obediently in front of the altar. At any other time, the sight of the little dog communing with the great god of war would have made Pomponia laugh out loud. But not now. Now, her heart was hammering in her chest and her stomach fluttered with a strange mixture of apprehension and arousal.

All at once, Quintus came toward her. His strong arms enveloped her, drew her in, until her face rested against his solid chest. Her body flooded with warmth and she felt a strange hardness pressing into her midsection.

"That is my desire for you," he said, for once speaking without even a trace of derision or impudence. "I am not ashamed of it." He moved his head so that his face was pressed against the nape of her neck. "You belong to Rome now," he said into her hair. "But I swear on the black stone that you will belong to me one day."

He pulled back and clutched her face in his hands. "Mars protect you while I cannot."

She put her hands on top of his and felt the blood on his palm drip down her cheek. He had offered his own blood to Mars. To protect her. “Vesta bring you home,” she said.

And then he was out the door and all she could hear was his receding footfalls and the scratching of brooms on cobblestone.

CHAPTER XII

AURIBUS TENEO LUPUM

(I HOLD A WOLF BY THE EARS)

EGYPT & ROME 32 BCE

Queen Cleopatra sat on the glassy blue edge of the pool in the palace courtyard and gazed thoughtfully into the turquoise water. The *weet weet weet* song of a sandpiper echoed somewhere in the marshy waters of the expansive gardens, and she smiled languidly at the pleasant sound. She had reason to smile today.

She could imagine Octavia's face when her brother gave her the news: *Your husband Marc Antony has forsaken you. He has married the Egyptian Queen.*

It had been a hard-won battle for Cleopatra. Antony had not been as pliable as she had expected. Despite his boyish and boorish nature, he had proven to be a Roman through and through. Every time he read a letter from his Roman wife Octavia, his sense of Roman pride and obligation had sent him scurrying across the sands back home to her bed. And every time he did, his alliance with Octavian was renewed and strengthened.

Those damn letters. They had always found a way into Antony's hands, no matter how many guards Cleopatra had assigned to intercepting them in the shipyards, in the desert and in the palace itself. The queen suspected Octavian's man Quintus was responsible. What a cheerless puritan that man was.

Cleopatra hadn't written any letters to Antony. She had sent messengers to Rome instead – it was a much more personal and persuasive approach. She had chosen these messengers with care.

First, they were selected from among the most strikingly beautiful women in Egypt. They were then trained in the dramatic arts: their tears had to be genuine and their words had to be sincere. They wept when they described how a heartbroken Cleopatra was only a breath away from opening her wrists and how their loving children, Alexander Helios and Cleopatra Selene, shed tears day and night for the return of their great father.

But their training went beyond their ability to act, for they all carried a very personal message to Antony, one directly from the lips of the queen. And when he was alone in his Roman bedchamber, they would bend to their knees before him and deliver it with their own lips.

It had worked. Antony had returned to Egypt. And this time, Cleopatra was determined to make him stay for good. She had to. Her life, the life of her children, and her throne depended on it.

Her spies in Rome had told her all about Antony's wife Octavia who by all accounts was the ideal Roman matron. Obedient. Docile. Subordinate to her husband. Free of vice or ambition. Virtuous and proper in every way. Apparently she dressed the part, too. When she wasn't in a white stola, she was in a white tunica. Had she not been sullied by her husband, she could have been a Vestal Virgin.

Instead of trying to compete with Octavia's submissive and accommodating nature, Cleopatra did precisely the opposite. Where Octavia would have bent to Antony's wisdom, Cleopatra challenged it. Where Octavia would have soothed him, Cleopatra scolded him. Where Octavia would have quietly slipped away when he became drunk, Cleopatra poured more wine and played drinking games with him.

Instead of the dowdy Roman matron wrapped in layers of white cloth, Cleopatra chose vibrantly-colored dresses that clung to her every curve. Her earrings grazed her bare shoulders and her necklaces dipped down between her breasts, drawing Antony's eyes to the places she wanted him to focus on. Her exotic perfume filled his nostrils and quickened his breath.

When he finally took her, she didn't lay silently in virtuous submission to his desires as her spies had told her Octavia did. Rather, she cried out in shameless pleasure, struck him across the face and climbed on top of his body. It had been a risky strategy, but it had worked like a charm.

Yet the most effective strategy she had employed was the one that worked on every man she had ever known and doubly so on Roman men: she inflated his ego.

She told him, time and time again, how that upstart runt Octavian was no Caesar, but rather a mewling little weakling who was no match for Antony's strength and ability. She told him, again and again, how Octavian's child-general Agrippa was no match for Antony's military genius.

How dare those spoiled little boys tell the great Roman general Marc Antony what to do! How dare they send to Egypt and demand that he account for grain or coin!

It had lit a fire of indignation and a growing desire for violence in Antony's stomach.

She heard a shuffling behind her and turned her head to see Antony – completely naked but only partially drunk – strolling into the courtyard. He spotted her by the pool and hiccupped as he made his way toward her.

"Hello, my love," she greeted, "come rest your head in your loving wife's lap." He obeyed, and she stroked his hair. "You should not walk naked through the palace," she said. "The servants may mistake you for Hercules and forget their duties."

"You have the mouth of a snake charmer, Cleopatra."

She scratched his scalp with her fingernails and he moaned in pleasure. "A thought occurred to me today," she said, "a thought about Julius Caesar's will."

"What of it?"

"Caesar had great affection for you. He told me so on many occasions. He relied upon your military skill and your personal devotion to him. Is it not strange that he made Octavian his sole heir?"

"It is not so strange. Caesar was not one for sentimentality."

"Nonsense," she gently challenged. "He regarded you as a son. By comparison, he barely knew the boy Octavian."

"Your point?"

She pursed her lips and slid her soft palms over his cheeks. "I have long suspected that Caesar's will was forged."

"Impossible. The will was kept in the Temple of Vesta. It was inviolate."

"Perhaps," she said, and then spoke on as though the thoughts were just occurring to her now, "but then again, Octavian's sister has always had a friendship with the Vestal Pomponia. There is no telling what could have happened to Caesar's will behind the closed doors of the temple."

"I've known that priestess for years," said Antony. "There's no way."

"As you say," Cleopatra replied lightly. She shifted her eyes to Charmion who stood silently by the pool. The slave nodded discreetly in understanding and left.

A moment later, Charmion returned with a platter of delicacies and a fresh jug of wine. Although Antony was in no condition to notice it, the wine was still swirling from the tincture of opium that had been added to it. He sat up and drained two cups, one right after the other.

Cleopatra waited patiently. And then she tried again.

"I remember how Caesar used to speak of you," she said, "with such fondness and acclaim. When I heard that Octavian was made heir in his will, I could not believe it. I said to myself, 'Cleopatra, surely some mischief has been done here. Surely some ambitious and unscrupulous person has forged the will.' The Caesar I knew and loved had planned to leave his legacy to his closest friend and ally, Marc Antony."

Antony squinted at her. "It is odd," he said, "that I was left nothing."

"Octavian has no scruples."

"He has no balls, either," said Antony. "He's just the sort of gutless weasel to get a woman to do his dirty work. And my wife...I mean my ex-wife...well, she always was his eager little handmaiden. If he asked her to get Caesar's will from the temple, she would've pissed on Vesta's fire to make it happen."

"Ah. Now Rome's great general thinks clearly."

Antony jumped to his feet, suddenly infused with violent energy. "I hold a wolf by the ears," he said. "I control the grain. I decide whether Rome eats or starves." He shook his head as the thoughts ran through it. "But at some point I must let go of the wolf. And when I do, it will bite."

Cleopatra wrapped her arms around his bare legs. "My love," she said, "we will kill it before it can bite us. And when the wolf that is Rome is dead, Egypt shall rule the world."

He squatted down and took her in his muscular arms. "You have it wrong," he said. "Antony and Cleopatra shall rule the world."

* * * * * *

He had been gone for a year. Yet his letters faithfully arrived at least once a month, always carried by the same discreet Egyptian slave Quintus had bought in Alexandria, always addressed to the Vestalis Maxima and always secured with Caesar's seal.

Quintus's duties in Egypt permitted him the use of Caesar's seal, and that small piece of stamped red wax was the greatest secret-keeper Pomponia could have asked for. After all, the punishment for breaking Caesar's seal wasn't just death – it was death by means of the most painful, gruesome ways Rome's executioners could dream up. And they were a creative sort.

Pomponia sat at her desk and opened the scroll. Quintus always wrote to her on the finest Egyptian papyrus and many of his letters were accompanied by small gifts. A pack of exotic spices. A tiny cat or doll made of reeds. Dried flowers or herbs. Small garnets, carnelians or smoothed lapis lazuli.

Once he had even sent a dead scarab beetle. No doubt he had thought the Egyptian insect would interest her; however, when the black creature had unexpectedly tumbled out of the scroll onto her lap, she had shrieked and knocked over a lit beeswax candle on her desk, nearly setting the scroll on fire before she had even read it.

Now, she opened his scrolls more carefully.

My dearest love,

These Egyptians are not right in the head. Their gods are beasts on top and men on the bottom. Yet their temples are as magnificent as any in Rome, may the gods forgive me for saying so. You would be tempted to crucify their priests and priestesses, though, since I have discovered the trickery they use – a sort of temple magic – to compel devotion to their gods.

I have seen the colossal statue of Isis at the great temple. The goddess weeps real tears from her eyes, yet after a few minutes of devout prayer from the gathering, the flow of tears stop. The people are convinced that their faith has pleased the goddess. Yet soon enough, the tears start again and the people are compelled to pray even more.

I am angered to say that at first I fell for the scam myself, but then I followed the priest into the sanctuary where all was revealed. The statue has a hidden hole at the back of its head. The priest adds a magic substance to a jug of water and then fills the statue's head with it. At first, the substance does nothing, but soon it solidifies to plug the passage of water for a short time. It would be ingenious were it not such a sacrilege. Nonetheless, I have sent you some of this substance – it comes from the inside of a certain leaf – so that you can see it for yourself.

It is similar showmanship at the Temple of Horus. When a pipe plays music, the hawk-headed god's arms open wide and a massive pair of feathered wings emerge from them. When the music stops, the wings fold back into the god's arms. The effect is masterful and truly a sight to behold. I have heard of other temples where the statues actually throw spears but I have not seen this with my own eyes. I cannot decide whether the gods should curse or applaud such dupery.

Earlier this month, I had reason to visit the old Egyptian city of Giza. It is an ancient place with the most unbelievable monuments imaginable. There is a sprawling necropolis upon which sits three pyramid structures that are so large the visitor must lift and move his head to take it all in. The eye cannot see it all at once. No one seems to know what these pyramids were first used for. Some say they were the tombs of ancient pharaohs. Others say they match the positioning of the stars in the firmament above and therefore are a message to the gods. I have even heard it said that when the wind blows a certain way, the pyramids make a sound that speaks to the gods.

Near these pyramids is an enormous monolith of a Sphinx, which is a monstrous creature with a human head and a lion's body. The local population calls this creature the Father of Dread. It is said that the Sphinx and the pyramids are over two thousand years old! Even the black stone is not believed to be so ancient! My slave Ankhu is very talented and I had him paint the entire scene for you on the skin of a camel (a most obnoxious beast, by the way). Alas, it will not be dry when I send him off with this letter, so I shall send it next time.

My beloved Pomponia, do not think that I enjoy such exotics. They only pass the time and I only take them in so that I may later write of them to you. Most of my time is spent trying not to burst into flames from the Egyptian sun, wrenching the fabric of my tunic from the claws of the queen's wretched cats, or toiling over the abysmal state of the royal treasury and grain stores. Bona Dea! How strange that these Egyptians excel in astronomy, mathematics, science and philosophy, and yet cannot load a ship with grain for Rome!

I awoke this morning and for a moment I thought I caught the scent of your hair. But then I realized it was only the scent of some lotus flowers through the open window of my bedchamber. The experience gave me pause, though, for the Egyptians believe that the strong fragrance of a flower means that a goddess is close by. It is no wonder I thought of you.

I sacrifice to Mars every week for your safety. I pray to Venus for your love.

Quintus.

Pomponia finished the letter. And then she read it again. And again. In person, Quintus could be as ill-natured as the Minotaur. On papyrus, however, he could be as romantic and lyrical as Cupid in love.

Once she had all but committed his letter to memory, she rolled it up and dipped the edge of the scroll into the flame of the beeswax candle on her desk. As the papyrus burned, the words flew up to the goddess. Pomponia had no secrets from her.

She dropped the scroll's cinders into a silver bowl and then uncurled the blank papyrus Quintus had included with his letter, taking up her stylus to write.

Quintus,

How strange and wonderful the pyramids and the Sphinx must be! I doubt I shall ever stand before them, but your letters let me see them through your eyes and that pleases me greatly. As for the temple magic practiced by the Egyptians – well, I suppose that is for the gods to judge. Although I must say that such antics smack of comedy more than piety.

You sound well, Quintus, although frustrated by the Egyptian queen. Fear not, you have good company in this regard. As I am sure Caesar has told you, Roman sentiment continues to mount against Cleopatra. The people are convinced that she has cast a spell on Antony and that is why he remains in Egypt. The people have always loved Antony and even as their bellies growl they make excuses for him. I must often bite my tongue, for even with the grace of Vesta I am not so forgiving. It is hard to see the people go hungry and the poor get the worst of it.

Your daughter Quintina continues to thrive at the Temple of Vesta. I often marvel that she is Vesta incarnate: her face grows lovelier each week and she masters any ritual or rite the first time she sees it. Her tutors are constantly amazed by the sharpness of her mind. I am happy to report that she has none of your surly or sullen nature – what a relief! – but is rather cheerful and inspiring at all times. She is a blessing to the temple and to me personally, Quintus. I have come to love her dearly and I will take the liberty of saying that she loves me, too.

Quintina tells me that she has written to you about the welfare of her younger sister and has requested guardianship of her until you return to Rome. I know you do not know your daughters that well, Quintus, and that you have been gone a long time; however, I urge you to accept counsel from Quintina. She is a young woman of fourteen now, although her wisdom and judgment exceed her years.

The unpleasant truth is that the girls' mother has immersed herself in the cult of Bacchus. It is well-known in our circle and in higher society that she engages in scandalous behavior with other Bacchants including certain bodily rites that are not becoming to a woman of her class. Your younger daughter is only a few years from marriage and her reputation must be upheld if she is to obtain a quality husband. That is all I will say on the matter, as it is not my place. I only mention this so that you take the words of your eldest daughter seriously.

I make daily offerings to Vesta so that she may bring you home and I thank you for your sacrifice to Mars. You need not burden Venus with too many prayers, for my affection is as it should be.

Pomponia.

She set down the stylus and re-read her words as the ink dried. Quintus openly spoke of his love for her in his letters, at times with a lovesick abandon that she would never have thought him capable of; however, her replies to him were always more measured. The two of them had already had one close call and if their relationship were suspected of being an intimate one – especially a physically intimate one – the punishment would be unthinkable for both of them.

Plus, she was the Vestalis Maxima and despite her feelings for him, she had a duty to the goddess, to the Vestal order and to all of Rome. No matter how her heart fluttered when she thought of him, that duty had to come first.

Anyway, it doesn't matter what I write, she thought as she rolled up the scroll, sealed it and slipped it into a scroll box. *Quintus will read the words he wants to see. He knows the secret love I have for him.* She smiled, despite herself, at his characteristic presumptuousness and called for his Egyptian messenger slave.

* * * * * *

It was the Vestalia, Vesta's annual public festival in June, and none of the priestesses had enjoyed a full night's sleep in over a month. The time leading up to the Vestalia was as busy as the festival itself.

One reason for this was the production of the sacred wafers: water had to be collected in the proper way and purified, flour had to be milled, salt had to sanctified. And all had to be done according to the same strict and sacred rituals the Vestals had honored for centuries.

Once finished, the sacred wafers would be distributed throughout the city of Rome. Considering the fact that the city's population was well over a million people, that was no small task.

In years past, people had simply come to the temple to receive mola salsa wafers; however, the traffic in the Forum had become too congested during the Vestalia and Fabiana had ultimately arranged for city-wide disbursements instead. It reduced congestion and supplied the sacred wafers to those who did not have means to visit the temple.

It was just one of the many ways that the former Vestalis Maxima had updated the practices of the Vestal order.

While the sacred wafers were used as offerings to Vesta during all public rituals and ceremonies, their most ancient and fundamental use was still as a private household offering to the goddess. That hadn't changed over the centuries.

At its heart, Vesta was still a home-focused tradition. People across the Roman world burned candles and oil lamps on their lararia, knowing that Vesta resided in the flame. They made offerings into the flame – sacred wafers, loose salted flour, olive oil or wine – not just to honor or feed the goddess, but to symbolically nourish their home and family, too.

The presence of Vesta's sacred flame in the household made every home a private Temple of Vesta, and the people adored the virgin goddess who chose to live with them and their families, regardless of whether they lived in a palace, hut or apartment.

She illuminated and warmed their homes, she sanctified their marriages and she embraced their children as her own. She brought focus and meaning to their lives. The people's devotion to her was as profound and perpetual as the sacred fire, and her priestesses were charged with preserving and spreading her flame.

Nonetheless, Pomponia always felt a little exposed on the first day of the Vestalia. Normally, flames from the eternal fire were placed in bronze fire-bowls in front of the temple for those who wished to make an offering or take embers home to burn in their own hearth. Only Vestals were permitted to view or enter the inside of the temple; however, the doors were opened on June 7th, the first day of the Vestalia, to reveal the inner sanctum and its sacred hearth.

Moreover, women of all classes were allowed – on this day only – to enter the consecrated inner sanctum. They came in droves, dressed in the finest of silks to the roughest of tunicas, and left their sandals at the base of the temple's marble steps to enter the sanctuary barefoot.

They carried plates of food to offer the goddess: some contained rich delicacies, others dry crusts of bread. They bowed their head in reverence as they stepped onto the white tile floor of the sanctum, saw the eternal flame burning in the hearth and felt its heat on their faces.

As the fire crackled and snapped, they set the plates of food on the floor along the curved inner wall of the temple. They said a silent prayer, bowed to the Vestals who stood watch by the fire, and then left.

As high priestess, Pomponia had spent most of the day inside the temple, standing beside the sacred hearth with Priestess Tuccia and accepting the prayers and offerings of Vesta's faithful.

Needing a breath of fresh air, she arranged for Nona to take her place and descended the temple's marble steps. As she did, she was rejuvenated by the fresh scent of the laurel and flower garlands that wound around the temple's columns and hung from its roof.

Priestess Caecilia stood in front of one of the bronze fire-bowls outside the temple, busily handing out the sacred wafers and accepting the blessings of a public eager to show their reverent respect to the Vestal order – and to meet a Vestal priestess face to face. Pomponia approached her for a quick word.

"Rome is getting too big," she said. "I think we need to make a change next year. I am going to propose that we keep the temple open for several days during the Vestalia. The crowds are too thick and I hear many people complaining they aren't able to make it inside to leave an offering.

"I think that is wise," said Caecilia. "A necessary change." She glanced at Fabiana, seated on a cushioned chair several feet away. "Although you might face some opposition."

Pomponia grinned. "Perhaps," she said, "but Fabiana seems to care less and less about custom these days. Just look at her! A reverent day like this, and there she is with that foul-smelling creature soiling her robes. What holy precedent exists for that?"

They both looked at Fabiana who sat by the temple with a royal purple canopy stretched overhead to protect her from the worst of the sun's heat. Curled on her lap was Perseus. He raised his head like a white furry god to regard each man, woman and child who knelt before Fabiana in turn, each asking her blessing or praying to the goddess with her.

Pomponia knew – all the priestesses knew – this might be the last Vestalia the ailing Fabiana would share with them. The former Vestalis Maxima seemed to know it too, which is why she had forced herself from her cool bedchamber to sit all day in the sun by the temple. She appeared to be greeting and blessing visitors, but many suspected it was really her way of saying good-bye to the people of Rome.

Pomponia rocked on her heels and looked around. Priestess Lucretia was moving among a crowd of men and boys who held out plates of food to her. Only women were permitted in the temple; however, the Fates took many women in childbirth which meant that some families no longer had a wife or mother who could make a temple offering to Vesta.

The men and boys in such families would therefore wait outside and ask a Vestal to make an offering for them. Such was Lucretia's duty today. She was fulfilling it tirelessly, even as the hot sun beat down on her white-veiled head.

In front of another bronze fire-bowl, Quintina stood on a step and leaned over into a large terracotta pot – it was almost as big as she was – that contained an excess of the loose salted-flour mixture used to make the sacred wafers. She emerged with a ladleful of the mix and poured it into a chipped bowl held by a hungry-looking boy.

"Don't give all of this to the goddess," she told the boy. "Vesta is full. Eat it yourself."

"Yes, ma'am!" The boy bowed in gratitude and moved aside to let the next person in line approach with their empty bowl.

Somewhere down the line a bit of roughhousing between two or three men had started, causing a little girl to fall onto the cobblestone. She stood up and a woman brushed the bloody debris from her knees.

A grim-looking Praetorian guard – one of many positioned around the temple to assist the regular guard – cast the men a warning glare and put his hand on his sword. "Get to the back of the line, you shit-eaters!" They hung their heads like pouting children and did as they were told.

Pomponia regarded the bustling Forum beyond the Temple of Vesta. As was customary, garlands of bread and flowers hung from shops, basilicas, the Rostra, as well as other buildings and temples. Similar garlands decorated private homes throughout Rome as well; however, Pomponia had noticed that this year there were more flowers than bread.

A sudden swell of excited shouts and applause caught her attention and she looked down the Via Sacra to see Caesar's grand litter slowly making its way through the throngs of people toward the temple.

Coins flew out of the lectica onto the cobblestone and people scrambled to gather them up. Others waved in awe and lifted their children onto their shoulders to catch a glimpse of Caesar and his sister Octavia.

Concordia's mercy, thought Pomponia, *just when I thought I had Chaos in chains.*

The litter set down near the temple. As several Praetorians surrounded it, Octavia stepped out of the lectica followed by her brother. Some people clapped and called out, but others merely stared, their eyes expressionless at best and accusatory at worst. Hunger had dulled their good will toward Caesar. He could throw all the coin he wanted to: there was no bread to buy with it.

Octavian greeted Pomponia first. He pointed his chin at two women fighting over a denarius in the street. "It is unfortunate they cannot eat silver," he said, seeming to read the Vestal's mind.

Octavia, dressed in a snow-white stola, bowed her head to Pomponia. "I have come to make an offering to Vesta," she said. She held a simple terra cotta plate upon which was a selection of fruit and bread dipped in oil.

"The goddess will be pleased," said Pomponia.

A moment later, another figure emerged from the lectica. Caesar's wife, Livia. Unlike her modest sister-in-law, she wore a vibrant green dress with earrings that dripped down to her shoulders. Clutching a gold plate stacked with exotic meats, she stepped gingerly onto the cobblestone and bowed her head to the Vestal.

"Priestess Pomponia," she said, "I hope our presence does not add to your labors today. We shall make our offerings and leave."

"Nonsense," said Pomponia. "Make your offering to the goddess, and then we shall all have some lemon water in the courtyard."

As the two women removed their sandals at the base of the temple's steps and moved reverently through the open doors into the inner sanctum, Pomponia studied Livia. She had known many ambitious men and women in her time with the Vestal order, but there was something about Caesar's young wife that had always stood apart. Something about her smile and the way every expression, every word, seemed strategically chosen for a reason that only she knew.

Livia was as a river of ambition, yes. But there was something below the ambition: insecurity. It was the unseen but unstoppable undercurrent of her ambition and Pomponia had a sense that it would wash away anything that crossed its path.

After the two women had made their temple offerings, Pomponia escorted them and Caesar into the courtyard of the House of the Vestals. The gardens offered a semi-shaded refuge from the relentless sun and febrile heat, and she gestured to two canopied couches by one of the pools. She and Octavia sat on one, Octavian and Livia on the other.

"Lemon water," Pomponia said to a house slave. "With ice, if we still have it."

"At once, Domina."

"I cannot recall a time when the heat came so early," said Octavian.

"It makes the people petulant, Caesar," Pomponia noted. "It's been orderly today, despite the heat, but I can feel it in the city."

"Hot and hungry," said Octavian. "An unhealthy combination, especially when it comes to public order."

It was Octavia who said what everyone was thinking. "My husband is to blame for it."

"How are you coping, Octavia?" asked Pomponia.

"Good days and bad, my friend. Juno gives me strength."

"I am happy to hear so." Pomponia shook her head in frustration. "The day Julius Caesar was killed, Antony came here to hide. He stood right here, at this water, and drank. It was here that I gave him Caesar's will...oh, if only I would have known what he would become. I would have had Quintus open his throat at Vesta's feet. Forgive me, the heat inflames my anger. I do not like to see my friend suffer and I do not like to see the people starve."

"We all feel it," said Octavian, "and we have all said and thought much worse." The slave arrived with lemon water – ice chips already in the glasses – and he took a long draw of the cool liquid. "The problem is that many of the common people do not believe Antony would let them starve. He has always had the love of the people."

"If only there was a way to prove Antony's disloyalty to the people," said Livia.

Octavian crunched an ice chip between his teeth and glanced at her. His wife was not yet as smooth as he or his sister.

Pomponia looked Octavian in the eye. "What are you asking me to do, Caesar?"

"Antony's will is in the temple. I have no doubt that it will show his allegiance and affection lie with his Egyptian wife and children, rather than his Roman ones."

Octavia took Pomponia's hands. "Once the people see that Antony is loyal to Egypt and not to Rome, they will lose their love for him. They will know who truly keeps the bread from the mouths of their children."

"And what good will that do?" asked Pomponia. "It will not change him. It will not make the grain come."

"No," said Octavian, "but it will give me the justification I need to kill him and to get the grain myself."

"I have no sympathy for Antony," said Pomponia. "I have never had much use for the man. But you know that I cannot do what you ask. The temple is sacrosanct. Rome's most important men have entrusted the Vestal order with their wills for many centuries. I will not be the Vestalis Maxima who breaks that tradition." She squeezed Octavia's hands. "I make this decision out of sacred duty. If I were at liberty to make it out of friendship, it would be a different decision."

"Of course," said Octavia. "Forgive us."

"Yes, forgive us," Octavian echoed. "The request was an improper one borne out of desperation. We shall find another way to do what must be done."

More lemon water and small talk followed until Livia exhaled heavily and stood up. "Husband," she said, "and sister, I fear that the heat is quite getting the better of me."

"We should go," said Octavian. "I apologize again for my misguided appeal, Lady Pomponia. It was not fair of me to put political pressure on our most sacred order."

"There is nothing to apologize for," said Pomponia. "You are Caesar and you are doing the work of Caesar."

Livia bowed her head to the Vestal. "Thank you for taking the time to visit us on this busy day. I wonder if you might come dine with Octavia and I at Caesar's house after the Vestalia? Our new cook prepares the most exquisite dormice you have ever tasted, does he not, Octavia? He is the mortal son of Edesia, I'm sure of it."

"Yes, I would like that," said Pomponia. "Our dormice taste like boiled leather. I've just bought a new cook from the country, though, so we have high hopes." She walked them out of the courtyard and back into the Forum where Caesar's litter awaited by the temple.

They exchanged partings, and Livia stepped into the lectica followed by Octavia. Octavian paused. He looked as though he was going to say something with weight, but then offered Pomponia a light "good-bye" and stepped in after his wife and sister. As the high priestess waved and walked back toward the temple, he closed the red curtains of the lectica.

"I told you she wouldn't do it," he said to Livia.

"It was worth a try, husband."

"Perhaps." He didn't sound convinced.

Octavia wiped away a tear and then rested her head on her sister-in-law's shoulder. Livia felt her chest tighten in irritation – the woman had become insufferably whiny since Antony had married

Cleopatra – but she suppressed her annoyance and stroked Octavia's hair tenderly. "There, there, dear sister," she said. "We shall find a way to make that barbarian husband of yours pay for his infidelity."

"We shall indeed," said Octavian. "One must admire the high priestess, though," he continued thoughtfully. "She is a virtuous woman and devoted to the goddess, yet clearly she favors us politically. Perhaps that will be enough to endear Vesta to our cause."

Livia's chest tightened even more. *Bona Dea! The Vestal refuses you, but yet your regard for her grows?* She licked her lips. She had fully expected the Vestalis Maxima to refuse Caesar's request for Antony's will; however, she had hoped the refusal would have tainted her husband's affection and admiration for the Vestal Virgins. To her dismay, it seemed to have had the exact opposite effect.

"Who is this Quintus the high priestess spoke of?" she asked innocently. "Is it the same Quintus you sent to Egypt? The one with the Bacchant wife?"

"Yes, the same," said Octavian.

"I did not know they were such good friends," said Livia. This was worth remembering.

But her husband didn't hear her. He was already distracted, sifting through a basket of scrolls and growling about overdue taxes, clogged public latrines and an epidemic of sexual blisters in the brothels of the Subura. All Rome's problems seemed to rise up to Caesar.

"Apparently I am to blame not only for their hunger pangs," he muttered, "but also for the warts on their cocks."

"I see." Livia felt Octavia's head grow heavy as the slow, rhythmic movement of the litter rocked her to sleep. Instead of pushing her off, however, she made a cooing sound and continued to stroke her hair. Caesar was always impressed when his wife showed sisterly love toward Octavia.

Octavian busied himself with his scrolls until they arrived at the portico of his house. Still preoccupied by the business of Rome, he stepped out of the lectica and was barking orders to his secretary before Livia had even shaken Octavia awake.

"Oh I'm sorry, Livia," said a blinking Octavia. "I think the heat got to me, too."

They followed Octavian inside and then went their separate ways: Octavia to bed, Livia to the slaves' bathhouse where Medousa was overseeing the preparation of Livia's latest gift to her husband: nine virgin girls, one for each night of the Vestalia.

Five of them sat emerged in a bath, doing their best to communicate with each other in various foreign tongues, while three others sat quietly as their long hair was cropped short. One stood in the center of the room, her arms and legs open, as the cosmetic slave removed her body hair.

"How are these ones, Medousa?" asked Livia.

"They are very good, Domina. Caesar will thank his wife."

"That's the idea."

Medousa hesitated, and then risked it. "Did you see the Vestalis Maxima today?"

"Yes."

"How did she look?"

"She looked as she always looks," Livia grumbled. "Very white."

"Yes, Domina." Medousa cursed herself. It was pointless to ask her mistress anything.

Nonetheless, she felt a bitter-sweet swell of nostalgia as she imagined Pomponia and the other Vestal priestesses tending to the sacred flame and navigating the crowds of faithful that descended upon the temple on this day, the first day of the Vestalia.

The Vestalia was always a busy but blessed time at the Temple of Vesta. And although only a slave, Medousa had been entrusted with many important duties. She had found great joy in serving the goddess in her own way and even the elderly Fabiana, who had disliked Medousa from the beginning, always personally commended her on her conduct during the Vestalia.

Things were different these days. She had spent the last few of Vesta's festivals purchasing and preparing virgin girls to be deflowered by Caesar. It was an insult to the goddess. And every time a girl emerged from Caesar's bedchamber, dishevelled and weeping, Medousa begged forgiveness from Vesta.

Livia put her hands on her hips and scrutinized the naked girl in the center of the room. Under her watchful eye, Medousa and another slave wrapped the girl's body in a pure white stola and covered her short hair with a white veil. A tear rolled down the girl's cheek.

"Juno, give me strength!" groaned Livia. "I have had my fill of sobbing women today." She let her arms drop to her sides and then looked contemplatively at the other eight gift girls in the bathhouse. "If my husband keeps going through virgins at his current rate," she said, "we'll be staffing the temple with whores by the kalends."

* * * * * *

My dearest Pomponia,

The Egyptian sun continues to persecute me. There are only two types of weather here: oppressive heat and oppressive heat in a sandstorm. Today is the latter. My eyes string from the whipping of sand they took this morning so if my letters are written sideways you will know the reason.

In honor of the Vestalia last month, Queen Cleopatra permitted an altar fire dedicated to Vesta to burn at the Temple of Isis. Many Roman soldiers and officials came to pray, including myself. A few officials have their Roman wives here with them, and these women spent the day making offerings into the fire on behalf of the men. They asked Vesta to bring home all of the Roman men in Egypt. I found that I missed you very keenly when I heard these prayers.

While at the temple, I spoke privately with several of Marc Antony's soldiers. There is growing discord in the ranks and many men are losing patience with their general. They say that Cleopatra is a fatale monstrum – a fatal omen – who has cast a spell on Antony and who will be his undoing. They despise her. I have even heard some of them say that she poisons his mind with an exotic compound that makes him her creature.

It is a strange thing to see them together. Were I not cursed with a cynical nature, I might say it is a true love match. Cleopatra is shrewd beyond measure and Antony regards her judgment as highly as his own. Then again, Antony has a history of choosing women who think they are as capable as men. It is no wonder he has forsaken the Lady Octavia. She is a virtuous Roman matron who knows her place and his soldiers have not looked kindly on his abandonment of her.

It is common knowledge among the people here that Antony and Caesar grow more openly hostile with each other every day. Yet Antony and Cleopatra sit on their golden thrones as though they are king and queen of the world. It baffles me, but Cleopatra has both the support and the love of her people. She tells them that Egypt is not merely Rome's bread-basket, but a great independent nation with its own gods and history. What gall that painted harlot has!

I have found your news about my daughters' mother to be useful and have given Quintina legal guardianship of her younger sister.

My gift for you this month is a silver amulet of a shen ring. I acquired this from a priestess of Isis. The circle symbolizes eternity. When I was told that, I thought of the love that I have for you and the eternal fire in your keep.

Quintus.

Once she had re-read his letter and burned it in the candle's flame, Pomponia picked up her stylus and chewed contemplatively on its end. There were still times she didn't know what to make of Quintus. He could be bitter as iron in one sentence – grumbling about how a woman should know "her place" – and then sweet as honeycomb in the next: *I thought of the love that I have for you.*

She looked at the silver amulet on her desk, warmed as she imagined him choosing it for her, and then put the point of her stylus on the papyrus.

Quintus,

The gift is beautiful as always. But does Ankhu not weary from carrying so many letters between Rome and Alexandria, and so quickly? Either he is winged Mercury or he rides Pegasus over the sea. I do not complain. No woman in Rome is as happy as I to greet the messenger. You should know that Ankhu is reliable and your letters always arrive in perfect condition.

I am glad to know that Quintina will assume the care of her younger sister. She anticipated your approval and has already been making arrangements for Quintina Tacita Minor to live with your brother and his wife. I am told they are fine people who are above reproach and hold true affection for their niece.

What a lovely image you have given me of Vesta's sacred fire burning in the Temple of Isis. Her cult has spread to Rome and I understand the goddess to be a kind and wise one. Surely a sister to Vesta in spirit. I have been told that a small temple has been built to honor her in Rome, but I have yet to attend. I shall do so soon and think of you baking unhappily in the Egyptian heat.

How I wish the situation between Antony and Caesar would resolve itself, one way or the other. Perhaps a battle is better than this infernal uncertainty and tension. It keeps both Rome and Egypt on the edge of a knife and it keeps us apart.

I fear it has put a strain on my relations with Caesar and his sister Octavia, as well. Would you believe they asked me to give them Antony's will from the temple? Caesar believes its contents will cause the Roman people to lose their love for Antony and support a war against him. I had no choice but to refuse him. My duty is to the goddess, not to Caesar.

Of course, Caesar was as politic and gracious as ever in the face of my non-compliance; however, only the goddess knows what he is thinking or what he will do. I fear he is the wolf in sheep's clothing that the Greek storyteller Aesop speaks of in his fables. I fear I hold that wolf by the ears. If I show any sign of weakness as Vestalis Maxima, he will enter the temple and tear the heart out of its sanctity.

Rome is also abuzz with talk about Cleopatra's power over Antony. I saw for myself many years ago, when Julius Caesar loved her, what influence the Egyptian Queen can have over Roman men. Perhaps if Roman women were permitted to rule themselves as Cleopatra rules herself, the Pharaoh's charm and resourcefulness would not hold such novel appeal to our men.

But enough talk of politics and philosophy. Let us instead pray to Vulcan that the smoke of these days soon clears, and that the skillful god can forge a bridge of iron to bring you home.

Pomponia.

CHAPTER XIII

De Fumo in Flammam

(Out of the Smoke, Into the Flame)

Rome February 31 BCE

The newsreader stood on his platform in front of the Rostra, bellowing the latest developments from Egypt to those gathered around him in the Forum.

The moment he finished one announcement, and before he could even start with the next, the news began to move through the city as people ran up and down the cobblestone streets, spreading the official reports as quickly as they normally spread rumor. News – good and bad – travelled quickly in Rome.

"From the immoral sands of Egypt," the newsreader called out, "Queen Cleopatra's binding exotic spell on the once great General Marc Antony holds fast. Caesar's spies tell us that the Pharaoh is as decadent as she is cunning, having performed sexual favors for one hundred of Antony's soldiers!"

"Tell Caesar's spies to send grain," shouted an angry woman, "not this smutty gossip!"

A heated cheer of consensus.

The newsreader ignored her. Hecklers were nothing new.

"By order of the Senate and Caesar," he continued, "no vandalism of public buildings, disruption of public ceremony, interruption of religious ritual, or public acts of sexual indecency are permitted during the Lupercalia. Any such acts will be considered treason and those found responsible will be committed to the Carcer for public flogging or execution." He ran a finger across his throat like a blade and opened his eyes wide for effect. "No exceptions!"

A low grumble of complaints.

"And lastly," he pointed into the Forum to nowhere in particular, "citizens are advised to avoid the brothels in the Subura district at least until the Veneralia," he dropped a hand to cup his genitals, "on account of severe venereal outbreak." He cast a warning glare into the crowd, handed the scroll in his hands to his secretary, and stepped off the speaker's platform.

Valeria watched the newsreader cross the cobblestone to a wine vendor in the Basilica Aemilia. She wrapped her wool palla around her shoulders. It was a cool, wet day. Perhaps not the most enjoyable weather for the Lupercalia, but rain was always auspicious during this time. It symbolized a cleansing, a sort of purification, which promoted the health and fertility of Rome.

The Lupercalia – the festival of the wolf – honored the she-wolf, called the Lupa, who suckled Romulus and Remus, twin sons of the Vestal Rhea Silvia and the god Mars.

Valeria used to love the spirit and celebration of the Lupercalia. It used to give her hope, for it was believed that a woman who conceived during the Lupercalia would be sure to give birth to a strong son. She swallowed a rise of sadness at the memory of her little grey son lying in his death basket.

She walked along the Via Sacra, paying little heed to the crush of people doing business, visiting the magnificent multi-colored temples, kneeling in prayer before makeshift shrines or shopping at the many vendor carts and storefronts that lined the streets of the Forum.

She stopped briefly at a public fountain for a drink of clear water, but a rough heavy-set woman shouldered her aside and thrust a pile of dirty laundry into the basin of clean water.

"Who do you think you are, missy," the woman cackled, "Queen Salacia? Drink up and move your fancy ass out of the way. Some of us have work to do."

In days past, Valeria might have hit her with the water ladle. These days, she just didn't care.

She walked until she reached the foot of the Palatine Hill to the site of an ancient cave within which it was believed the she-wolf had first found the twin boys. Here, she had raised them. Here, she had suckled them and nourished them to adulthood, filling Romulus with the wolfish ferocity and fierce devotion it would take to found the great city of Rome.

The Pontifex Maximus Lepidus and two other priests were already presiding over the somber public sacrifice to the Lupa – a sacrifice which consisted of two male goats and one dog – before a massive gathering of men, women and children.

Valeria spotted a few of her fellow Bacchants leaning against a large fluted column and talking a bit too loudly. She moved through crowd to stand closer to them. The wine spilled over the rim of their cups as they began to openly mock the public ritual that was being carried out at the mouth of the ancient cave.

As the sacrificial dog collapsed into a pool of its own blood, the Pontifex Maximus bowed his head to a white-veiled figure who stepped forward toward the fire that burned brightly within a large bronze bowl. The Vestalis Maxima Pomponia lifted a handful of sacred wafers over her head and then lowered them into the fire as offering to the gods.

Valeria gave the Vestal the evil eye. She was so busy giving it, in fact, that she didn't notice the soldiers who had surrounded her and her rowdy companions. The soldiers grabbed the troublemakers by the scruff of their necks. Only one had the poor judgment to put up a fight, for which he quickly received a helmet to the face and a nose that fractured into a particularly gruesome arrangement.

Valeria made a run for it. She wound her way through the crowd, darting behind columns and hiding behind a snorting barrel-chested donkey until she saw a clear path to the street. She lifted her dress and scampered over the cobblestone, ignoring the mud and waste that accumulated on the bottom of her sandals.

Finally, she saw a shelter of sorts – a public latrine. She slipped inside, lifted her dress above her waist and quickly chose a toilet beside a seated mother and daughter who appeared to be having some kind of argument over the daughter's boyfriend while they relieved themselves. She was safe: only the most zealous of soldiers would follow a simple rabble-rouser into the unpleasantness of the public toilets.

Unfortunately for Valeria, the soldier who had given chase did suffer from a streak of zealousness. He barged into the latrine like the Cretan Bull, seemingly oblivious to the profanity-laden shrieks of the mother and daughter, and hauled Valeria out over his shoulder as if she were Pasiphae.

"Put me down," she yelled, "I am a noblewoman!"

"You're a drunken woman, that's what you are," said the soldier, "and you're disrupting a public ritual. I have my orders."

He carried her to a metal-barred prison cart that stunk of vomit and tossed her inside. She tried to stand up, but forgot that the bottoms of her sandals were coated in mire. She slipped and hit her head hard.

The soldier's voice was strangely muffled and a ringing sounded in her ears before the world went silent and black.

Slowly, her hearing returned. The clang of metal. A dry, hacking cough somewhere in the distance. The rattle of chains and the click of a steel lock. The sound of men's voices echoing in a confined space.

Her vision came next, blurry at first but then clear. The space around her was dim. Solid. The ceiling seemed too close, too heavy. Her head ached and her throat was dry.

"Have some water, Lady Valeria."

She pushed herself up to a sitting position and met eyes with the Priestess Pomponia.

The Vestal handed her a cup of water. She accepted it and drank.

"You are in the Carcer," said Pomponia. "You have been arrested for public disorder. It isn't your first arrest for this and you will likely be sentenced to death this time. The priests of the Lupercalia will see the disruption of their ritual as a bad omen and recommend execution."

Valeria said nothing.

"Your daughter Quintina is waiting outside in the litter. Would you like me to send her in?"

"No." Valeria shook her head. "I don't want her to see me like this." Her dress was bunched at her waist and she pulled it down, not wanting to think about what might have happened to her while she was unconscious. "Does my husband love you?"

Strangely enough, the blunt question did not surprise Pomponia. "Yes," she said.

"Have you coupled with him?"

"No. I would never break my sacred vows to Vesta. He would never ask me to."

"But if he loves you..."

"Love is not forbidden to a Vestal," said Pomponia. "Coupling is."

Valeria pushed her messy hair off her face. "He never loved me," she said matter-of-factly. "Do you think he loves his daughters?"

"There is no doubt of it."

"How are they?" asked Valeria. "How are my girls?"

"They grow like roses in May," said Pomponia. "They are happy and cared for."

Valeria stretched her back and cringed at the pain that shot down her spine. "I wasted too many years trying to make Quintus love me," she said. "What a fool I was." She laughed. A bitter laugh. "I sound like an actor in a Greek tragedy. Self-awareness only comes at the end."

"It need not be the end, Valeria. I can pardon you, but you cannot stay in Rome. Your vices are well-known and you have become the subject of ridicule. Neither Quintina nor the Vestal order can be caught up in scandal. Exile is the only option. It has its benefits. You can have a new life, a fresh start, and I will permit letters between you and Quintina. Who knows what the Fates will spin for you? Perhaps one day you can be part of your daughters' lives again."

"Why would you do this for me?"

"Quintina is the brightest young priestesses our order has seen in many years," said Pomponia. "I have been going back through the scrolls and there hasn't been a girl with her capacity for ritual and understanding in generations. Perhaps it is in her blood from the Vestal Tacita. Regardless, Mother Vesta chose you to bring her to us. You must hold yourself to a higher standard. You have your own duty to the goddess."

"Yes."

The Vestal stood. "I will make the arrangements. You will be released shortly. Go home and await news of your departure." As she walked out of the prison cell and disappeared down the dark corridor, a guard slammed the steel-barred prison door closed.

"You have some fancy friends, lady," he said.

Valeria leaned back against the cold stone wall of the cell and closed her eyes. The next thing she knew, the steel-barred door was once again open and the guard was shouting at her.

"Come on already," he said. "Wake up. It's time to be on your way now, lady."

And then the blue sky was overhead again, and it was almost as though the last few hours – the most terrifying, emotional and surreal hours of her life – had never happened. As she so often did, she found herself walking along the cobblestone streets of the Roman Forum.

She wanted to go home. She wanted to wrap herself in her bedsheets like a caterpillar in a cocoon and wait until the knock at the door came and a ship sailed her off to a new life in a new land. She had to get out of Rome. But first, there was something she had to do.

The sounds and sights of the Lupercalia swirled around her as she made her way down the Via Sacra to the Temple of Vesta. Garlands of fresh laurel leaves and white flowers wound around the temple's fluted columns, base to top, as they did every festival. Thick smoke from Vesta's eternal fire billowed out of the tiled roof, drifting up to the goddess. The flames that burned in the bronze fire-bowls outside the temple crackled and snapped.

Valeria walked past the temple, continuing along the exterior of the House of the Vestals until she reached the rear of the Vestal's expansive house. She looked up at the marble façade of the rear wall until she saw what she was looking for. A block of marble with a deep chip in it.

Standing on her tiptoes, she reached up and pulled at the chip until it came loose to reveal a small hole in the stonework behind the façade. She slipped her fingers inside the hole and poked around until she felt it. She pulled it out: the curse tablet she had placed there eight years earlier.

"What do you have there?"

Valeria spun around. It was the same soldier who had arrested her during the Lupercalia ritual. His streak of zealousness had extended to following her on foot, just to make sure she went straight home as the high priestess had instructed.

"It's nothing," Valeria stammered. "None of your concern."

"I'll be the judge of that." He yanked the lead tablet from her hands and uncurled it.

By this time, a small crowd had gathered round. An elderly woman wrapped in a black palla pointed at the lead scroll in the soldier's hands. "That's a curse tablet!" she shouted. "She put a curse on the Vestals!"

"No," exclaimed Valeria, "I was removing it! I was revoking it!"

"Read it out loud," someone yelled to the soldier.

As he read the words pressed into the lead, the soldier's face blanched and his hands began to tremble. "I call upon black and shaded Pluto. I call upon dark and hidden Persephone. *Hoc nomen dare infernum:* the Vestal Virgin Pomponia, white-robed harpy. I curse her food, her drink, her face, her laughter, her virginity. I curse her watch over the sacred fire and her service to the goddess. I divorce her as a bride of Rome and marry her to Pluto."

When the soldier looked up from the tablet, the crowd had grown from a few to a few dozen.

The old woman in the black palla pointed a crooked finger at Valeria. "You cursed the Vestalis Maxima! You have made the goddess forsake us! You have reduced Rome to a starving dog that must beg for food at Egypt's door!"

The crowd surrounded Valeria like a pack of hungry wolves circling a wounded animal. When the first stone struck her, she didn't even feel the pain – such was the shock. But then more stones followed, as did the pain and panic. Bodies closed in on her from all sides. There was nowhere to run. *Who knows what the Fates will spin for you?* For the second time in one day, a ringing sounded in her ears and the world went silent and black.

The soldier drew his sword, but didn't know where – or who – to strike. Should he stab the old woman? The patrician man in his expensive toga? The bejeweled matron? The pleb boy? The merchant? The bearded Jew? He had just decided on the bearded Jew when someone shouted "She's dead!" and the crowd broke apart and scattered into the Forum.

As he bent down to pick up the body of the woman – he couldn't just leave her there, could he? – the old woman in the black palla knelt on the cobblestone and began to scratch the words off the lead tablet with the sharp edge of a stone.

A younger woman who was similarly wrapped in a black palla knelt down beside her elder and poured a small vial of salt that hung from around her neck onto the lead tablet. Both women rubbed the salt into the lead with their hands while murmuring soft incantations to Persephone, gently pleading with her to revoke the curse.

"Will that work?" the soldier asked them, the dead woman's body slung over one shoulder.

"It will remove the curse," said the younger woman, "but only the gods know when."

* * * * * *

The more Livia stared at the coarse black hair of her younger son Drusus, the more she suspected he was the product of that hairy pig Diodorus.

"How old are your sons now, Domina?" asked Medousa.

"Oh I'm not exactly sure, Medousa. The block-headed fat one is ten or eleven and the little hairy one is seven or eight."

"How delightful, Domina."

Livia thought about whipping the slave for a moment, but couldn't be bothered. In the eight years she'd lived with Medousa, she had learned to let a lot go. Had she not, Medousa would have been lashed to shreds years ago and her own hands would be raw from holding the whip.

The block-headed Tiberius and the hairy Drusus ran up to her with mischief in their eyes. Tiberius opened his hand and in the center of his palm the black body of a spider – only two of its six legs still intact – flopped around. "Look what I did, Mother," he said.

"What a prince you are," said Livia.

It was that moment that Octavian's daughter Julia wandered into the triclinium. She peered into Tiberius's palm, scowled, and pushed his chest so hard that he fell onto his bottom. "You are a cruel and petty boy, Tiberius," she said. "No wonder my father hates you so."

Tiberius picked himself off the floor and glared at Julia, his temper threatening to boil over. He lifted a fist as if to strike the little girl, but she laughed in his face. "As if you had the nerve," she said, smirking at him over her shoulder as she left the room.

He stood rigidly, his jaw clenched in anger. Like his mother, he had despised his step-sister since the day he had first seen her pompous little face asleep in her cradle.

"Tiberius, go outside!" snapped Livia, "and take Drusus with you." Grumbling, he grabbed his brother's arm and ran off, no doubt in search of more spiders to take out his frustrations on.

Livia cursed her ex-husband Tiberius for bringing the boys here, to Caesar's house. Normally, she visited them at their father's house. On those occasions Tiberius wanted the boys gone, Livia would arrange for them to be sent to her sister Claudia's house so that she could visit them there.

Not that she was particularly interested in visiting them at all. When it came to her sons, she was caught between Scylla and Charybdis. If she didn't see them, she came across to Caesar as a cold and uncaring mother. Yet if she did see them, Caesar was reminded of her former marriage and the fact that she had children by another man but none by him.

She reclined on a couch in the triclinium as Medousa brought a bowl of grapes, and a guest, into the richly frescoed room. "Domina, your sister Claudia is here."

Claudia turned up her nose at the mud on the floor as she entered the triclinium, dressed in one of her trademark purple dresses. "I assume the darling demons are visiting?" she asked drily, resting on the couch beside her younger sister.

"That wretch Tiberius," fumed Livia. "He knows that I hate it when he drops them off unannounced. He does it just to goad me, you know. It's his pathetic way of waving his cock before Caesar."

"It's still early," Claudia replied. "Perhaps he'll send a litter to retrieve them before Caesar returns."

"I doubt it. There is no senate business today, so I expect him home earlier than usual."

"Has he warmed up to them at all?" asked Claudia.

"He tolerates Drusus, but he despises Tiberius."

"Do you think he suspects?" Claudia lowered her voice. "That they may have different fathers, that is?"

"I think he does his best not to think about it at all," Livia replied, "and so do I. You've heard how he drones on and on about the virtues of the Roman matron and the importance of pure sexual morals. Never mind how many of his friends' wives he's screwed in the pantry during his dinner parties or how many virgin slave girls he's pierced, the man would choke on his moral standards if he knew how hard Diodorus used to drill it into me."

"Sexual hypocrisy is the luxury of manhood, dear sister."

Livia exhaled heavily and turned onto her back, suddenly pensive. "Still...the boys are so different from each other, Claudia, it's hard not to wonder. They're both beasts, to be sure, but Drusus at least has some ambition. Unless Tiberius turns him into a drunk or a catamite, he might actually make something of himself."

"Hmm. Let's hope." Claudia placed a bunch of grapes in her palm, plucked a plump one, and popped it into her mouth. She spoke as she chewed. "I heard that the grain rations were increased for the Lupercalia. Has Antony sent a shipment?"

"No. The Senate ordered the increase. Caesar didn't oppose it, but he wasn't happy about it. He said that a full stomach one day means an even emptier stomach the next day."

"And he still refuses to take Antony's will from the Temple of Vesta?"

"As far as my husband is concerned, the sun shines out the asses of the Vestals."

Claudia chewed another grape. "And the virgins? Does he tire of that yet?"

"Does a fox tire of the hen house?"

"Hmm." Claudia spat a grape seed onto the floor. Truly, her sister would try the patience of Clementia. Here she was, the wife of Caesar, and already out of his bed.

Claudia couldn't let the situation deteriorate any more. After all, her own fortunes were tied to Livia's and she quite enjoyed the adulation of being known as Caesar's sister-in-law. She rolled a grape between her fingers. "Seems to me, sister, that it's time your husband lost his idolatry of the Vestals."

"Nice thought, but I doubt that will happen. I thought he would be angry with the high priestess when she refused to give him Antony's will, but instead his admiration of her only deepened. I couldn't believe it!"

"He admires their virtue," said Claudia. "The more virtuous the behavior, the more he reveres them. His reaction therefore wasn't surprising."

"Whatever you say."

"You're not listening to me, Livia." She leaned forward. "That means the opposite is also true. The less virtuous the behavior, the less he will revere them. Your husband must see that the Vestals are not the chaste guardians of the sacred flame that he thinks they are."

Livia sat up and faced her sister squarely. "I'm listening now, Claudia."

* * * * * *

My beloved Pomponia,

Today I have seen three sights that I could never have imagined. The first concerns Marc Antony. This morning one of the greatest generals that Rome has ever known emerged from his dressing chamber wearing the cosmetics of a woman.

It is customary for Egyptian men to wear make-up on their faces and Antony has taken up the practice. He wears some kind of black coloring that covers his eyelids and makes his eyes look like those of a cat. I hope I do not sound womanish describing this to you. I am uncomfortable discussing it but I wanted to tell you. He has also taken to drinking beer over wine, as the Egyptians do. I have tried the stuff but cannot stomach it.

The second thing concerns Caesarion, son of Julius Caesar and Cleopatra. You may still think of him as a young child of two or three years, the age he was when Cleopatra was in Rome, but time flies and he is now sixteen years old.

Although I have been in Alexandria for two years, today was the first time I saw Caesarion on Egyptian soil as Cleopatra only lets Romans who have sworn an oath to her and Antony be near him. The encounter was by accident. I was to travel in a litter with one of Antony's men, but there was some confusion and I stepped into a lectica within which sat the Queen and Caesarion.

I must tell you, Pomponia, looking at the boy was no different than looking at Caesar. Although Caesar never acknowledged him and there has always been speculation the child was not his, I am convinced there can be no doubt of parentage.

Antony's men tell me that Caesarion has the makings of a capable leader. He has his mother's undeniable intelligence and his father's even temperament. But alas, if Octavian Caesar ever comes to Egypt with sword in hand, the young Caesarion will not be long for this world. I cannot imagine the adopted son of the divine Julius would let the true blood son live.

The third thing I saw this day was the making of a mummy. One of the Queen's favorite astrologers died and Marius – one of Antony's soldiers I have become friends with – petitioned the priests to let us watch the process. Marius has become quite friendly with the locals and has adopted many Egyptian customs (other than wearing make-up for which I am very grateful).

Now Pomponia, you may think that you have seen some disturbing things in your life, but nothing compares to mummification. While we Romans are reasonable in our knowledge that only the spirit travels to Elysium, the Egyptians believe that their physical bodies go to the afterlife. They therefore need to preserve the body to house the spirit.

I urge you to sit down while you read this process lest the description weaken your womanly constitution. After the priests have made their incantations to the gods, the embalmers remove the brain from the body, bit by bit, by means of a sharp hook inserted through the nose. If the brain is stubborn, an embalmer strikes the body on top of the skull to dislodge it. Once the brain is out, the embalmers pour liquid resin into the nose to fill the space where the brain was.

The body is then cut in a ritualistic fashion and the stomach and other organs are removed and set in an urn. Only the heart is left in the body. The Egyptians believe that their spirit and all that they are resides in the heart. The embalmers then wrap the body in white gauze, using strange smelling unguents to hold the fabric in place, while the priests chant and place amulets along the body to ward off evil spirits.

The body is then put in a sarcophagus and buried deep in the earth with items it will need in the afterlife, such as food and drink. This confused me above all for I had to wonder how the Egyptian afterlife could be so poorly stocked that the dead must bring their own sustenance. More strangely, no one left a coin with the body to pay the ferryman. The priests said they did not believe in such things, but Marius and I suspect they simply did not want to part with any money. I left a coin by the sarcophagus when no one was looking.

The Lupercalia will be over by the time this letter reaches you, but I trust it will arrive before the kalends of March and the renewal of Vesta's eternal flame in the temple. My greatest wish is that I could once again watch you perform the sacred ritual with my own eyes.

For now, I shall light a candle on the kalends and make an offering to the goddess. I will tell her of my love for you, and surely she will light my path home very soon.

Quintus.

P.S. I have written to Valeria and divorced her. You have six years left in the Vestal order. When I return to Rome, I shall make arrangements for our future.

Pomponia set the letter on her desk and leaned back in her chair. She often felt dizzy after reading Quintus's letters. Invariably, they were full of contradictory emotions and messages: warmth and affection in one sentence, haughtiness and condescension in the next. Today, the dizziness was stronger than usual.

She re-read the post script: *You have six years left in the Vestal order. When I return to Rome, I shall make arrangements for our future.*

How typical. It was not a declaration of love or a humble marriage proposal, but rather an order.

She loved Quintus. That much was undeniable. Yet she had given little thought to whether she would leave the order at the end of her thirty years of service. It gave her joy to know that Quintus felt such love for her, yet as always he assumed she was his to rule over as he pleased. Her wish to rule herself didn't just irritate him, it baffled him.

She read the post script again before rolling the scroll back up and dipping the end into the flame of the beeswax candle on her desk. As the papyrus burned, the words flew up to the goddess and Pomponia wondered what she would make of them. What would

Vesta want her to do? Become the bride of Quintus or remain a bride of Rome?

The idea of a private life with Quintus was compelling. They had shared intimate moments that had foreshadowed the pleasures he could give her.

Many times she had thought upon the press of his full lips, the feel of his breath and strong arms, and the sound of his loving whispers in her ear. These moments had been shadows of a life that one day she might see more clearly.

For years, she had longed to know him in a way familiar way. In the way that Valeria knew him.

Valeria. Quintina had written to Quintus about her mother's death, but clearly the letter hadn't yet arrived. Pomponia had to wonder how Quintus would react. He had never shown affection for her and it was no surprise that he had chosen to divorce her now, when both of his daughters were out of her care. But would news of her death spark some kind of guilt or regret?

Pomponia's face reddened at the thought of Valeria: a high-born woman, the mother of a blessed priestess, and yet found with a curse tablet that threatened a Vestal's watch over the sacred fire. Did she not care what misery and death such a curse could bring to Rome and her people?

It was Vesta's sacred fire that kept the barbarians out of Rome and kept Roman citizens out of slavery. It protected Roman wives and children from raping invaders, and watched over Roman men on the battlefield. It sanctified the home and, at life's end, it led the spirits of family members through the darkness so that they could be together again in Elysium.

To cast such a curse was unforgiveable and Pomponia could spare no pity for the violent way Valeria had crossed Pluto's threshold.

As if giving sound to her anger, Pomponia heard a loud banging in the corridor outside her office. A swell of loud voices. Quickly, she burned Quintus's letter and went to investigate.

The moment she turned the corner into the atrium, she was met by the unexpected face of a man. Lepidus.

He was accompanied by two Praetorian guards who stood uncomfortably at his side. Their heads were bowed and they avoided making eye contact with the two priestesses – Tuccia and Lucretia – who stood in front of them, their hands on their hips in angry indignation.

"Pontifex," said Pomponia. "Are you mad? What is the meaning of this trespass?"

Lepidus rubbed his temples and then shook his head. "I cannot believe it."

"What is it? What has happened?"

"Lady Pomponia," said Lepidus, "It is my most grievous duty, but I must tell you that a credible accusation of incestum has been made against the Vestal order."

The blood drained from Pomponia's face. "Against which priestess?"

He paused and licked his lips before handing Pomponia a scroll. "Against Priestess Tuccia."

Tuccia put her hands to face and slumped to the floor. "*Tu etiam protege me, dea*," she breathed. "Goddess, protect me!"

Lepidus took a step toward Pomponia and lowered his voice. "I am sorry, it gives me no pleasure to say so, but she must come with us. She cannot remain near the sacred fire. It may be her incestum that has caused the goddess to forsake Rome. People are starving and Egypt grows powerful as Rome weakens. We cannot take the chance."

"Pomponia, no!" cried Tuccia. "It is not so, I swear it is not true!"

Pomponia forced herself to think. What was the protocol for this?

"Stand up, Tuccia." It was Fabiana's voice. The elderly priestess walked past the guards and the Pontifex Maximus as if they weren't there and looked down at Tuccia. "Remember what you are and stand up at once."

Tuccia stood up. Her legs were shaking, but she faced Lepidus with sudden dignity.

"You will go with them," said Fabiana. She looked at Lepidus. "Take her to the house of the former Vestal Paulina on the Palatine Hill."

"Yes, Priestess."

"We will see what must be done and send word to you tomorrow," Fabiana said to Tuccia. "Mother Vesta goes with you."

Tuccia folded her trembling arms across her chest and followed the Pontifex Maximus and the Praetorians out of the House of the Vestals. As she left, she crossed paths with Nona and Caecilia who had just come from the temple to investigate why the Pontifex Maximus – with soldiers, no less – would possibly be attending the House of the Vestals, and at this hour. They watched Tuccia walk by them, but her eyes were fixed on the scarlet cloak of the Praetorian in front of her and she did not look at them.

The Vestals stood silently together, waiting for the initial wave of astonishment and disbelief to pass. Pomponia thought about chastising Nona and Caecilia for leaving the temple to the care of novices, even for a few moments and when it was under guard, but then she thought again. Right now, a show of unity was needed. Plus, she had never felt justified in correcting the elder Nona, not even now that she was the chief Vestal. She opened the scroll in her hand.

"Tuccia is accused of incestum with someone named Gallus Gratius Januarius."

"I know him," said Lucretia. "He's a chariot racer."

Pomponia swallowed hard. Tuccia's love of the chariot races was well-known in Rome and she openly befriended several racers. It was a bad sign. Pomponia kept reading the scroll. "Her accuser is Claudia Drusilla," she said.

"Why does that name sound familiar?" asked Caecilia.

Nona clucked her tongue. "She is the sister of Caesar's wife," she said, "and a gossiping, maneuvering little trollop if there ever was one."

The younger Vestals raised their eyebrows at the pious senior priestess. Every now and then, when it really mattered, Nona could spit out a spark.

Lucretia wiped a tear from her cheek and they all fell into a sober silence until a soft clicking on the marble floor made them all glance down the corridor.

Perseus trotted up to Fabiana, gave a bored yawn, and sat at her feet. The mighty hero, come to slay the beast and save them. Caecilia picked him up and placed him in Fabiana's arms.

"Let's go to the temple," said Fabiana. "I have a story to tell you."

CHAPTER XIV

THE STORY OF THE VESTAL LICINIA

ROME FEBRUARY 31 BCE

It was a cool February night and five priestesses walked barefoot up the marble steps of the white Temple of Vesta in the Roman Forum.

As they moved through the bronze door, the black, starry canopy of the night sky gave way to the soaring circular dome of the temple's inner sanctum. The eternal fire roared and crackled in its marble and bronze hearth, and the sacred smoke rose upward, billowing out of the oculus at the dome's apex and ascending to the goddess.

The temple was lit not just by the eternal fire, but by a number of olive oil lamps fixed to the marble columns that encircled the sanctum. They cast flickering shadows on the rounded walls. The white tiled floor was cool and it felt good below the Vestals' bare feet.

Pomponia dismissed the novices who were tending the hearth and they left noiselessly, their eyes full of fear and confusion. Using a pair of iron tongs, she then chose a few rocks of coal from a decorated marble bowl and carefully placed them in the sacred fire, nudging them between criss-crossing logs of wood. Lucretia stoked the fire with an iron and it roared up anew, fresh sparks flying out and snapping loudly in the air.

Pomponia looked into the fire. When she was a child Vestal, the eternal flame had still been fueled by wood alone, but the addition of black coal in the hearth seemed to nourish the embers and sustain the fire more than wood alone. Still, some of the senior Vestals had resisted the change. They didn't want to break with tradition; however, Fabiana had persuaded them.

"*Tempora mutantur, nos et mutamur in illis*," she had told them. "Times change, and we change with them."

Fabiana had been a natural Vestalis Maxima. She had always been able to balance ancient custom with new ideas. She had always been able to withstand any crisis, political or religious, with grace and competence. Pomponia silently thanked the goddess that at ninety years old Fabiana was still strong enough to help her navigate the wicked storm that had descended upon them.

The priestesses sat on simple wooden chairs beside the hearth. Fabiana stroked the old little dog that slept on her lap, and everyone sat quietly waiting for her to speak. When she finally did, her words mixed with the snapping fire and reverberated against the marble walls. Pomponia had the sense that the goddess herself was listening.

"When I was a novice Vestal of only eight years old," began Fabiana, "my favorite priestess was a young woman named Licinia. Everyone loved her. Her father owned a large apiary in the country and he used to ship giant crates of candied honey to her for the Vestalia. She would hand these out to the novices and the children of Rome. Oh, I remember it well. The honey was sticky and so delicious. Sometimes you could taste just a little of thyme or rosemary. The children would swarm the temple like bees during Vesta's festival and wait for hours for a single piece.

"Licinia was a bit of a trickster. This endeared her to the novices and the public, but often found her out of favor with the Vestalis Maxima, who at that time was Tullia. You all know of Tullia. Her statue has stood in the peristyle for decades. Tullia was a diligent chief Vestal and a true servant of the goddess. She felt her most important duty was to uphold the dignity of our order and she could be quite severe when faced with any deviation from sacred custom, no matter how small.

"Licinia was of the wealthy and noble family Licinius, which in those days was much richer and grander than it is today. The Licinii owned some of the finest land in Italy and Licinia added to her own wealth by purchasing an expansive villa at Frascati and another on Capri. I remember she once took all the novices to her house in Frascati and we had the most delicious sweetened ice you could imagine.

"In those days, Cisalpine Gaul was a torment. There were some good-sized Roman settlements, but these were always under attack. The worst of the barbarians was a Germanic tribe called the Cimbri who threatened to invade Italy itself. Now, you know your history: the consul Gaius Marius and his legate Sulla ultimately defeated the Cimbri and stopped the invasion, but for a while victory was not assured and it was a frightening time with the constant worry of invasion. The high priestess Tullia was forever offering to Vesta for Rome's safety.

"Even though the war was won in the end, there were some early losses. One of the worst military defeats happened to the legions of Gnaeus Artorius Cotta. Were I not on consecrated ground right now, I would spit on the floor at his name. Cotta was an incompetent fool who marched nearly one thousand Roman soldiers straight to their death at the hands of barbarians.

"Upon his return to Rome, Cotta was expelled from the army and reviled for his foolishness and loss. He retreated from public life for a few months and went to holiday at a friend's villa on

Capri. This friend was named Gaius Sempronius Calidus and his villa was adjacent to Licinia's villa.

"I never saw Licinia's villa on Capri, but everyone said it was much better than the villa owned by Calidus. It was on the coast and grew the finest grapes. It had a huge olive press and Licinia often had the oil sent to the temple for use in sacred rites. There were rumors that the Sirens rested on rocks that could be seen from Licinia's shore, and that on the hottest of summer nights they could be heard singing of the Fall of Troy. This would cause the house slaves to rush around and close all the windows in fear.

"Ah, where was I...oh yes. Now I remember. When Cotta returned to Rome, he wasn't alone. His friend Calidus was with him. They went straight to the Senate and asked for the floor. Of course, they were denied but they assured the senators that Rome's very existence hinged on what they had to say, and such were their dramatics and portends of doom that they were heard.

"Cotta told the Senate that the battle he lost was not his fault. Rather, it was the fault of an unchaste Vestal – Licinia. She had been seen consorting with one of his legionary soldiers, a man named Marcus Sergius Rufus. With shaking hands and moist eyes, Cotta swore that the priestess's incestum had caused Vesta to turn her back on Rome.

"He cried that her betrayal had broken the *pax deorum* – the agreement between mankind and the gods – and warned that his military loss would be only the beginning if the priestess was not made to atone for her broken vows. For without the protection of Vesta, the invasion of Rome and the enslavement of her people would surely follow.

"Of course, no one believed him. They had known Licinia since she was a novice of only six years old. Yet Cotta said that he had quality witnesses and Calidus, a wealthy landowner, was one of them. Calidus testified that on more than one occasion he had visited the Vestal's villa at Capri on neighborly business and had seen her in the embrace of the same legionary soldier. The two men also had a Greek priest present a Sibylline prophecy that supported their accusation.

"Now, some people at last began to wonder. It was true that Licinia was a favorite of this particular soldier's legion and had been since she was a child. Many of the soldiers gifted her with spoils from their campaigns in exchange for the goddess's blessing. Yet other legions did the same with their favorite Vestals. Such had been the custom for as long as anyone could remember.

"However, the timing of the accusation was fatalistic. It came just before another defeat by the Cimbri in Gaul and the threat of invasion seemed imminent. A wave of panic began to spread throughout Rome. The people needed a sacrifice. And that sacrifice was Licinia.

"I was only a girl of eight years, but I remember the men coming into our sanctified house in the middle of the night..." At the memory of it, Fabiana's voice cracked and trailed off. She wiped away a tear with her palla and scratched Perseus's ear.

"The Pontifex Maximus was with them. Tullia threw a statuette at him. I remember because I thought the Pontifex would be angry, but he wasn't. He apologized and told her that Licinia had to come with them. Licinia came out of her room to see what all the noise was about. She was holding a cup of water and when they told her what was happening, she dropped it onto the floor and it shattered. I was such a child. I remember thinking, 'they're going to make me clean that up.'

"Poor Licinia, that lovely young woman...they took her to the ancient Temple of Jupiter when it still stood on the Capitoline, before fire destroyed it. It had several underground chambers and it was there, in those dark caverns, that she was scourged. They had to bring in a man from Judea to do it. No Roman would do it, not even those who condemned her.

"The high priestess Tullia had all of us, even some of the novices, wait outside the Temple of Jupiter. We had an oil lamp lit with the sacred flame and we all prayed over it. I saw Licinia when they brought her out. Her white dress was torn to strips and rivers of red blood ran down her legs. She could not walk, but was dragged along by two priests of Jupiter.

"They had a cart and horses ready to take her to the Campus Sceleratus. She looked at us – oh, I will never forget her face – as they bound her wrists and put her in a box. That was the last time I saw her. The high priestess and Priestess Flavia refused to ride in the lectica and climbed up into the cart with the box. Flavia sat on her knees and put her mouth to the box. She must have been speaking to Licinia through it.

"Then the cart left and we all stood there for a long while, just watching it disappear down the street. Cassia, do you remember what you said? You said – " Fabiana caught herself. "Oh, what am I thinking? Priestess Cassia is dead, of course." She stroked Perseus as the Vestals exchanged heartsick glances.

Pomponia took one of Fabiana's hands and held it tightly. "Tell us the rest. What of the soldier?"

Fabiana nodded sadly. "Rufus had been a legionary soldier for fifteen years. He was a large man, even for a legionary. His wife had died in childbirth and his son lived with Rufus's sister and her family. He was a proud man, too. When the Pontifex Maximus asked if he wanted to beg the goddess's forgiveness for his crime, he asked the Pontifex whether he wanted to beg his wife's forgiveness for having such a small cock.

"They stripped him and tied him to a post in front of the Rostra. He was flogged more times than I could count. I saw a large mass of skin on his back peel away and slide down his back, like rain slides down a wall. He called out his dead wife's name and then never made another sound. His murder was as revolting to the goddess as Licinia's was.

"When Tullia and Flavia returned from the Campus Sceleratus, we were all still in the temple praying for Licinia. Flavia went to her bedchamber, but Tullia came into the sanctum. "She stood by the fire – " Fabiana pointed her finger " – right there, by that chip in the hearth. I can still see her standing there. She said nothing, but she began to weep." We were all shocked. We had never seen the high priestess cry, not even when her sister had died earlier that year.

"She wept like a child. She was inconsolable. The more she cried, the more we knew that whatever she had seen at the evil field was beyond horror, beyond sorrow. A year passed before she could talk about it. She told us how Licinia had cried out to the goddess for protection, but how she had regained her dignity and climbed down into the black pit as bravely as Perseus had faced the gorgon. She told us that she had sent the sacred flame down into the pit with her."

Lucretia brushed tears from her face. "What of her accusers?"

"Ah, of course," said Fabiana. "Those men, demonic larvae both. Cotta was no longer considered a disgraced general but now the savior of Rome. The tide of the war eventually turned in Rome's favor and many said it was Cotta's discovery of the Vestal's incestum that saved the city and her people.

"Calidus also had reason to be pleased. Licinia's properties were sold off and he was able to acquire her villa on Capri for a song." Fabiana snorted. "At the time of Licinia's murder, there was a shipment of olive oil on its way to the temple. Would you believe that demon tried to charge Rome for it, claiming it was his property?"

Fabiana sighed. Her shoulders dropped, as if releasing some of the tension and bitterness she had been holding inside. "But Veritas always swims out of her dark well into the light of day. You see, Rufus had a loving son. He did not believe the accusation against his father and it wasn't long before Rome realized what it had done. And the horror of the truth was even worse than the lie had been.

"The younger Rufus presented evidence that proved the innocence of his father and of the Vestal. It started with the discovery of several letters written by Calidus to Licinia in which he offered to buy her villa at Capri. He wanted to add her property onto his own. She declined the offer, but he kept sending letters, each one more aggressive than the last.

"And then there was the Greek priest who had presented the Sibylline prophecy. It turned out the man was not a priest after all, but rather the Greek freedman of a true priest. The man knew just enough to sound believable. He cracked like a nut under interrogation.

"But the spark that truly set fire to the men's funeral pyre was the return to Rome of a man called Laenas. He was a respected centurion in Cotta's legions. During the battle that had disgraced Cotta, Laenas was one of the few officers who had maintained his men's respect. There were many accounts of his bravery and how he risked his life to save even the lowliest of the men under his command. At the time the accusations were made, he was fighting with Sulla's legions in Gaul.

"When word of what had happened reached him, Laenas returned to Rome like a thunderbolt thrown by Zeus, angry and at lightning speed. What he said shook Rome. He said that he had overheard a drunken Cotta telling a now-dead soldier that, if he lost the battle, he would blame it on the broken vows of a Vestal, even if he had to screw the priestess himself.

"So for the second time in one year, I watched a man scourged in the Forum. Flavia chose to stay and tend the sacred flame in the temple, but Tullia insisted the rest of us go to witness it, even the youngest novices. I remember it vividly. Tullia set her chair an arm's length away from the post they tied Cotta to. When they flogged him, the blood spattered her stola. She never took her eyes off him the whole time.

"When he was near dead, Tullia called out for the flogging to stop. For a moment we thought she would grant mercy. Instead, she ordered that he be taken to the top of the Tarpeian Rock and flung from the cliff to his death. It was done. So much for Cotta.

"But Calidus escaped the executioner's lash. The man was as rich as Midas and he bribed his way out of the Carcer, although he probably wished he hadn't. The younger Rufus knew he would try it. He and some men followed Calidus into the countryside on horseback. They captured him and crucified him along the Via Appia. The story came back that it had taken two full days for Calidus to perish and that Rufus and his men drank and celebrated the entire time. They left his body hanging for the crows.

"For months, people came to kneel before the temple to beg forgiveness not just of the goddess, but of the priestesses, too. The Pontifex asked Tullia to make a public statement of forgiveness on the Rostra but she refused.

"Flavia left the order less than a month after her thirty years of service were completed. She married an ex-consul about a year later and if I remember right they had a daughter who later married a young kin of Sulla. She bought a country house outside of Pompeii and swore to never return to Rome, not even for her daughter's wedding. Everyone had to go to Pompeii for the ceremony."

Fabiana sighed heavily and put her hands on the arms of her chair. "Lucretia, help me up."

"Yes, Fabiana." The younger Vestal lifted Perseus off Fabiana's lap and set the little dog on the tile floor as she helped Fabiana to her feet.

"I'm tired," said the old priestess. "I leave the matter with you, Pomponia. But I will say this: the black pit in the Campus Sceleratus is filled with enough of our bones. And although we serve the goddess, you cannot rely on her intervention. Tuccia's life depends on you." Tapping her leg to call Perseus behind her, Fabiana shuffled out of the temple.

The Vestals sat in silence for a long time, the only sound the crackling of the sacred fire in the temple's hearth. Finally, Pomponia spoke: her voice sounded stronger than she had expected it would.

"Our beloved sister Tuccia has been disparaged by a scheming little shrew," she said. "But fear not. Pluto will have to go through us to get to her. Let me think on this tonight. We will speak in the morning."

She stood and took a handful of loose salted flour from an earthenware bowl, tossing it into the sacred fire. The flame surged upward as it consumed the offering.

Leaving Nona and Caecilia behind to tend to the hearth, she led the other priestesses out of the temple and back to the House of the Vestals where they each returned to the privacy of their own quarters and their own thoughts.

Pomponia went to her office and sat at her desk. Outside her open window, she heard the sweeping of a broom on the cobblestone of the Via Sacra as the street-cleaners moved through the Forum, doing their work by torch light in the still of night.

The sound always made her think of Quintus and the night before he had left for Egypt.

The night he had held his bloody palm to her cheek before the shrine of Mars and sworn on the black stone that they would be together, and she had stood inside the Regia as he departed, listening to the sound of his receding footfalls and the scratching of brooms on the cobblestone.

The memory of it, and her longing to once again see his face, caught as a sob in her throat. She looked at the silver bowl of ashes on her desk and then her eyes moved over some of the gifts he had sent her in the two years he had been gone: a small painting of the pyramids and the Sphinx, a shen ring, some gemstones, a jar of exotic plant extract used for temple magic.

And then Pomponia, High Priestess of Vesta, had a most unholy idea.

CHAPTER XV

Tuccia & the Sieve

Rome February – March 31 BCE

It was a clear, warm day for February; however, Gallus Gratius Januarius had no way of knowing that. He sat hunched in the corner of a cold black hole in the stone-walled Carcer, twelve feet below the living world.

Gallus wasn't a man who was accustomed to such soundless solitude. His world was a loud one, full of hooves pounding thunderously on sand, chariots roaring down the track and the frenzied cheers of thousands of spectators.

The soldiers had arrived at his house in the middle of the night. The pounding on the door had sounded like a battering ram. Gallus had wrapped himself in a cloak and stood in front of his wife who held their infant son to her breast in fear as his house slave opened the door. He could still vividly see the look of shock on his wife's face as the accusation was read: a charge of incestum committed with the Vestal Virgin Tuccia.

He covered his face with his hands. This wasn't happening. Despite the ghost stories about Vestals being buried alive, that just didn't happen. There had only been a few accusations of incestum throughout the long history of the Vestal order and those were more legend than reality.

Even if a Vestal were so inclined, she'd have a hard time finding a partner in crime. There were plenty of women to be had. No point losing the skin on your back and the head on your shoulders for one that Rome and the gods had deemed off-limits.

Gallus chewed at his fingers. Claudia Drusilla. Who in Hades was she? A woman he had wronged in some way? Perhaps a misguided or obsessive fan of a competing chariot team? Outside of the racing track, he had no enemies that he knew of. He owed no debts.

He scratched anxiously at his head as a memory came to him. *No...could that be it?* He picked at an insect that had attached itself to his scalp and cursed himself.

At the end of the last games, Priestess Tuccia had been asked to present the victory palm to the winning charioteer. That had been Gallus, of course. The Vestal's love of the races and of a particular horse on his team – Ajax – was common knowledge, and she had even visited the stables on occasion to fawn over him.

As she had presented Gallus with the victory palm, he had surprised her with the gift of Ajax's golden bridle. The crowd had gone wild. Now, Gallus wondered whether the innocent gesture had been seen by some as a sign of a greater guilt.

A scraping noise sounded above him and he sensed the barred grating at the hole's entrance had been slid open. A moment later, a dark figure landed heavily at his feet and the grating scraped closed again.

The man at his feet groaned once and then fell silent. By the scarce light of the single torch that burned in the hole, Gallus could see a dark pool of blood spreading out from the man's skull. A white bone protruded from one leg. Gallus pushed himself up and stepped away. He crouched in another corner and waited, like an animal locked in the pit of the arena, to see what his fate would be.

He had no way of knowing that the Fates were spinning their thread at that very moment.

It was happening in the Forum Boarium along the banks of the Tiber River. On any ordinary day, the Forum Boarium was a bustling mass of people and stock animals. It was Rome's main riverside hub of trading and commercial activity and every day a multitude of cattle, donkeys and pigs were bought and sold.

Every day, blacksmiths noisily hammered at hipposandals and horseshoes and farriers broke their backs fastening them to the hooves of high-strung horses and muscular working oxen. Every day, wooden carts packed with hay, straw, feed or manure rambled and rattled down the cobblestone and a dirty child could be seen running to catch an escaped goat or chicken.

But not today. Today, the Forum Boarium was closed for business; however, it was still packed with people who had come to witness one of the most inconceivable spectacles anyone could have imagined would happen during their lifetime.

A Vestal Virgin, accused of incestum, was going to call upon the goddess to decide her fate by either proving her innocence or guilt.

The agitated crowd stood at a distance from a circular temple located beside the Tiber. Their rowdy excitement was held at bay by a long line of no-nonsense soldiers whose polished armor reflected the light of the sun and whose hands rested menacingly on their swords.

This particular temple was a multi-use structure dedicated to both Hercules and Vesta. Although the eternal flame did not burn within it, it nonetheless served an important function for the Vestals. It was here that water collected from the Tiber was sanctified by rites so that it could be used to prepare the sacred wafers and clean Vesta's temple in the Forum Romanum.

Standing closer to the temple was a throng of senators, various officials who fidgeted in nervous expectation, and the city newsreader with his secretary.

They exchanged whispered words with the Flamines Maiores, the High Priests of Jupiter and Mars, as the augers looked on with sober interest. Even the priests of Pluto were present, their black robes and somber chants adding an even greater sense of dread to the occasion.

The Pontifex Maximus Lepidus raised his arms to quell the chatter and command attention as the Vestal litter approached the temple and set down before it.

An apprehensive silence descended over the Forum Boarium as High Priestess Pomponia stepped out of the lectica, followed by the elder Priestess Nona and finally the Priestess Tuccia.

All three were dressed in the impressive ceremonial robes and headdresses of the Vestals. A young novice wearing a simple white dress and veil stepped out of the lectica after them and quickly dropped to her knees to straighten the bottom of their stolas. She then reached back into the lectica, first pulling out a round wooden sieve which she presented to the Vestalis Maxima, and then an earthenware jug which she gave to the Vestal Nona.

Pomponia faced the crowd, casting the same superior but indignant look to everyone, whether respected priest or state official, wealthy citizen or common slave.

"We, the faithful priestesses of Vesta," she began, "who keep the eternal flame in the temple, who offer our youth to the goddess and to Rome, come before you today to answer a sacrilegious charge of obscene incestum against the virtuous Priestess Tuccia."

After she was certain that all eyes were on her, Pomponia held out the sieve with extended arms. As she did, Nona poured the water from the jug into the sieve. The water ran straight through to create a large puddle on the ground.

Pomponia took a step to stand beside Tuccia. "Only the goddess can judge the purity of her priestesses," she said, and then passed the sieve to Tuccia.

Tuccia held the sieve above her head. "Mother Vesta," she called out. "If I have always brought pure hands to your sacred fire and ancient rituals, make it now so that with this sieve I shall be able to draw water from the Tiber and bring it to your temple. Let the water remain in the sieve as my vows remain unbroken."

At that, Tuccia walked toward and then past the temple to where a stone staircase descended directly to the banks of the Tiber River. She walked down the steps as the Pontifex Maximus and the high priests of Jupiter and Mars followed her, everyone else jostling to see what they could.

The newsreader muttered to his secretary who feverishly transcribed his words. Regardless of how this ended, he knew he'd be shouting out the news for days in the Forum.

Pomponia remained beside Nona and Quintina in front of the temple. Her face wore an expression of cool certainty, but her heart hammered against her chest in doubt and fear.

Tuccia stopped at the bottom of the steps on top of a white marble platform that extended into the river and that allowed the Vestals to collect clean flowing water from the Tiber. A gold plaque had been affixed to its center. It read: *On this holy spot, the Vestals collect the sacred water.*

She gently immersed the sieve in the river, left it submerged for a moment, and then lifted it out. The Pontifex and the priests nodded in confirmation: the sieve was indeed full of water.

Yet – though they could not believe their eyes – the water did not drain through, but instead remained in the basin and splashed against the high wooden rim of the round sieve, even as Tuccia walked back up the steps.

Still holding the sieve full of water – from which not a drop had drained – she quickly walked the short distance back to the temple to stand before the mesmerized crowd in the Forum Boarium.

The Pontifex Maximus stood beside her and looked into the sieve. He cupped his hands, filled them with water, and took a sip. The crowd drew in a collective gasp of amazement.

"Mother Vesta," said Tuccia, "your priestess is as pure and faithful as always." She passed the sieve to the Pontifex Maximus and, almost immediately, water began to drip through the sieve. A moment later, the pool of water in the sieve gushed out the bottom to drench the chief priest's sandals.

The Pontifex Maximus held up his arms. "*Lure divino,*" he shouted, "divine law has proven the priestess innocent!" As the crowd erupted into a chorus of cheers, applause and prayers that all flowed into one jubilant song, he pointed to a centurion. "Go immediately to the Carcer and free Gallus Gratius Januarius."

Pomponia felt pressure on her hand. Tuccia was clutching it. Her eyes were wet and her chest was heaving with deep breaths. She had the face of one who been too close to death, one who had already stepped into Charon's boat but at the last moment been pulled out by an unseen hand.

As she gripped Pomponia's hand in relief and gratitude, Tuccia's eyes grew questioning. She had followed Pomponia's hasty and cryptic instructions without thinking. There had been no other choice than to put her life and her trust in the hands of the Vestalis Maxima.

Gently fill the sieve with water from the river and then bring it back. Walk quickly. The goddess will not permit it to drain and you will be proved innocent. Don't think about it, just do it.

But how? Had the goddess truly intervened? That was doubtful. Had there been a deception? A collusion? Had some kind of trick saved her from the evil field?

Pomponia saw the questions and squeezed her friend's hand. "*De duobus malis, minus est semper eligendum,*" she whispered, as they stepped into the lectica with Nona and Quintina.

Of two evils, the lesser must always be chosen.

* * * * * *

After Vesta's show of divinity by the banks of the Tiber, the renewal of the Eternal Flame of Vesta on the kalends of March had been a more joyful ritual than it had been in years.

Despite its hunger pangs and the ongoing hostilities between Caesar in Italy and Antony in Egypt, all of Rome had embraced the ceremony with particular zeal. As the sacred flame had been reignited, the people's faith in the gods, the Vestal order and the future of Rome had been renewed.

Following the renewal ceremony, as was customary, a few Vestals remained in the temple while others left to participate in rituals and ceremonies elsewhere in Rome. This year, Lucretia and Caecilia remained, while Fabiana had surprised Pomponia by saying she wanted to go. The former Vestalis Maxima hadn't seemed well enough to Pomponia, but it was pointless to argue.

Along with Fabiana, Pomponia made sure that it was Tuccia and Nona who accompanied her to these other dedications and celebrations.

As the Vestals who had stood by the Tiber together only a week earlier, she wanted a show of solidarity. The more they could be seen in public – proud and confident – the sooner the incestum ordeal could be wiped from the public's memory.

The chariot races in the Circus Maximus provided the perfect opportunity for such a display. Tuccia was determined to act like nothing had happened and to cheer on her beloved Blues as she had done since she was a young girl. In fact, she had gone a step further by inviting the wife of Gallus Gratius Januarius, who was currently in the lead chariot, to sit beside her.

As Tuccia and Gallus's wife shouted and waved the blue ribbons in their hands, Pomponia chatted comfortably with Medousa. Despite Pomponia's refusal to give him Antony's will from the temple, Octavian had remained as friendly and accommodating as ever and often brought Medousa to events he knew the Vestalis Maxima would be attending.

Yet the day had its tensions and the largest of these was named Claudia Drusilla. She sat beside her sister Livia, clearly determined to reclaim her position in high society by being seen socializing with the Vestals. Dressed in vibrant gowns of purple and blue, and dripping with gold and gemstones, the two sisters couldn't have looked more different than the white-robed priestesses who sat a few rows ahead of them.

Following Tuccia's astonishing show of innocence, Claudia had issued a public apology to her and to the Vestal order. She had retracted the accusation, claiming that it was only her profound love of the Roman people and her sorrow over so many empty stomachs that had compelled her to see guilt in the innocent interactions between the charioteer and the priestess, and to worry that breach in the pax deorum had caused Vesta to forsake Rome.

Along with the apology, she had donated a significant amount of grain from her personal stores to some of Rome's poorest districts, all in the name of Vesta. The quick gestures of contrition, along with her status as Caesar's sister-in-law, seemed to have saved her skin.

Of course, none of the priestesses believed the remorse was genuine. Even if had been genuine, it would change nothing. The damage had been done and forgiveness from the Vestal order would never come.

Claudia was beginning to suspect as much. She leaned over to whisper to her sister, but was forced to speak a bit more loudly as a swell of ear-splitting screams from impassioned spectators filled the stadium.

"How much grain must I part with before I am back in their good graces?" she asked.

"You could hand them Egypt on a silver platter and they still wouldn't forgive you," Livia said under her breath. "They are not changeable." She fidgeted angrily with a gold and ruby bracelet on her wrist as she watched the horse-drawn chariots peal violently around the circular track. "Medea's hot cunt, what a mess the whole thing is! The incestum charge was supposed to make Caesar see the Vestals as impure, but now he sees their purity as *divine* and sanctioned by the goddess. Worse, he now openly asks me to send virgins to his bedchamber and grows sullen if I don't send one nightly. The gods know when he'll bother to get between my old legs again."

"And what of war with Antony? Is he any closer to declaring it?"

"No. He says the people will hate him for it. They still don't believe it is their beloved Antony who is withholding the grain. Antony has men in Rome and they spread the rumor that Caesar is sinking shiploads of the stuff just to turn the people against the great general." Livia folded her arms across her chest. "I wish Antony were dead. I would be first woman in Rome if he were dead. No more playing second woman to that snivelling prude Octavia."

"Hmm." Claudia drummed her fingers on the wooden arm of her chair. "You need Antony's will from the temple."

"Caesar will never forcibly take it," said Livia, "not after that miraculous display by the Tiber. It would be political suicide to violate Vesta's temple, especially now." Exhaling an irritated sigh, Livia straightened her back and craned her neck to look around. "Where is that ugly slave with the wine? I don't know why we bother taking slaves to the Circus Maximus. They pretend to be busy when really they've snuck off to watch the races. We'll see if they think it's worth it when their backs are bleeding tonight. Never mind, I'll find the wine myself. I need to stretch my legs anyway."

Livia stood up and left her seat. A moment later, Priestess Fabiana sat in it. Of all the people in Rome, the former Vestalis Maxima was the last one Claudia expected to find sitting next to her.

"Are you well, Lady Claudia?" asked the elderly Vestal.

Claudia smiled. She would not let this old woman rattle her. "I am, Priestess."

"That is good to hear," Fabiana said pleasantly. "The priestesses and I have been so worried about you. That regrettable business with Tuccia." She shook her head to emphasize her concern while, at the same moment, Pomponia and Tuccia instinctively turned to look at Claudia with thin smiles. "We want you to know that we forgive you, dear lady. We know that your motive for making the accusation was as pure as your own heart. We know what an honorable woman you are."

Claudia's felt a burning heat on her face. "Thank you for saying so, Priestess."

"Not at all." Fabiana folded her hands on her lap. "The Vestal order considers you a friend. Not that we have any enemies of course. We shall forget the entire thing."

"Priestess, I sincerely hope we can." Claudia's voice sounded more desperate than she would have liked it to. "I am beside myself with regret about the whole fearful misunderstanding."

"Now, now," said Fabiana. "Nothing can stand in the way of forgiveness between true friends. And we are true friends, nay?" Fabiana smoothed the back of Claudia's purple veil. Gently, she took Claudia's hands in her own and raised them to her lips, placing a soft kiss on the back of Claudia's hand.

The moment lasted uncomfortably long and Claudia gave a slight tug to withdraw her hand. As she did, she thought she saw a whispered prayer – or maybe a malediction? – pass over the old Vestal's lips.

But then Fabiana looked up with a pleasant smile. “Oh, here is your sister.” She stood up to give Livia back her seat. “I was just speaking with your delightful sister, Lady Livia. How alike the two of you are! Like Helen and Clytemnestra. Now if you will excuse me, I think I must return to the cool comfort of my bedchamber. Good bye.”

“Good bye, Priestess,” said Livia. She sat beside Claudia and handed her a cup of wine. “It took me forever to find the wine slave,” she grumbled, “hiding behind a column and watching the races, just as I suspected.”

“Hmm.” Claudia took a sip of her wine. And then another. But no matter how much wine she drank, her mouth still felt dry.

CHAPTER XVI

Lux Lucis in Obscurum

(A Light in the Darkness)

Egypt & Rome April 31 BCE

Sunrise was still a few hours away, but Quintus didn't care. He had spent over two years in this beast-worshipping desert wasteland where women ruled men and men wore make-up. It was time to go home. But first, there was one last Egyptian wonder to visit: one that would hold special fascination for Pomponia as chief priestess of the sacred fire.

The monumental Lighthouse of Alexandria stood on the small island of Pharos in the Alexandrian harbor and towered some 450 feet into the sky, making it the tallest structure in the world. It had a broad platform of white stone atop of which a three-part lighthouse – square at the bottom, octagonal in the middle and circular at the top – reached higher into the heavens than anything made by mortal hands should reach.

The massive white stone structure was adorned with statues of the ocean gods Neptune and Triton. Each time Ankhu had set sail from Alexandria to bring a message to Pomponia, Quintus had stood in the shipyard and looked out at the lighthouse in silent prayer to both of these gods, but especially to Triton, messenger of the sea, in the hopes that he would blow his horn and calm the waters enough for the ship to travel with speed.

During the day, the lighthouse used mirrors to reflect sunlight and serve as a beacon for ships at sea. It was rumored that these mirrors could generate such intense beams of light that enemy ships could be set on fire long before they reached the shores. *Egyptian delusions of grandeur,* thought Quintus. *How typical.*

A fire also burned day and night at the top of the lighthouse. During the day, it created black smoke that was released through the lighthouse's apex to form a thick column of smoke that could further navigate ships safely into the port. It reminded Quintus of the plume of smoke that billowed from the apex of the Temple of Vesta.

At night, and throughout the dark hours until dawn, this fire burned more fiercely to produce a vibrant orange flame that could be seen from great distances by ships trying to navigate the sea and enter the port. It was this fire that Quintus wanted to see up close. After all, was it not a type of eternal fire? And would that not be of interest to a Vestal priestess? He felt a smile spread across his face as he imagined Pomponia's fascinated expression as he told her all about it – but then he forced himself to stop smiling. *Stop being so damn womanish,* he told himself.

It had been a moonless but starry night and the stars were still bright in these quiet hours before dawn. Quintus and Ankhu had climbed the spiral stairs of the lighthouse all the way to the second observation deck – some 300 feet above ground – where they had stopped to catch their breath and wait for Marius who had bribed some person or another to gain them access to the very top of the lighthouse.

Quintus leaned over the edge of the observation deck and gazed upon the sleeping city of Alexandria. The Royal Library was clearly visible, some of its windows flickering with light. No doubt those annoying Egyptian academics and philosophers were already busying themselves debating the mysteries of the gods and creating more scrolls to join the hundreds of thousands that were said to fill the bibliotheca.

He turned his head to look down at the shipyard in the Alexandrian port. It was mostly quiet and still at this hour, although there were a few early risers working by torch light to load crates, freight and trading goods into ships for whatever voyage awaited them.

In just a few hours, he would be on one of those boats on his way home. He allowed himself a smile as the raucous cries of sea birds, the splashing of black waves against the rocks and the roaring of the great fire above him sounded in his ears.

Quintus faced Ankhu. "You remembered your supplies, correct? I want you to paint the fire and the view from the top when we get up there. I want the priestess to see it."

"Yes, Dominus."

"Good." Quintus reached into his goatskin sack and pulled out a scroll, handing it to Ankhu.

"What is this, Dominus?" Ankhu uncurled the scroll – and gasped.

"It's your manumission," said Quintus. "I've freed you."

"Dominus..." the slave stammered. "By all the gods and goddesses of Rome and Egypt, I thank you, I cannot express my – "

"Oh stop sputtering, you fool. I don't have time to sell you for any profit so I might as well set you free. Finish your paintings and then you can do as you like. You can come to Rome and work for me, or stay in this sand-blown version of Hades, it's no concern of mine."

"Yes, Dominus! Of course, Dominus."

Quintus rolled his eyes at the tears running down the former slave's face, and then waved as he spotted his friend Marius emerging from the lighthouse to limp onto the observation deck.

"*Salve*, Quintus," panted Marius. "I have a big heart because you are leaving Egypt this morning, but it is not big enough to forgive you for making me climb these steps before I've had my breakfast. I'm winded." He struggled to catch his breath. "You said you were departing early, but I didn't think you meant before Ra rose in the sky."

"You and your damned Egyptian gods," grinned Quintus.

"Pray Isis, I have been converted," Marius smiled back. "Now let's keep moving upward. If I stop now, I won't be able to get going again."

The three men – two Romans and a freed Egyptian slave – labored up the last spiral staircase to the very top of the lighthouse. As they ascended into the uppermost chamber, they felt an unexpected swell of heat on their faces from the fire that burned in the middle of the circular space. The snapping and crackling of its flames were surprisingly loud and echoed in the round chamber.

Yet most dazzling and unexpected to Quintus was the way the vibrant orange flames reflected off the multitude of mirrors that encircled the inside of the chamber. The effect was spectacular and like nothing he had ever seen before. He raised his eyebrows and nodded to Ankhu. Yes. It was worth climbing the thousand stairs. This would *definitely* impress Pomponia.

Quintus appreciated the fire for a few long moments, and then took several cautious steps over the mirrored floor to peer out one of the wide slotted openings through which the fiery orange beacon was made visible to ships at sea. With the heat of the fire on the back of his head and the cool ocean air on his face, he again felt a rise of excitement in his gut. He was going home.

He turned to say something to Ankhu, but furrowed his brow as he caught an expression of sudden fear on the slave's face. A moment later, his insides burned with a searing heat that he could not have imagined possible. He clutched the solid instrument that had impaled him – a red hot iron stoker from the fire – and tried to pull it out of his body, but then the pain crippled him entirely and he collapsed onto the mirrored floor.

Movement. Someone was lifting his body – was it Marius? – and then a feeling of falling.

Or perhaps it wasn't falling. He wasn't sure. He was suddenly confused and disoriented. No, not falling. Sailing. He could feel movement below him. Water? *I'm on the boat,* he thought, *the one in Alexandria.* But then he realized it looked different.

This wasn't the boat in Egypt. It was Charon's boat. The silent black-cloaked figure stood at the prow, but someone else was in the boat, too. A white-robed woman stood above him. She turned to place a coin in the ferryman's hand and then looked down at Quintus. The boat moved forward. Fast. And the faster it went, the clearer he could see where they were going.

He could see the shores of Italy, the cypress trees that lined the road to Rome, the cobblestone of the Via Sacra and the smoke billowing out the dome of the white circular temple in the Forum. He could see her white dress, her smile as she greeted him, her body as they made love and her hand in his as they walked through the green fields of their home in Tivoli.

He blinked at the orange glow of the sacred fire before the light in his eyes went out.

* * * * * *

Pomponia was working at her desk when a slave escorted the messenger Ankhu into her office. She dismissed the slave and rose to greet Ankhu as she always did, holding out her hand for Quintus's letter.

"Please sit down, Priestess," he said. His face was drawn. His normally impeccable dress was dishevelled.

She sat down, suddenly unable to take a deep breath. Ankhu's voice sounded muffled and distant, like she was hearing him speak through a thick wall.

Quintus was dead, stabbed in the Lighthouse of Alexandria by one of Marc Antony's men. His body had been thrown from the top of the tower to fall from the sky like a sea bird struck by an arrow. Murdered on the very morning he was to return home.

Ankhu had been marked for death as well, and had only escaped by running for his life and finally jumping into the sea.

The Egyptian allowed her a moment to absorb the shock of his words. He had to make sure she understood what he was telling her. She said nothing, but gave a slight nod of her head.

He pressed on, gently. "My master gave me strict instructions to follow in the event of his death in Egypt," he said, "I was able to retrieve his body and I followed his instructions with all diligence. First, I was to cremate his body and return his remains to you." He placed a round funerary urn on Pomponia's desk.

The Vestal stared at the urn, but still said nothing.

"Also," continued Ankhu, "I am to present you with this ring, which you are instructed to wear as the wife of Quintus Vedius Tacitus." He set Quintus's gold intaglio ring, the one with the carnelian seal of Vesta, on her desk.

This, the Vestal picked up.

Ankhu folded his hands together. Of course, he had always suspected the relationship between the Vestal and Quintus was an intimate one. He had learned enough of Roman law and religion to know it was a forbidden one, too; however, his duty was to his master, not to the foreign gods of Rome.

"Finally, I am to paint images of the fire atop the Alexandrian lighthouse as well as the view. I have not had occasion to complete this task, but I will do so."

For several long moments, the Vestal said nothing. Finally, she reached for a purse on her desk, removed several coins and placed them in Ankhu's hand. "Is there anything else I should know?"

Ankhu lowered his head. "My master had freed me shortly before his death. The manumission paper was lost when I jumped into the water."

"You shall have your freedom, Ankhu. You have earned it. Come back in a few days."

Ankhu bowed deeply and then slipped out of her office, leaving Pomponia to stare at the intaglio ring in her hand. *I am to present you with this ring, which you are instructed to wear as the wife of Quintus Vedius Tacitus.*

Typical Quintus. She slid the ring onto one of the gold chains he had sent her from Egypt, and then fastened it around her neck. One way or another, she always ended up obeying him.

She felt the grief swell inside her and she knew the tears would soon come. They would be as insistent and unstoppable as the flood waters of the Nile, that great deluge Quintus had described in his letters. Compelling her breaths to remain steady, she removed the lid from the urn.

On top of the mix of grey ash and bone sat a lock of Quintus's dark hair. She suspected that was Ankhu's idea. It seemed too sentimental a gesture for Quintus to think of.

She removed the lock of hair and placed it in her desk drawer, and then poured the ashes from the silver bowl on her desk into the urn with Quintus's remains. His body and his words together. She would take them to the temple and put them in the eternal fire.

Vesta would accept the offering. After all, she had answered her priestess's prayers by bringing Quintus back home. It just wasn't in the way that Pomponia had expected. But the gods had their own way of doing things.

The grief flooded over the banks now. Her throat tightened and tears welled in her eyes, even as she heard the muted sound of voices in the corridor outside drawing closer to her office. How would she explain such uncontrolled sorrow to the other priestesses?

But then the goddess gave her a way. Quintina swung open her office door and ran inside, her cheeks wet with tears.

"You must come at once, Pomponia," she said. "Fabiana is dead."

CHAPTER XVII

Letting Go of a Wolf

Rome April 31 BCE – July 30 BCE

The former high priestess Fabiana lay in state in the courtyard of the House of the Vestals. Her body had been washed and prepared by the priestesses, and then dressed in the formal white robes and headdress worn by the Vestalis Maxima. A coin had been placed in her mouth.

Countless friends, family, aristocrats, politicians and religious colleagues had come to pay their respects. Every person present had known Fabiana, either personally or by reputation, for their entire life. Indeed, almost every person alive in Rome knew of her: she had served with the Vestal order for an unprecedented eighty-four years.

Octavian had already announced plans to commission a new mausoleum for the Vestal order in Fabiana's name, and it was he who would be delivering the funeral eulogy speech on the Rostra later that day. Another high-profile death, another opportunity for self-promotion. After the service, Fabiana's body would be placed on its funeral pyre and set alight. Wine would be used to douse the embers and her ashes would be collected.

Word of Quintus's death had not yet reached Octavian, although it would within a day or two. Octavian would be offended – how dare Antony order the killing of Caesar's delegate! – but otherwise he wouldn't care. Quintus's death was hardly important enough to start a war over.

Quintina and her sister were similarly unaware of Quintus's death. For now, that was good. The delay gave Pomponia time to manage her own shock and sorrow, and it would help Quintina portion the grief of suffering two losses so closely together.

The little dog Perseus scratched at Pomponia's leg and she bent down to pick him up. He smelled better than usual. No doubt one of the house slaves had bathed and perfumed him. *Small mercies,* thought Pomponia.

Despite the people and activity in the courtyard, the space seemed strangely empty to Pomponia. The two people she had spent her happiest times with here were gone and their absence was painfully palpable. All the things that were so familiar – the statues in the peristyle, the double pools, the statue of Vesta in the water, the trees and flowers in the gardens – all seemed so unfamiliar in a world where Quintus and Fabiana no longer existed.

But then the familiar form of Medousa arrived, trailing respectfully behind the stately Caesar and his ornate wife Livia, and Pomponia felt more grounded.

Livia spoke first, rushing ahead to wrap her arms around Pomponia as if they had been the best of friends for all their lives. "Oh Priestess Pomponia," she said, "I was heartbroken to learn that our great priestess has crossed the black river. What a loss this must be to you. Vesta and Juno give you strength."

"Thank you, Lady Livia."

Octavian lowered his head in respect. "We have lost a true friend," he said, "and Rome has lost a beloved guardian. We mourn with you."

"I know you do, Caesar. Thank you both." She gestured to Fabiana's body. "You may say good-bye if you wish," she said.

"We shall."

"If you do not mind," said Pomponia, "I would like to borrow Medousa for a moment."

Livia blinked to squeeze a strategic tear from her eye and then touched Pomponia's arm with affected sincerity. "Of course," she said. "I know she is a comfort to you. We will leave you to grieve in private." She took Octavian's hand and they made their way across the courtyard to Fabiana's body and the somber gathering of senators, Vestals, priests and nobility that surrounded it.

When they were out of earshot, Medousa let out an exasperated sigh. "That woman's tears are pure poison. I'm surprised they don't burn through her cheeks." She glared at Livia across the courtyard. "And who in Hades wears *pink* to a funeral?"

"Come with me, Medousa." Pomponia led her through the peristyle and into the house, taking tired steps over the marble floor to the privacy of her office. She closed the door when they were inside, sat down on a couch against a blue frescoed wall, and began to cry.

"I am sorry about Fabiana," said Medousa. She sat down beside Pomponia and gently brushed the hair off the Vestal's drawn face.

"I do not weep for Fabiana."

"For who then?"

"Quintus Vedius Tacitus."

Medousa sat straight up. "Why would you weep for him, Priestess?"

"He is dead. Killed in Alexandria by one of Antony's men."

"I have heard nothing of this..."

"Caesar doesn't know yet. No one knows, not even Quintina. The news will arrive in a day or two."

"Then Priestess," said Medousa, "how is that you know this information so soon?" She shook her head. "Although I think I already know the answer."

Pomponia stood up quickly and faced Medousa. "I do not answer to a slave," she said, a burst of anger suddenly mixing with the sadness.

Medousa stood up and embraced her. "Forgive me." She forced the words out of her mouth. "If there was affection between you, I am sorry he is dead."

"He is *murdered* and it is Marc Antony who did it." Pomponia wiped the tears from her eyes and walked to her desk where she removed a cylindrical silver scroll box from a drawer.

She allowed her eyes to rest on the lock of Quintus's hair that lay within the open drawer before closing it with renewed purpose and holding the scroll box out to Medousa. "Give this to Caesar as soon as you can be alone with him."

Medousa wrapped the scroll box in her palla. "What are you doing, Priestess?"

"I'm letting go of a wolf, Medousa. One that I hope will tear open Antony's throat."

* * * * * *

"How goes the war against Antony, sister? Has your husband won yet?"

"Oh, General Agrippa just won some big naval battle in Actium. Caesar says it is the beginning of the end for Antony and Cleopatra. Medousa! Bring more wine. And something for us to eat."

The auburn-haired slave carried a tray into the triclinium of Caesar's house and set it down before Livia and Claudia.

She had no sooner taken a step back than Livia's sons Tiberius and Drusus snatched pieces of glazed baked bird and melons off the tray with grimy hands and raced into the courtyard, nearly knocking over the cups of wine she had just poured for the two sisters. She mopped up the spill. "Is that all, Domina?"

"Yes. You can go." Livia let her head hang over the edge of the scarlet-colored couch and grinned at her sister. "Thanks be to Fortuna, it looks like I will soon be first woman in Rome *and* Egypt, Claudia."

"Your husband was right," said Claudia. "Antony's will was his death warrant."

"Honestly, what was the man thinking?" Livia asked. "He divorces Octavia and marries Cleopatra, renounces Rome and embraces Egypt, and disowns his Roman children so that he can leave the eastern provinces to his Egyptian children by Cleopatra. His will was a checklist of reasons to go to war. The people turned on him faster than a cornered cat turns on a mad dog."

"It was a remarkable turn of events," said Claudia, frowning at a wine stain on her purple dress. "I never imagined the people could have such hatred for the general."

"Hate comes easy when you're hungry." Livia bit into a baked bird. "Or so I hear." She wiped her mouth with the back of her hand. "But the worst part of the will by far, at least as far as my husband is concerned, was Antony's declaration that Caesarion is the true heir of Julius Caesar and should rule Egypt. The boy is doomed. Caesar will never let him live."

"Your status and fortune rise as never before," said Claudia. "Rome now loves your husband Caesar with as much passion as they hate Antony." She slurped glaze off her fingers. "I hope you are mindful to share your fortune with those who have helped you acquire it."

Livia stopped chewing. "Speak plainly, sister."

"I want an estate in Capua." Claudia's thoughts turned to Fabiana. To the way the old Vestal had squeezed her hand and kissed the back of it. She still wondered: what whispered words had passed her lips that day? What were the other priestesses whispering? She needed to get out of Rome. Soon.

"Claudia, Rome is at war. Caesar is off wading through Greece and Egypt with his armies. The treasury is as empty as the grain bins. I cannot now be seen granting an extravagant estate in Capua to my sister. The people would rise up and my husband would be livid with me. Have patience."

"Patience is not one of my virtues, Livia."

"Then you must learn it."

"I will learn patience when you learn gratitude." Claudia threw the meat in her hand onto the tray. "If it weren't for me, Livia, you wouldn't just be out of Caesar's bed, you'd be out of his house, too. You'd be begging for scraps at your block-headed ex-husband's door or whoring yourself out again to that hairy Greek pig you love to hate."

"Sister, calm down."

Claudia sat up and thumped her chest. "You have me to thank for your good luck, sister, not Fortuna. I was the one who helped you convince Caesar that his wife Scribonia was unfaithful so that he would divorce her. I was the one who figured out a way for you to be useful to Caesar. I was the one who risked everything to accuse the Vestal. I was the one who advised you to bribe Antony's man in Egypt and have him kill Quintus Vedius Tacitus. That is the only reason the high priestess gave your husband Antony's will and you know it. I have risked all, and I want my reward. Those Vestals are a vengeful nest of vipers, sister. I want an estate outside of Rome. It is for my safety."

Livia looked unmoved.

Claudia took a deep, calming breath.

"It is in your best interests, too. It will look good if you are seen to be sending your sister away from Rome. The people will assume you are doing it out of respect for the Vestals. Your husband will approve of that, no doubt."

Livia raised her eyebrows. "Ah yes, you have a point there. Caesar would like that."

Claudia inwardly fumed. She remembered Fabiana's words: *How alike the two of you are! Like Helen and Clytemnestra.* Indeed.

"Yes," Livia decided. "I will find you a fine villa in Capua. Do not misunderstand my words, sister, but it would be best if you left Rome as soon as possible. I would think you could return in two or three years, after the wounds of the incestum accusation have healed. I will miss you terribly, of course."

Satisfied, Claudia settled back onto the couch as Medousa returned with fresh wine and delicacies. The two sisters met eyes but remained silent as the slave busied herself. It was only when Medousa had left the room that Claudia spoke again.

"Take one last word of advice from your older sister," she said. "You are a fool to keep that slave around. I swear by the secret keeper Jana, she keeps snakes under that white veil of hers. And each one slithers to the temple after dark to hiss into the ear of Priestess Pomponia."

* * * * * *

The vomit basin by Medousa's bed was full yet again. The slave Despina hastily replaced it with an empty one, only to have Medousa lean over and heave more of her curdled stomach contents into it.

Despina looked into the basin and furrowed her brow. She looked at a subordinate slave. "Go fetch the physician. There's blood in it now and the retching is getting worse. It should be easing up by now."

"She doesn't need a physician, Despina." Livia strolled casually into the room, talking through a mouthful of fresh fig. "She just needs to rest. The physician will only afflict her with a cure that is worse than the ill." She wrinkled her nose. "Leeches, bleedings...why should we put our beloved Medousa through such torment?"

Despina turned back to the retching auburn-haired slave and wiped her forehead with a cloth. "Tell me again, Medousa, what did you eat?"

"She ate what the rest of you ate," snapped Livia, "bread, wine and figs from the garden."

Medousa rolled onto her back and the sight of her blanched, sunken face gave Despina a start. The whites of her eyes were yellow and the bedsheets were soaked through from her profuse, foul-smelling perspiration.

"I had some fish from the kitchen," Medousa moaned, "but only one or two bites." She had no sooner spoken than she vomited again and then passed out from exhaustion.

Despina stared into the basin. "It had to be the fish. Only rancid meat could do this. But she said that she only had a bite or two..."

Livia shrugged. "You know what they say, Despina. Fish and company go bad after three days." She turned to the other slave in the room. "Go to the kitchen and make sure cook throws out the fish. You'll be scrubbing the floors for a week if he serves it for dinner."

"Yes, Domina."

Medousa made a whimpering sound and woke up, her eyes wide open and already in search of the vomit basin.

Despina held it to her mouth and Medousa ejected into it again. Brown sputum, bright red blood and yellow bile. Medousa sighed, rolled onto her back, and fell into a still sleep.

Thank Juno, thought Despina. *She needs a few moments of relief.*

But then Medousa's fingers began to twitch in the most disturbing way, followed by her arms and legs. A moment later, her entire body erupted into a violent seizure that caused her to bounce up and down on the bed. The Medusa pendant around her neck clinked with the fierce movement and her eyes rolled back in her head.

The spasm stopped as unexpectedly as it had started and Medousa's body lay unmoving. A strange exhalation escaped her lips.

Despina placed her ear on Medousa's chest and floated her hand over her mouth, feeling for breath.

"She's gone."

Livia spat a fig seed into the vomit basin.

"Now aren't you glad we didn't send for a physician?" she asked. "It's a priest that we need."

CHAPTER XVIII

Damnatio Memoriae

(damnation of memory)

Egypt August 30 BCE

Cleopatra VII Philopator, Queen and Pharaoh of Egypt, peered out a high widow of her heavily fortified royal palace. She felt another thud of panic against her ribs. Panic had become an all too familiar feeling in the last few days.

Caesar's forces had surrounded the Royal Palace. They struck battering rams against the reinforced doors. They tried to scale the side of the palace to enter through windows. They hacked at the walls with axes. And they were making progress. She turned from the window to address Charmion and Iras.

"It is time," she said. "Tell Apollonius to send Caesarion away now. Through the tunnels."

Iras nodded. "It shall be done, Majesty." She quickly scurried away.

Charmion put her hand on Cleopatra's back. "Are you sure you don't want to know where they will take him?"

"No," said Cleopatra. "It is for his own safety. If I am tortured by Caesar..." She put her face in her hands.

"Caesar would never violate the Queen of Egypt."

"Caesar would *gut* the Queen of Egypt with his own hands," spat Cleopatra, "and then lick the blood off his fingers."

A moment later, Iras returned and offered the queen a nod. Caesarion was safe. Behind the slave, however, stood a Roman centurion. He wore the same heavy silver armor and blood-red cloak they all did, but he held his red-crested helmet in his hands.

Cleopatra smirked. A rare show of Roman humility.

"Majesty," said Iras, "this man has a message from Caesar."

Cleopatra stood as straight as she could. "What is it, boy?"

The centurion looked her in the eye. So much for Roman humility.

"Caesar says that if you give him General Marc Antony, he will spare you and your children. He gives his personal assurance that you will keep your throne, although a Roman presence will remain in Alexandria to ensure you do your duty to Rome. Caesar wishes no further disruption in Egypt. You have until morning to comply."

Without waiting to be dismissed by the queen, the centurion turned on his heel and left.

Cleopatra collapsed onto the green-leaf tiles of the marble floor. Charmion knelt beside her. "See? He wants Antony, not you."

"Nonsense," said Iras. "He will never let her live. Or the children. He just doesn't want the Egyptian people seeing him hack their queen to death in the sand." She also knelt on the floor beside Cleopatra. "Majesty, he knows you want to live. He knows you want your children to live. He gives false hope so that you will give him Antony and do his job for him."

The queen took Iras's face in her hands. "But what if it isn't false hope, Iras? What if it is true? What if I can save the lives of my children? What if I can keep my throne, even if it is just as Caesar's puppet? Is that not better than death?"

Charmion nodded and then looked harshly at Iras. “Caesar hates Antony. If he can kill him, he will be the top man in Rome and that is all he cares about. He has nothing to lose by keeping Cleopatra alive, especially if he leaves a detachment here. It is in his best interests to have her remain a figurehead on the throne. The Egyptian people support her reign. It ensures stability and avoids more bloodshed.”

Iras shook her head. “You know what he has said about her,” she countered. “He has said that she practices the black arts and can cast spells on Roman men. He has said that she wants to rule Egypt and Rome, to enslave the Roman people and watch them starve. This is what his people believe of the queen. He cannot leave her on the throne or he will be seen as weak.” She stroked Cleopatra’s hair. “And what of Caesarion? Majesty, you know he will never let him live. Caesarion is the true blood son of Julius Caesar, while he is only the adopted son. Think on it, Majesty. You know I speak the truth.”

Cleopatra sprawled herself on the floor and fell into an open sob. “I know it, Iras,” she wept, “but still I want to live. I want my children to live. If there is any chance...”

“Then we shall try,” said Iras. She met eyes with Charmion. “Send word to Antony that the queen has committed suicide,” she said. “He will follow her.”

“He will want to see her.”

“Tell him it is forbidden. The queen’s body cannot be seen by anyone but the priests.”

Charmion stood and was about to leave, but Cleopatra gripped her ankle. “Wait,” she said, “do not send word.”

“Majesty, I know you love him. I know he is – ”

“Do not send word,” said Cleopatra. “He will not believe it. Deliver the message yourself.”

Charmion nodded gravely. “Yes, Majesty.” She left the queen’s chambers without looking back.

Marc Antony was in his strategy room – his war room, he called it. He sat on the base of a colossal statue: a red, bronze and gold lion with its front foot resting regally on a turquoise globe, the kingly master of the world. He wore an Egyptian tunic with Roman sandals.

A giant map of Italy, Greece, Egypt and Africa hung on the wall and he was staring vacantly at it. The back of a heel rhythmically thumped the base of the statue.

"General Antony," said Charmion. "The goddess Isis sends word. Cleopatra is with her."

Antony looked at her sideways. "What in Hades are you talking about, woman?" But then the light of realization shone in his eyes. He swallowed hard. "Take me to her."

"It is not permitted. Only the priests can see the queen's body."

"I don't give a shit about the priests," he said. "Take me to her."

"They have already taken her away," said Charmion. "I do not know where. The location must be kept secret so that Caesar does not find her. Her body must be prepared for the afterlife. It must be done properly, you see."

Antony's body jerked forward and he slid off the base of the statue, slowly lowering himself to the floor. Charmion approached him. The fallen general wrapped his arms around her legs and a long, low howl of pain escaped his lips.

The slave bent down and pulled the dagger out of the gold sheath that always hung from Antony's left side. She gripped the blade so tightly that blood ran down it, and then held it in front of his face.

"The queen orders you to follow her," she said. "Now."

Antony ripped the dagger from her hands and scrambled to his knees. "*Futuo,* you cursed gods," he seethed, and in one fast, hard motion thrust the blade upward into his chest to pierce his heart.

Except that the blade didn't pierce his heart. Blood pooled on the floor and spurted from his nose, but he didn't die. Instead, he rolled in agony on the orange and brown tiles, his grunts and groans of pain mixing with gasped sobs of despair.

At that moment, the door flew open and Cleopatra rushed inside the war room. "Antony, no! I was weak and frightened, I changed my – " She took a few faltering steps and then dropped to her knees at the sight of his writhing, bloody body on the floor and crawled to his side, nuzzling her nose into his hair.

Antony's legs twitched and straightened as he struggled to look at her. *Alive?* His blood-soaked hands reached up to wrap around her neck. "You lying little Egyptian bitch!"

"My love," she cried. "I am sorry. I am – "

His hands tightened around her neck and, with breathless alarm, she tried to pry off his fingers. Charmion knelt down to help her queen wrench Antony's death grip from her throat, both of them slipping on the blood-covered floor. Finally, Cleopatra broke free and fell back as a shout – in Latin – echoed off the walls.

"*Cleopatra regina*!" barked the same centurion she had spoken to earlier, "stand up and step away from the general. You are under the authority of Caesar."

The queen turned her head to see what appeared to be an entire legion of Roman soldiers filling the war room. They had entered the palace. It was indeed over. Caesar had won.

She stood up slowly to avoid slipping in blood, her eyes fixed on Antony. Her husband. His eyes stared blankly at death and his mouth hung open. His body had stopped moving. He was dead.

He died hating me, thought the queen. *He will not meet me in the afterlife.*

All pretense gone now, the centurion grabbed her arm and pulled her back toward her chambers as Charmion followed. Iras already sat rigidly on a couch inside the room and the centurion pushed Cleopatra and Charmion in as well.

"You will await Caesar's orders," he said, and then slammed the doors.

On the other side of the closed doors, the trembling women could hear the deep voices of the guards as they talked and laughed. It was a happy day for them. They would soon be going home. And as victors. No doubt their fellow soldiers were already moving through the Royal Palace, filling their sacks and helmets with Egyptian gold, gems and ancient treasures.

Cleopatra and Charmion hadn't moved – they still stood in the center of the room holding each other and exchanging frightened looks with Iras – when the doors again opened and Octavian strode in wearing the polished armor and red cloak of the Roman commander.

His expression was cool, confident, even casual. As if conquering a nation and taking its queen captive was an everyday occurrence in his life. He stood in front of Cleopatra and smiled thinly.

"Antony is dead," he said. "Thank you for your cooperation. I can assure you that your children by him will not be harmed."

"And Caesarion?"

"My little brother," said Octavian. "What would he have to fear from me?"

Cleopatra's hatred for him swelled and swirled in the pit of her stomach.

"I have other business to attend to now," said Octavian, "but we shall speak again soon." His eyes moved over the bloody fingerprints on her neck and he cast the queen a knowing glance. "Rest now, Cleopatra."

He left her chambers and the guards closed the doors behind him, locking them from the outside and falling into muffled chatter. Cleopatra fought to regain control of her breaths. She spoke as levelly as she could. "What will happen now?" she asked her advisors.

"You will be taken to Rome and marched before the Roman people in Caesar's triumph," said Iras. "And then you will be publically executed. Perhaps strangled or beheaded."

Cleopatra looked at Charmion, waiting for her opposing opinion. The queen had spent her entire life depending on the alternating advice, an insightful process of back and forth strategizing, that her two wisest advisers were known for.

Charmion only nodded. "It will be so," she said.

The queen's face contorted into a fearful sob. "And what of the children?"

Again, it was Iras who spoke. "He will likely let your children by Antony live. It will be seen by his people as an act of mercy and respect for the children of a once great Roman."

"And Caesarion?"

"Caesarion will only live if Caesar cannot find him. But he will tear Egypt apart until he does find him."

Charmion nodded in sober agreement.

"Isis holds her hand out to me," said Cleopatra. "It is truly over." She walked slowly through her chambers, past a colonnade of palm-tree columns and lay down on her bed. The exhaustion of the past weeks, the guilty horror of Antony's death, the threat to Caesarion and the hopeless finality of her situation all combined to rock the queen into a sudden, strange sleep.

* * * * * *

She awoke with a start. The same impudent Roman centurion as before was in her chambers. He stood above her holding a platter of food and drink in his hands, and was in the midst of a heated argument with the unyielding Charmion.

He set the tray on the bed when he saw Cleopatra open her eyes. "You haven't had anything since yesterday," he said. "You need to eat and drink."

Cleopatra ignored him. "Is it tomorrow?" she asked Charmion.

"Yes, Majesty."

"What has happened? Where are my children?"

"They brought Alexander Helios and Cleopatra Selene to the doors early this morning," said Charmion. "We could not wake you, Majesty. But your children live and are unharmed. Iras and I both saw them."

Cleopatra looked at the two women. She wanted more. She wanted news of Caesarion.

"No other news," said Iras.

The centurion pushed the tray closer to her. "Eat."

"I am not hungry," said Cleopatra.

The centurion brought his lips close to her ear. "You will eat this bread," he said, "or Caesar will eat your children." He smiled at her, studying her face. For a fleeting moment, she thought he would risk an insolent kiss. What better bragging rights to spread among his fellow soldiers than a stolen kiss from the Queen of Egypt? But then he seemed to think twice and merely lowered his head with mock respect and stood back, waiting for her to eat.

"Why should Caesar care if I eat," she muttered.

"You need your strength," said Charmion. She glared at the Roman soldier. "He cannot march you to your execution in his triumph if you've already starved yourself to death."

"Caesar only has your health and well-being in mind," the centurion said unconvincingly.

Cleopatra slid off the bed. As she rose, Charmion and Iras instinctively fussed over their mistress's dress and hair, making sure they were arranged properly. The queen positioned herself in front of the Roman soldier and studied him as he had studied her.

"Tell Caesar I will do all that he asks," she said. "I am his Egyptian prize and I will shine as he wishes me to. But first I wish to anoint Antony's body in the mausoleum."

"I will inform Caesar," he said. "I am certain that can be arranged."

Not caring that his heavy cloak brushed indecorously against the great Queen of Egypt, the centurion turned and left Cleopatra's chambers, slamming the doors behind him.

Iras was the first to speak. "Majesty, it should be the priests and embalmers who anoint Antony's body," she said cautiously, "the linseed oil can heat and char the skin if not properly applied and – "

"I know that, you foolish woman," snapped Cleopatra. She spoke urgently, under her breath. "Do you not remember what is in the mausoleum? You put it there yourself, Iras."

The gravity of the queen's meaning descended upon her. "Of course, Majesty."

Moments later, the doors to the queen's chambers opened again. The centurion stood outside and cocked his head at Cleopatra. "I am to take you to the mausoleum," he said. "Caesar trusts you will perform as promised afterward."

Perform. The word struck Cleopatra. *Indeed, I will perform for Caesar,* she thought. She smiled at the Roman soldier. "The queen will do all that Caesar requires."

The centurion and what seemed like a full cohort of Roman soldiers escorted Cleopatra and her two advisors out of the palace where the glaring light of day pierced their eyes. They walked along a sand-covered limestone path under the searing heat of the Egyptian summer sun until they reached the seven-meter high door of the mausoleum.

The door was built of pure granite and it took a small army of Roman soldiers to open it. After all, it was meant to be closed once and never re-opened.

Rays of light illuminated the interior of the luxurious, gold-gilded tomb and Cleopatra strode inside without waiting for permission from her Roman captors. Almost immediately, she brought her hand to her mouth. The body of Marc Antony lay naked on a marble table. His flesh gleamed with the oil that had already been applied by the embalmers.

Cleopatra had known his body would be here; however, she had not known that Caesar had permitted Antony to receive the Egyptian funerary rites he had dictated in his will. The sight of his body being prepared for the afterlife refreshed the sorrow of his death.

She walked slowly to his body as the door of her tomb closed, sealing the mausoleum from the outside world of sunlight and sound. The oil on Antony's bare chest, arms and legs reflected the flickering light of the oil lamps that were affixed to the walls of the tomb. She touched his skin. It felt as warm in death as it did in life. But he did not move. He did not rouse and reach for her in the way he always did when she touched him.

She leaned over to kiss his mouth. "I am coming, my love," she whispered. Cleopatra looked over her shoulder at Charmion and Iras who stood trembling but dutiful behind her. They would follow their queen into death. "I am ready," she said to them. "We must move quickly."

Charmion nodded and moved to open a cabinet decorated with lapis lazuli, removing a jeweled diadem and gold robe. She placed the crown on Cleopatra's head while Iras wrapped the queen in her royal robe.

Cleopatra sat on a golden couch as Iras retrieved a large pottery bowl within which lay a coiled cobra. The skin on its long body twitched when the lid was removed, but otherwise it seemed unperturbed even when Iras reached into the pot and gingerly pulled it out. It yawned and moved lazily through her fingers.

"Give it to me," said Cleopatra, "it must bite me first."

The queen held the cobra in her hands. The creature was waking up now and becoming more interested in its surroundings. It glided through Cleopatra's fingers and wrapped around the wrist of her left arm.

A sound at the door of the tomb. The soldiers were returning. They would not risk leaving the queen – their master's Egyptian prize – unattended for too long.

Cleopatra pinched the cobra's face and it bit her on the wrist, its curved fangs sinking into a blue vein so fast that she didn't even see it happen. The bite was hot and sharp, but otherwise she felt nothing. She dropped the cobra onto her lap.

A moment later, it began. A sudden shortness of breath. The queen inhaled deeply, yet her lungs still felt empty. She tried to draw in another breath, hungry for the feeling of full lungs, but she could not. She held out her hands and Charmion and Iras took them, interlocking their fingers with hers.

Cleopatra lay back on the golden couch as her breaths became shallow and then stopped.

Iras put her face to the queen's lips.

"It is done," she said to Charmion. "Isis took her quickly."

More sounds from the door of the tomb. Any moment, the door would open and the light of day and realization would fill the tomb.

Iras picked up the cobra and pinched its mouth as Cleopatra had done. It struck her in the crook of her elbow.

Wordlessly, she passed the snake to Charmion who hesitated for a split second before seeing a slant of daylight pierce the darkness of the tomb and then also coaxing the cobra to strike her.

It bit her on the back of her hand, but its fangs lodged in her skin and she had to pry its head off of her. She dropped it onto the floor and it slithered away, utterly indifferent to the drama unfolding around it.

Sunlight blazed into the tomb as more than a dozen Roman soldiers rushed inside. The same centurion who had brought Cleopatra and her advisors into the mausoleum was the first to see the sight: Cleopatra lying dead on a golden couch, dressed in royal attire, with her advisors Iras and Charmion lying at her feet.

"Pluto's withered cock!" he shouted. He took off his helmet and threw it hard against the wall of the tomb, and then kicked over a large amphora. It fell over, broke, and spilled oil over the floor. Taking an angry step closer, he saw that Charmion still clung to the last of life.

"Are you happy now, Charmion?" he asked bitterly.

"Happier than you, Roman," she said. "I fulfilled my duty." She rested her head on Iras's stomach and joined her friend and her queen.

The centurion ignored the parting gibe but, just when he thought the situation couldn't get any worse, heard a swell of shouts and marching footsteps behind him. Caesar was coming. He muttered another obscene curse to the gods of the underworld and reluctantly turned toward the approaching Caesar – now the sole and undisputed leader of the Roman world – to explain why he had failed in his duty.

"Caesar," he began, "we only left her for a matter of minutes, as instructed. We did not – "

Octavian held up his hand for silence. He walked slowly, dreadfully, to Cleopatra's body and stared at it for a long while. *You lying little Egyptian bitch,* he thought.

General Agrippa appeared at his shoulder. "Ah," he said, as he assessed the situation. He knew exactly what Caesar was thinking: his triumph just wouldn't have the same flair to it. "It is a lost opportunity," he admitted, "but I have news that will lift your spirits, Caesar."

"Oh? What's that?"

"We found the boy Caesarion. I decapitated him myself."

Pomponia sat on the Rostra next to Livia, Octavia and the young Julia as Caesar, wearing a crown of laurels and standing only an arm's length away from her, regarded the Roman mob that spilled into every street, peristyle and portico in the Forum, and that sat perched on top of temples and statues.

Red banners flapped regally in the wind and the horns sounded, although they were drowned out by the crowd's victory cheers.

A parade of spoils from the palaces and temples of faraway Egypt rolled through the streets and people swarmed to catch a glimpse. There were giant painted statues of foreign gods with the heads of animals: a falcon, a jackal, a ram. A particularly strange one – which had the head of a black scarab beetle and the body of a man – received more than its share of jeers and finger-pointing.

But then along came a procession of mummies propped up in jeweled sarcophagi and the beetle-headed god was forgotten.

Another round of cheers as the mummies gave way to a golden couch, upon which reclined an effigy of Cleopatra. It had been outfitted with the queen's jeweled diadem and gold robe. Its arms were crossed over its chest, showing the Egyptian Pharaoh in death.

Following close behind the effigy of the dead queen were her two living children by Marc Antony: Alexander Helios and Cleopatra Selene. They walked slowly with their heads down. What was there for them to see? Ahead of them was the effigy of their dead mother. Around them were the faces of their foreign conquerors.

Yet Caesar had kept his word and allowed them to live. In fact, he had placed them under the care of his sister Octavia who continued to bear the dictates of the Fates and her powerful brother with regal composure. Pomponia had never known anyone who accepted their fate so willingly.

Octavian stood and the crowd roared even louder. Octavian. Then Caesar. Now Augustus.

Following his defeat of Antony and Cleopatra, the Senate had bestowed upon him the honorific title Augustus. It meant "the great one." Pomponia smiled to herself. The man sprouted more names than the hydra sprouted heads.

The month of Sextilius had also been renamed: it was now known as August in honor of Rome's savior and it was only fitting that it followed the month of July which had been named after his divine father. The son follows the father.

"Citizens," shouted Caesar. "I now give Rome a gift. The death of Antony and Cleopatra!"

At that, the main attraction rolled before the Rostra: a massive prison cart decorated in the style of the Royal Palace in Alexandria.

Inside the cart, a man was dressed in the style of an Egyptian male, complete with garish make-up on his face. A woman was dressed as the Queen of Egypt, complete with diadem and royal robes. Antony and Cleopatra.

Or more accurately, inside the cart were two slaves whose greatest misfortune in life had been the striking resemblance they bore to the Egyptian queen and her Roman lover. They sat facing each other, each fastened to the very golden thrones that Antony and Cleopatra had ruled from in Alexandria.

Caesar nodded to the executioners and the performance that everyone had come to see then began.

Four men dressed as snake-charmers carried heavy baskets to the prison cart. They tipped the baskets through the bars – careful to stand back as far as possible – as hundreds of snakes spilled into the bottom of the cart.

The mob of people moved, weaved and climbed whatever they could to get a better view.

Inside the cart, the man and woman tied to the thrones began to buck in their seats and scream as snakes of every shape, size and color swarmed around their tethered feet. To add to the drama, the snake-charmers used long sticks with hooks on the end to grab snakes from the bottom of the cart and place them on the bodies of the couple – on their laps, heads, shoulders, even shoving them under their clothing.

Pomponia grimaced and looked away. Her thoughts were wandering. They moved from Vercingetorix to the Carcer, from the Carcer to Quintus, from Quintus to Antony, and then to Antony's will.

Hunger, the threat of war and the fear of Egypt's growing strength had made Rome shake in its sandals. The question of how Caesar had obtained Antony's will wasn't one that many people were asking. Or if they were, Caesar was finding ways to stifle their curiosity. It didn't matter to Pomponia. It was in the past. Roman stomachs were once again full and peace had come. The Queen of Egypt had imperiled Rome and had needed to die.

At the same time, Antony had deserved to die for turning on his people. But it wasn't Antony who had killed Quintus. He didn't deserve to die for that. Someone else had killed Quintus.

Pomponia turned her head and smiled amiably at Livia Drusilla. Caesar's wife wore a green dress with a teal veil, her hair sparkling with gemstones and her teeth bared in a wide smile as she beamed at her powerful husband and basked in her newfound status as the first woman in Rome.

The Vestal turned to her and spoke lowly. "Tell me, Lady Livia, how does your sister like her new villa in Capua?"

"She likes it very well, High Priestess. Perhaps too well, since she has not replied to the last three letters I sent. I think country life has gotten to her."

"Maybe she ate some bad fish," said Pomponia.

Livia felt a sudden hot flush in her cheeks, but resisted the urge to make eye contact with the Vestal.

"It is such an important day for your husband," Pomponia continued, "and for you as well."

"The gods bless us."

"Not all the gods."

"Oh?"

"Vesta does not bless you," said Pomponia. "Neither does Juno. The divine sisters have not blessed your home by giving you children with Caesar. They have not blessed your bed. I am told that common slave girls and the wives of other men spend more time in it with your husband than you do."

Livia bristled. "Priestess..."

"I know all your secrets, Livia. I could have you fed to the lions in the arena for some of them. Your husband could easily find another slave trader to staff his bedchamber."

"Caesar would never – "

"Oh hush now, Livia," Pomponia said. "Caesar would push you off the Tarpeian Rock himself to stay in the good graces of the Vestal order. We are an asset to him. You are becoming a liability."

"Caesar knows my worth." The words came out weaker than she would have preferred and Livia exhaled out her nose. She hadn't expected this. Her blood quickened with anger. No matter how many stinking beasts she sacrificed to Fortuna, no matter how many backs she managed to clamber over, there was always some tart in the way. Unfortunately, this one had the high ground. Yet again, she found herself caught between Scylla and Charybdis with no escape, no option. Not yet. Not with a barren belly. "What do you want, Priestess?"

"You've spent years trying to reduce the Vestal order because of your own ambitions and petty insecurities. Now I want you to do the opposite. I want you to elevate us as never before."

"I would be happy to do so."

"Good." Pomponia lifted a disapproving eyebrow at Livia's garishly-colored dress. "You will begin by wearing white for all public occasions. No make-up. You're pretty enough, nay?"

She reached her hands behind Livia's neck to secure Medousa's pendant around it. "No jewelry, other than this."

Taking a break from the adoring mob, Caesar turned to smile at his wife sitting alongside the Vestal. The two women seemed to be getting along very well. The high priestess even seemed to be giving Livia a gift. Wonderful. He nodded at Livia in approval and she smiled tightly back at him.

Pomponia carried on. "You will mint Vesta on your coinage and adopt the modest dress of a Vestal in all your statuary. You will extol our order at all public sacrifices and festivals, and you will make an annual donation in the amount that I specify. In fact, I shall spend part of your first donation by commissioning a statue of Tuccia for the gardens outside the Circus Maximus."

Pomponia accepted a glass of ice water from a passing slave, took a sip, and then continued. "I must admit, it will be amusing to watch the public ridicule your attempts at purity. After all, the rumors of your purchases at the slave market are already the tastiest topic at every dinner party in Rome."

She swirled the ice in her glass until it made a clinking sound. "And then there's your own matrimonial history, of course. A divorced woman with children by another man. Or rather by two men. There is no question your elder son is the legacy of that square-headed Tiberius, but Drusus..." Pomponia shook her head and bit her lip in mock concern for Livia's welfare. "Caesar would recoil at how often Diodorus used you. And he'd do much worse if he knew you'd birthed a Greek bastard."

Livia's nostrils flared and she opened her mouth, but Pomponia spoke first. "Oh look, Livia. The general is making a run for it. Let's see how it all ends."

As the crowd roared anew, the slave who was playing the part of Marc Antony dramatically broke free of his restraints and tried to climb the wooden bars of the prison cart to escape the sea of snakes at his feet. He slid down the bars at every try.

And then in an act of pure desperation, he tipped over the throne upon which was tied the slave Cleopatra and scrambled on top of it.

The slave woman's face was buried in the moving sea of snakes. It moved and bobbed for a while, but then she succumbed to either suffocation or the venom of countless snake bites.

The mob loved every moment of it.

Pomponia stared at the unmoving body of the slave Cleopatra. She grew pensive and sincere. "Do you know what's strange, Lady Livia?"

"What is that, Priestess?"

"I think that you and I had more in common with Cleopatra than we think. I met her, you know. The last time was on the day I became a full Vestal."

"Oh? What was she like?"

Pomponia thought about this. "Overconfident."

When Livia didn't reply, Pomponia sat back in her chair. *Well, that's done,* she thought, *I now hold a she-wolf by the ears.* She took another sip of her ice water, feeling her face cool down from the confrontation, and watched the rest of the show.

The slave Antony was still balanced on the overturned throne of his queen. No matter how many snakes coiled and glided their way up to him, he managed to either avoid them or toss them off. If this went on much longer, the crowd would grow bored.

Caesar gave a quick nod of his head to a centurion who stood beside the prison cart. The soldier unsheathed the dagger that hung at his side, thrust his arm through the bars and stabbed the slave in the chest. The slave bellowed a cry of pain but then toppled over to land in the moving nest of snakes below him.

The show was over. But Caesar's triumph would go on.

More importantly to Pomponia, so too would the triumph of the Vestal order.

Following the defeat of Antony and Cleopatra, the people's love of and devotion to Vesta was stronger than ever. Of course, the goddess's flame had always burned in the temple and in the homes and hearts of those in Rome.

But now, the flame was spreading.

It was burning in lands beyond Italy: in Macedonia, Greece, Gaul, Africa, Asia, Syria and Egypt. Pomponia knew it would continue to spread: to Judaea, Britannia, Arabia, Germania and even to lands that had not yet been discovered, new lands the geographers said existed beyond the Sea of Atlas.

After all, the nature of any fire, even a simple one, was to spread.

That being true, surely a fire as blessed and eternal as Vesta's fire would one day illuminate every corner of the world. That being true, surely those who would try to extinguish the flame would find that, one way or another, its sacred embers would always rise from the ashes.

CHAPTER XX

Triginta Annis

(thirty years)

Tivoli 25 BCE

She wasn't fated to walk through the green fields of Tivoli with Medousa after all.

Neither would she walk through them with Quintus.

But she was walking through them just the same. That was something.

Pomponia sat down on a large stone and enjoyed the view of the beautifully ornate Temple of Vesta in Tivoli.

Surrounded by lush rolling green hills and vividly colored flowers, and boasting a well-regarded vineyard for libations to the goddess, the circular temple perched on the edge of a grassy cliff to overlook the roaring falls of the Aniene River.

A Vestal priestess named Cassia approached and sat beside her. Pomponia liked Cassia. She reminded her of Tuccia.

"Any decisions, Pomponia?" Cassia asked.

"I am staying with the order," said Pomponia. "Although I think I will stay here in Tivoli. I'm finding it harder and harder to leave my quiet villa for the noise of the city. The temple here is lovely and the Aniene falls are an excellent source of sacred water that I'd like to start sending to Rome." She picked a long piece of grass and twirled it around her finger. "I can do more good here, especially if Quintina stays with me. Tuccia has Nona and the other priestesses to help in Rome."

Cassia warmly wrapped an arm around Pomponia. I am not surprised," she said, "but I am happy to hear the words anyway. This will be big news for our little town. May I tell the other priestesses?"

"Of course."

Cassia made her way back to the temple. As Pomponia watched her go, she touched the Vesta intaglio ring that hung from a chain around her neck.

Her love and her loss of Quintus didn't blind her to the truth.

The marriage between the two of them would have been an unhappy one. Not at first, but eventually. He could not have changed his sullen disposition and she could not have tolerated it.

It was better she remained a bride of Rome. She could be Quintus's bride in the afterlife. Perhaps Pluto could make sure he was a pleasant husband to her.

She stood and walked to the edge of the falls. The rush and spray of the water was invigorating, and yet thoughts of the past – of Medousa, of Quintus – always made her melancholy.

It was fitting that she would find herself at the Temple of Vesta in Tivoli. It was a newer temple, newer than the ancient one in the Roman Forum at least, and it was the first temple that Fabiana had ordered to be built after being appointed Vestalis Maxima.

The sound of a dog barking in the distance filtered into Pomponia's ear and for a moment her heart longed to see the little dog Perseus scampering toward her, his nails clicking on the marble walkway and his tongue hanging out.

She had buried his thin white body in the flowers at the base of Fabiana's statue. How could she so dearly miss something that had tormented her so?

She smiled to herself. Did she not feel the same way about Quintus? About Medousa?

She heard laughter and turned toward the gardens of the white marble Temple of Vesta where Quintina was leaning against the trunk of a tall cypress tree. She was talking to a young priest from the Temple of Mars in Tivoli – what was his name? – oh yes, Septimus.

He said something to Quintina that Pomponia could not hear, but it made the young priestess put her hands on her hips and march away from him indignantly, straight up the marble steps and through the doorway of the temple where the eternal fire burned in the sacred hearth.

Septimus watched her walk away with a grin of self-satisfaction on his face. Yet instead of leaving once Quintina had disappeared into the sanctum, he stood where he was and stared at the closed bronze door of the Temple of Vesta.

Pomponia huffed. Could the foolish boy not be more discreet? But then she grinned despite herself as one of Medousa's plain and churlish sayings came to her mind: *Amor tussique non celatur.*

Neither love nor a cough can be concealed.

EPILOGUE

FATA VOLENTEM DUCENT, NOLENTEM TRAHUNT

(FATE CARRIES THE WILLING AND DRAGS THE REST)

SYRIA

24 BCE

She still wore the same royal purple dress she had been wearing that night. The night the men had burst through the doors of her villa and dragged her by the hair over the floor, outside into the stinking cart.

The night the grimy, toothless slave women in the cart had mocked her as she had shrieked her protests to her captors. *I am not a slave, you fools! Return me to my home at once!*

It hadn't taken long for her demands to turn to pleas. *Please! I am rich, I can pay you anything! My sister is a powerful woman! She will pay a fortune for my freedom!*

At one time, her dress had been the finest that money could buy. Now it was rags. Now she had to knot it in places to hold it together.

Sitting cross-legged on the ground, she bit into a crust of bread that was so hard it made her gums bleed. Her next bite was more cautious, but her mouth was too sore to chew. She tossed the bread aside with a thump.

She felt a sudden tug at her ankle and flinched in pain. The skin under the iron manacle was rubbed raw. Her captor – a fat, filthy, foul-mouthed man named Hostus – tugged the chain harder and she stood up. If she didn't stand up, he would just drag her. He liked to do that. She scowled at his odious bare chest with its black tufts of hair. Rain or shine, the madman never wore a tunic but scurried about with only a sagging loincloth, ratty sandals and a whip.

Hostus handed the chain to another man: well-dressed and composed, but not Roman. She knew the style – yes, Egyptian. He placed a gold coin in the slave owner's greasy palm and took hold of her chain. She followed obediently behind him.

Not that it mattered anymore, not that she really cared after these last years, but she found herself wondering where she was. The convoy of slave carts had been travelling for weeks. All she knew was that the sand stung her eyes and the landscape was more barren than any place she had ever seen.

Yet here in the middle of the barren desert, in the middle of nowhere, there stood a rickety arena held together by splintered wood and worn ropes. Through the uproar of cheers and jeers, through ruckus of shouts and sobs, through the crack of the whip against flesh, she heard a sound she had heard many times in the arena in Rome: the roar of a hungry lion.

She dropped to her knees, wrapped her fingers around the chain and pulled. "No!"

But her raspy voice was lost in the blowing sands as the Egyptian dragged her toward the arena.

Denarius depicting the
Temple of Vesta

Statue of a *Vestalis Maxima*

Original press photo of the Temple of Vesta after partial reconstruction in the early 1930's

Note from the Author

In 1989, when I was twenty years old, I had a chance encounter while visiting the ruins of the Temple of Vesta in the Roman Forum. The experience sparked a lifelong interest in ancient Roman history and religion, particularly the Vesta tradition.

In *Brides of Rome,* book one in *The Vesta Shadows* series, my goal was to bring the ancient Vestal order and religion to life in an engaging, realistic and respectful way. I say realistic and respectful, because unfortunately the way Vestal Virgins have been portrayed in the past (on those rare occasions they have been portrayed at all) is anything but. These important women deserve better.

Of course, this is ultimately a work of historical fiction. I have taken well-known figures, events and conditions from a variety of historical and artistic sources and I have blended them at times with my own interpretations, imagination and educated guesses. For readability and effect, I have at times written outside the strict timeline of history or adapted what ancient authors such as Suetonius or Livy have told us.

A few examples: While Pomponia is a fictional character, the story of the Vestal Tuccia and the sieve is true; however, the manner in which she performed her miracle is my own speculation. It is also true that the Vestal Licinia was condemned to death circa 113 BCE on fabricated charges and Sibylline prophecies; however, I took the motivations for the charges against her from other cases.

There is no note I could find of Livia having a sister; however, Roman naming convention suggests she was a second-born daughter.

Livia did publicly align herself with the Vestals. She was a major benefactor of the order and her statuary shows her dressed as a Vestal. No doubt this was for the mutual benefit of the order and her own political image. It also was rumored that she poisoned her adversaries and supplied her husband with virgins to deflower.

Octavian was given the honorific Augustus, although this happened a couple years later than it does in the book. The Emperor Augustus was also a lifelong friend and benefactor of the Vestal order, mentioning them more than once in the *Res Gestae Divi Augusti*, his autobiography.

Antony and Cleopatra – no doubt to Octavian's dismay – did manage to commit suicide before he could execute them during his triumph; however, the way he compensates with the murder of lookalikes is my own inference based on practices of the time.

In any event, I have presented a big picture that is far more fact than fiction, especially as it relates to the Vestal order and the historical background of this period. Classicists will know where I have taken liberties. If that's you, I hope you have tolerated the artistic license and simply enjoyed the read.

If you are new to ancient Roman history or religion, I hope you have enjoyed learning about this important period, as well as the remarkable people and events that have fascinated so many of us for so long.

Be sure to check out other or upcoming book titles in this series at VestaShadows.com.

Thank you for reading.

All the best,
Debra Macleod, B.A., LL.B.

Made in the USA
Lexington, KY
31 May 2018